*Requiem
for the Last Indian*

Also by
Ashis Gupta

NOVELS
The Siberian Odyssey of Hans Schroeder
Krishna, A Love Story
Rahul, A Different Love Story
Dying Traditions

SATIRE
The Acts of the Compassionates

POETRY
The Gospel according to Clarence Thomas
'For New Orleans' and Other Poems (Editor)

NON-FICTION
Ecological Nightmares and the Management Dilemma:
the Case of Bhopal
Indian Entrepreneurial Culture

Requiem for the Last Indian

ASHIS GUPTA

Copyright © Ashis Gupta 2015

Publication: October 2015

Published in Canada by
Bayeux Arts Digital-Traditional Publishing
119 Stratton Crescent, SW
Calgary, Canada T3H 1T7

www.bayeux.com

Book Design by Lumina Datamatics, Inc.

Cover Image: "As she sits on Ghost Island Rock - James Bay," acrylic on board and quills by Cree artist, Sheila Orr. With kind permission.

All rights reserved.
No part of this book may be reproduced or transmitted in any form or by any means, electronic or mechanical, without permission in writing from the publisher.

Library and Archives Canada Cataloguing in Publication

Gupta, Ashis, 1940-, author
    Requiem for the last Indian / Ashis Gupta.

Issued in print and electronic formats.
ISBN 978-1-897411-84-1 (pbk.).—ISBN 978-1-897411-99-5 (epub)

    I. Title.

PS8613.U68R45 2015   C813'.6   C2015-902612-1
                                             C2015-902910-4

The ongoing publishing activities of Bayeux Digital-Traditional Publishing under its varied imprints are supported by the Canada Council for the Arts, the Government of Alberta, Alberta Multimedia Development Fund, and the Government of Canada through the Book Publishing Industry Development Program.

Printed in Canada by Friesens

*For my friends in Chisasibi, northern Quebec,
for their kind hospitality and 1001 stories*

In memory of George Mackay Brown

We'll let blood build a bridge, over mountains draped in stars
I'll meet you on the ridge, between these worlds apart
We've got this moment now to live, then it's all just dust and dark
Let love give what it gives
Let's let love give what it gives

From *Worlds Apart*, a Bruce Springsteen lyric

Requiem for the Last Indian

We had been in a gray, smoke-filled room all morning. From time to time my thoughts moved around like a curious mouse and left me unable to follow the questions I was being asked. This led to long silences on my part, and a great deal of frustration on the part of my interrogator. The curious mouse — there was indeed a mouse scuttling around in one corner of the room — could understand the odour of perspiration hanging in the air, but couldn't trace the smell of stale sandwiches and donuts that mingled with it. I couldn't see any donuts around; maybe the donut remnants from some previous interrogation lay stuffed in some unseen trashcan inaccessible to the real mouse.

I ought to have been hungry, considering I had skipped breakfast, but the air conspired with my stomach to turn me away from all thoughts of eating. Instead, I found my thoughts unsteady, wavering between seemingly unrelated times and places separated by vast stretches of the ocean. I caught myself dreaming, or at least half asleep, with the grayness of the room often indistinguishable from the mist of blue cigarette smoke surrounding me like a womb. But the officer questioning me wouldn't let me be; he kept shredding my dreams. "Where was I?" I finally asked the man seated across the table, trying hard to disguise my weariness.

His florid face loomed large and bright as an egg yolk pinned to the wall behind him; his thick fingers rested like sausages beside a ballpoint pen and a pile of papers stacked on the metal table, its gray paint peeling at the edges, and twenty seven circles of coffee mug stains stamped on the surface. Twenty seven was as far as I could count before shadows spilled on the table and rolled quietly towards the white shirt and fleshy body softly rounded like a pig's against the other side.

"You were telling me about the tamarack trees that circled the bay and how they've been harvested so the moose have moved inland," he said, with only the slightest hint of irritation.

To his right, the opaque glass partition was alive with a constant parade of unknown figures marching to and fro. What were they doing, I wondered, all those uniformed officers scuttling like crabs on the ocean floor, or the mouse in the room where we were. I asked for another cigarette, and waited for the smoke to writhe upwards and dissolve in a pool of yellow light pouring down from above, trapping particles of dust in frenetic confusion.

I continued. I told my inquisitor how our heavy footsteps crunching over the gravelly sand had startled the geese feeding among the rushes and scattered them over the water with the chaotic, flapping sound of frightened, almost desperate, wings. I explained how we walked in silence, our eyes scouring the water's edge, gusts of cold wind whipping across our face. By the time we had approached the shore, the ripples had settled down to a languid rhythm and the rushes were swaying to the soft whisper of the birds' wings as they flew away from the land and into the heart of James Bay and beyond to Hudson's Bay. It was cloudy and damp, and the white specks in the distance looked like white sails daubed with mist as in some painting I must have seen somewhere.

I recalled that hollow, desolate day, our hearts numb with foreboding. The RCMP officer accompanying us had expressed his dismay at seeing icebergs — for that's what the white specks were — in mid-July. Larry was walking with us too, wielding a baseball bat like a stick. He pushed the scum away from a clump of weeds. "Never seen this shit here before they dammed the river," he said, "Now it's everywhere."

My interrogator smiled. I described to him how the officer had called us over with a wave of his hand: "Bingo," he whispered hoarsely, pointing to the body bobbing like a buoy face down behind a small boat tethered to a large boulder.

I watched them drag Pierre out of the bay, his face white as a pearl, a chain of puckered skin round his neck where a knife had left a deep incision, so delicate and precise it could well have been etched by a surgeon's knife.

The body had been found. Now it was time to flush out the killer.

As the day wore on, I grew more and more reconciled to what the police were after. In a manner of speaking, I had been one of them too, digging for clues, probing for give-aways, savoring occasional triumphs over unsuspecting foes. But that was in an earlier incarnation, until one day, standing on an icy clifftop four thousand miles away, I had decided that enough was enough.

It was another dismal day, and the end of my stay in the Shetland Islands. Maybe the sky's complexion was a reflection of my mood, maybe it had nothing to do with the laws of nature. In and around the bay, where they had found the body, it was always like this, I thought, as I parked my car beside the battered barn at the bottom of the hill. Maybe not. It didn't seem to matter. As soon as I shut off the engine I heard the wind sweeping down the hillside, whistling through the creaking frames and rusty panels surrounding an abandoned tractor from ancient times. It was the sound, not the relic from the past, that grabbed my attention. It was mournful and I suddenly felt distracted and afraid. Eight Shetland ponies gathered in a circle round a mud spattered feeding trough looked up at me, shook their heads several times, as if trying to fight off some unpleasant thought or vision or a pesky fly, then went back to their feeding. I knew the crofter who owned the place wouldn't mind my leaving the car next to the crooked, sad-looking gate he claimed to have cobbled together with pieces of wood, pipes and rope twelve years ago. "Still does the job," he said.

Over the past two weeks I had often come this way, my mind tossing between remorse, anger and self-pity, always in the company of others charged, like me, with the task of adding, multiplying, subtracting and dividing the damage caused by this latest shipwreck which had drawn me to Lerwick. On almost every occasion earlier, I had at least doffed my hat and said hello to the impassive, bearded farmer. I had never noticed what a work of art the gate was. Today, the gate struck me as a masterpiece, even as everything I had done in my own life seemed so wretched and pointless in comparison.

My sense of fear came and went inexplicably, but there was no escape from a deepening despondency. Today, I was glad the farmer wasn't around. Today, I wanted to walk alone, free of professional distractions, my thoughts uninterrupted by talk of estimates, bills of lading, and salvage fees. Today, walking by myself, I had all the time I needed for my own thoughts, and soon realized I had quite a long way to walk, much longer it seemed than on other days. The slope was gentle enough, but it looked at least a mile or more to the top. It must have been the relentless chatter of my companions, especially Sven, that made the distance appear shorter on other days.

I had walked only a few short steps past the gate when I was suddenly struck by the moss-covered ruins of a crofter's cottage which, strangely, was something else I didn't remember from my earlier visits. I might have cast a curious glance or two and walked past the ruins had not the wind blown the faintest notes of a song into my ears. Somebody seemed to be singing from within the ruins. It was a sad, haunting song, the notes rising and falling with sudden shifts of the wind. I stopped. Then, prodded by some sudden inner force, I started briskly up the rutted path towards the cottage. I had to slow down almost immediately, for the ground was covered with a thin layer of ice. It cracked under my feet, giving way from time to time, forcing me to stumble, slide and stop. Drawn as if by a powerful magnet,

I plodded along laboriously, stopping once in a while to try and understand the strange patches of shadows that kept popping up in the distance. I couldn't figure them out, and needed to focus my attention on the frozen tracks left in the hardened mud by the crofter's pick-up truck, simply to fix my eyes on something close and familiar. It helped calm my nerves. Over and around me, the wind slipped through unseen passages it carved for itself out of sheer space and filled the air with shrill, piercing cries, sounds that all but drowned out the earlier song but continued to deepen the gloom. Still, I was surprised by a sudden, momentary lightheartedness, a childlike expectancy of something about to happen. I looked up from time to time, prodded by wistful, fleeting reminders of earlier times. The sound of the wind that came and went brought back memories of the sheer joy I had felt from my childhood days every time, walking or cycling, I turned corners on hilly trails that I loved so passionately and which never failed to surprise me with slender streams or cascading waterfalls suddenly coming to life and vanishing beyond the next corner. I felt the same thrill every time until yesterday, or so it seemed. On this day, it remained a distant memory, quickly, strangely, replaced by sounds that touched me with the nearness of my mother, dead some years ago. Yes, the song returned, so disturbing, so tragic. How I loved her!

But the song stopped abruptly as soon as I stepped over the scattered stones. They were encrusted with dull orange and green and led into what was once a home, sheltered from storms driven by waves, warmed by sinuous fires affirming a crofter's defiance in the face of life's inescapable hardships. An ashen sky rested on the walls which once held up a roof of dark thatch. I found myself sharing the space between the shattered walls with a wispy sliver of gray mist which slowly drew away from me onto the field outside, filling me with even greater astonishment as it kneaded itself into the form of a woman clad in a billowy white dress. She glided away from me, held aloft in the air by her trailing cape of patched rags which fluttered in the wind like a sail and drew her higher and higher to the edge of the cliff. Her threadbare cape of faded colours was something I recognized right away, and the recognition made me even more nervous. She turned once, and I saw her face. I pray to God to spare me such visions, for there was such anguish in her face, such reproach in her eyes, that my blood ran cold. Surely I had failed her somehow. Surely, there was some reason why I felt the floodgates of guilt swing open inside my mind. While I imagined or believed — I was never certain — I had seen visions before, this was the first time I had come face to face with Isabel Gunn, my great great grandmother's apparition. I stopped in my tracks, uncertain about what to do next. But I couldn't stand still. A mighty force kept pulling me forward. In spite of it, as soon as I started to walk again, a sudden calm spread through my body, touching every limb, every extremity. My breathing became easier, the fear left me, and I was filled with a fresh expectancy. Maybe I was mesmerized. I continued to plod up the icy slope, following her. I kept my unblinking eyes fixed in front of me as the figure weaved in and out of the twisting, dancing mist. But she never turned to face me one more time. A ball of mist floated by and she was out of sight. What do you want from me? I cried, my throat parched, my voice hoarse. I stopped, waiting for a sign, waiting for some words to filter through the mist. I heard nothing, saw no signs. But what was it trying to tell me? My concentration broken, my gaze wavering from the spot ahead I had been focusing on, I was startled by the presence of hundreds of seabirds gliding above my head, a heaving, shifting canopy piercing the air with shrill discord.

Perhaps I would see her again if I kept on walking. Perhaps the mist would burn away. I did want to see her. I kept walking.

My interrogation resumed in the afternoon. Officer Pettigrew, for that was his name, waved a video cassette in his hand and asked, "We found this in your apartment," he said.

"Child pornography?" I asked.

"Worse," he said, taking no offence, as he walked over to a corner of the room where pieces of necessary equipment stood perched on a metal trolley. He switched off the single light-bulb illuminating the table and turned on the video.

We speak of a time when the heavens no longer showered pearls in the form of raindrops. And yet, men had all the wealth they needed, all that they really wanted. Nothing was rarer than food for winter, or lovelier than the animals that yielded such food. Moccasins and beads hardly excited anyone. One was a necessity, often lovingly crafted. The other was a plaything, not yet an object of barter. People never searched for anything which cannot be found, never tried to understand things better left as mysteries, or change that which was meant to be. Men never strayed far from the land, or from their women and children. They had no homes. They slept under the blue heavens, sometimes on mats of bulrushes and sometimes on the leaves of trees. Home was where the men happened to be, and the women always were. It was a time, a long time ago, when there was no such thing known to Indians as a people with white skin. Some called it the Age of Innocence; others, less kind, called it an age of hardship.

There are but few who remember those times, for it is not a thing of memory. Remembrance is a thing of the heart, and so many of us have lost ours.

One day, a group of Indians went fishing in the river. They fished until the bottoms of their canoes glistened like so much silver. By the time the sun was in the highest heaven, they had paddled to where the sea widens and tumbles down the edge of the earth. It was here that they saw, at a great distance, something remarkably large. It could be a huge fish, the biggest known to man. Or perhaps a monster from the deep.

The men paddled furiously up the river, spreading the word along the villages on the banks. Before long, the sides of the river became lined, first with women and children, and later with men, young and old, all chattering excitedly about what the fishermen had really seen.

Another boat came swiftly up the river. A young man paddled straight as an arrow and told the people gathered on the riverside that the object was moving in the very direction of the villages. Answering questions as he shot past, he declared the object to be made up of many houses of different colours. At this, the elders grew thoughtful. They huddled together at a central point and, puffing deeply on their yellow copper pipes laden with tobacco, decided that the description suggested the object as being a large canoe in which the great Mannitto himself was riding. They concluded that Mannitto, the Supreme Being, was probably coming to visit them.

Sometime later, the huge canoe lumbered up the mouth of the river and glided to a stop on the southern edge of the island of the Manhadoes. It presented itself to people far and wide, from the green shores of Scheyichbi, already in the shadows, to the forest-covered heights of Ihpetonga radiant in the golden evening sun.

Indeed, Mannitto had come, but not alone. He had come with many slaves, for a great number of men rushed up and down the length of the canoe on mysterious errands. They were all splendidly dressed, all splendidly white. It was only after the Indian chiefs had gathered in a half-circle at the water's edge to welcome Mannitto that the great one, resplendent in a garment of red, appeared in the midst of his men.

A large canoe set out from the shore and stopped alongside Mannitto's. Three of his servants dropped into the canoe before Mannitto also came down the ladder and joined them in the canoe. Marvelling at the rare privilege that had befallen them, the Indians paddled back towards the land, proud and smiling.

As Mannitto and his men clambered ashore, the chiefs quietly joined him in a circle. He saluted the chiefs with a wave of his hand and spoke words they could not understand. But the circle was one of friendship and honour. Mannitto's servants stayed outside of it, although their shining faces seemed to say they too were touched by the warmth that spread through the circle. When Mannitto had finished, the chiefs returned their own salutations.

One of the servants now stepped towards Mannitto and pulled out of his cloak a large flask and a small cup. He uncorked the decanter and poured a clear substance into a cup and handed it to Mannitto. After the Mannitto had drunk from the cup, he had the servant fill it up again, and then he handed it to the chief standing next to him. The chief received the cup, but only sniffed at it before passing it on to the next chief. He did the same. The cup passed through the circle without the contents being tasted by anyone.

"Time for a coffee break," said Pettigrew, rising abruptly from his chair and turning on the light.

Time stands so still in the imagination. I often surprised myself playing with long strings of thought, one thought leading whimsically into the other like the sudden recollection of sailing on a river in Scotland, dredging up a bottle of Perrier I had once tipped over on a glass table at the company president's house in Westmount, Montreal, to the memory of a sudden flash of surprise and amusement at a Robbie Burns birthday bash in Edinburgh where a hopelessly drunk tourist had lifted up my kilt to see what one wore under it. The time it took for this train of images to pass through my mind was a mere few seconds. But I never felt I was being miserly with time in my reveries. Nor did I ever feel guilty of wasting time, given how slowly it moved when I least expected it to.

Now a door clicked open in my memory. Everyone turned to look. It was Professor John Gage stepping out of the projection room at the back of the class. The students began to stir. I recognized a slender woman I remembered seeing somewhere as she stood up and stretched herself, sighing. I wished it was Rosie, but she wasn't. Larry raised his enormous frame like a lumbering elephant and, ambling over to a window, lifted the blinds.

The sun was going down, but there was hardly the riot of colours that one was accustomed to seeing over the bay where every sunset was a feast. A lone aircraft crossed the sky, leaving a slowly dissolving trail of vapour in its wake.

There was silence once more in the room. People looked at each other's faces absent-mindedly. A few stood looking out at the dull grey sunset sky framed by a large window. I remembered it all clearly as I walked up towards Sumburgh Head that weird and desolate morning. Remembered how the echo of the commentator's voice trailed away as the video came to an end. John Gage turned his head away from the window and looked at his class, waiting for the first questions and comments.

Larry was back in his chair laughing, his whole body rocking as he laughed. He was a large man with an infectious laughter and—as I was to discover later—a terrifying scowl. John turned to him with an amused smile. "What's so funny, Larry?" he asked.

"Well," said Larry, "I was thinking of all the movies where the only way to make it out with a woman, virtuous or not, is for someone to fill her up with booze. Seems to me it's a pretty ancient idea. They're screwing us the same way to this day, aren't they?"

Everyone burst out laughing until someone interrupted with the question, "Isn't there a kind of symbolism about the chiefs not drinking the stuff that's being passed around in the cup?"

"No," replied John Gage, his eyes narrowing in thought, "No symbolism at all. The stuff was totally foreign to them."

The class was drawing to a close on a less than serious note. Larry suggested that the aboriginals wouldn't be in their present predicament if only they had a good interpreter or a lawyer like Mr. Rochard or Donald McDonald present at the first meeting.

"I know Donald McDonald, a great friend of the natives, but who's Mr. Rochard?" asked John Gage with a sneer.

Larry replied, "He has taken over where McDonald left off. He's the lawyer who's billing the hell out of our Band Council up north. And they daren't do a thing because Rochard knows all about their own crooked deals."

One of the students nodded thoughtfully and pointed out to the class that had Mr. Rochard been around, he'd make sure Mannitto and the chiefs were still talking.

"Right," agreed a woman's voice, adding, "And still paying the legal bills." Most others in the class felt they had little to say. "Who wants to settle native land claims?" asked Larry, adding, "No one." The note of bitterness in Larry's voice affected them all. They were all natives, aboriginals; they didn't really care what one called them. They were all living under the shadow of the hot, troubled summer, everyone still talking about the March attack on the village of Kanesatake by the

Surete du Quebec, during which one of their officers died. Each side blamed the other for the officer's death. To me it didn't seem to matter whose bullet hit him, now that the man was dead.

All summer there were barricades by Mohawks that shut off access to Montreal through the Mercier Bridge. Whites burned the Indians in effigy, stoned their cars. During mid-August, twenty five hundred soldiers from the Canadian army moved into place opposite the barricades at Oka. Night after night, the blinding television lights sent chills through a happy, contented nation as they saw Canadian soldiers and masked Mohawk warriors, both fully armed, standing nose to nose in the woods, trading curses with each other. Many feared they could be safe no longer. Thousands rushed out to buy guns with which to defend their women and children against the impending calamity of Indians on the rampage.

Thanks to those days of frustration and anxiety, my 'education' had all but ground to a halt. This meeting with Larry in John Gage's class was my first since my visit to Chisasibi in May. During all that time, I hadn't seen Rosie even once. I missed our earlier conversations in Chisasibi almost as much as I missed Rosie. But this didn't bother me, even though I had been feeling a great deal of uneasiness and unhappiness since my last trip north with Pierre. My heart was telling me to take sides in the debate between the natives and the rest of the country, while my mind was warning me about the futility of it all. Besides, was it really my business—me, a passing visitor from Scotland whose only connection with Quebec was a job?

Luckily, Pierre himself — whose political zeal I found insufferable at times — seemed far less enthusiastic than before about the brilliance of Mr. Bourassa, the premier of Quebec's vision for the natives and for Quebec. On the other hand, I simply couldn't understand the unspeakable fury of the Mohawk warriors. It was in an effort to rid myself of some of this unease that I agreed to see the video John had booked for his class.

The Mohawk barricades came down early in September. But John Gage assured me, as we drove up for a visit to Oka after class, that the wounds would never heal. John thought I would find the visit useful — educational, as he put it.

"How come I didn't see Rosie in your class today?" I finally asked John Gage. It was the beginning of term at the university and I was hoping Rosie hadn't dropped out. My question took a lot of courage to ask, I still don't know why. Even as I spoke the words I felt my face turning red.

"She had to go back to Chisasibi," explained John. "Substitute teaching. The school's going through a crisis. Many teachers have become violently ill. I think it's the fish, and it's the fish that's going to make them extinct eventually," he added.

The lush, wooded approach to Oka belied the ugly violence that sputtered within the community for months, waiting for that single miscalculation that would set the place on fire. From the very beginning, John's friend and former student Barry had taken a firm stand against any talk of violence. For weeks he had gone from one barricade to the other, counselling patience, getting together support groups for those whose nerves were at an edge. So much so, that they had nicknamed him Gandhi.

Barry had argued: Why raise the Warrior flag? There's no future in it. Look how hard they hit the aboriginals at Aquasasne. What did they gain? Nothing. The only thing this country owes each one of us is a grave. That too may be hard to come by some day.

Barry was an artist, earning a modest salary as an illustrator for aboriginal school textbooks. The exhibitions, sometimes they brought him some money, very little at other times. He thought he had correctly argued, to himself at least, that he ought to take no part in any act of destruction. Walking now with John and me along the fringes of the quiet golf course, Barry suddenly stopped. Pointing in the direction of a row of towering pine trees, he said, "I was standing there beside a half dozen Mohawk Warriors. From the sound of the army vehicles, I could've sworn they were coming to kill us. When I saw the first column of armoured cars swing past those pine trees towards the village I stepped back and picked up a rifle without a moment's hesitation. I didn't regret it then, but I do now. I'm filled with remorse over every moment that the rifle rested in my shaking, sweating hands."

There were tears in Barry's eyes. I felt confused. John Gage, who had tremendous respect for Barry, put his arm round his shoulder.

Barry continued, "We were such a good community here. White Francophone families living side by side with us for years. Now their eyes seem to follow me everywhere. They follow me into the store, into the post office, everywhere. The whole town is sore at the troublemaking longhairs. And all over a stupid golf course."

"These trees seem to have been hacked down recently," I remarked, pointing to some stumps in front of us. Remembering my last trip up north, I wondered if these trees too—old and mature—had gone to the lumber mills.

"Yes," answered Barry, "the Surete took care to cut down some of the trees where their bullets had lodged the day they attacked us and said we had murdered one of their officers. The trees had bullet holes in them, they were evidence of how low they were firing, evidence pointing to the possibility that their own fire may've killed Lemay. Of course, the thinning out of the trees was explained as a strategy decision, purely defensive. You can't imagine what they've done to this forest. Gets worse as you move closer to the lake."

Sounding somewhat sentimental, John Gage said, "The land's so beautiful, Barry, that one is driven to possess it. Some of us would probably like to see the whole country transformed into a golf course, all the way from Vancouver to Halifax."

"But there's enough here for everybody," replied Barry. "Nature didn't intend to confine us to narrow, rectangular sections, drawn by municipalities."

We kept walking silently until we found ourselves back in Barry's house, a weathered clapboard cottage crying out for a coat of paint. "Let me make you some coffee," he said. "I can't offer you anything else because I have no money." Barry seemed to wait, to note the reaction in his guests, and then continued, "I found I just couldn't work, so I gave it up. At home, I became terrified of the phone ringing, of newspapers wanting to talk, cameramen wanting to shoot, even my own people visiting. When they came to speak to me, to pass on information about what other communities were doing, to strengthen the network as it were, I began to recoil within myself. They left me empty and exhausted. It seemed they were ripping something out of me, taking it away for themselves. I began to break out in cold sweats for no obvious reason. Most of all, I felt ashamed of myself for having picked up the gun. You see, I had little choice but to turn to my saviour, the bottle. And now I hate that too."

On the wall, there were some of Barry's paintings—mostly aboriginal faces. Having grown up with painted faces decorating the walls of my home, I actually felt drawn to some of the portraits. "You wouldn't be interested in selling some of these paintings, would you?" I asked.

Barry looked at me, surprised, and—as is usual with me after the event—I regretted having asked the question. Perhaps Barry thought I was feeling sorry for him. But he let me off the hook quickly.

"None of these are in a really finished state," he said. "You wouldn't really want them."

John Gage hugged Barry before we left. "Take good care of yourself, Barry," he said.

Barry seemed genuinely touched by the visit. "I will," he replied. "I just wanted to put you in the picture."

I asked John, on the drive back, why he hadn't offered Barry any money. To me, it seemed that was one of the things Barry was perhaps reaching out for.

"That's the last thing I'd want to do for him," said John. "We see so many aboriginals hanging around like beggars that we think that's all they need. We keep drumming the image into them. One of our Prime Ministers once said: 'They are simply living on the benevolence and charity of the Canadian Parliament and, as the old adage says, beggars should not be choosers.' Decades later, another Macdonald, a swaggering Rhodes scholar to boot, authored a complicated document on aboriginal land rights that showed the same disdain, the same Machiavellian contempt of Prime Minister Macdonald."

John went on, "But that's precisely the point. They're not beggars. And rightfully, they've got to be choosers. What I'm trying to say is that only Barry can straighten himself out."

"With all these Macdonalds charging around Canada," I asked somewhat ruefully, "are you wanting me to apologize for my Scottish origins?"

"That could be an interesting classroom discussion, Charlie," replied John. "We were all land-based creatures once. Trouble began with a few people—you could count them on the fingers of one hand—a few people born, destined I should say, to sail the seas, searching for elusive, far-away lands, wanting to conquer and impose their wills on others. Who knows what really moved them. They all came with good intentions, and left behind dreams that others have rearranged and embellished, and nightmares that'll be with us forever."

"Here we go," I thought to myself, with a sense of amusement, "It's maps that started it all. Now he will really start to torment me." It took me a while to think of what to say for I really didn't want to sound pompous or embarrassed. Finally, I said, "You've got me with a double whammy. My father worked most of his life for a firm of map-makers. And my great grandfather probably wouldn't have survived as a child without the help of a Cree woman. How do you expect I'm supposed to feel after what you've inflicted on me today, your contempt for Macdonalds?"

John started to laugh. "There seems to be a new side of you I knew nothing about," he said. "What's this about a Cree woman in your great grandfather's life? This is an absolutely brilliant revelation. We must investigate, no, celebrate. I think I'll get my whole class to your apartment for our Christmas party, and a formal initiation. You'll love it."

Then I began to tell him things I hadn't told him about Isabel Gunn earlier. "I guess I didn't tell you everything about her the last time we talked," I found myself apologizing. "She lived a while in Canada, went to work with the Hudson's Bay Company. Moose Factory, Rupert House, outposts along James Bay. The year was eighteen hundred and six or seven. My father said there was an Indian woman, someone like a witch-doctor or a shaman, who looked after Isabel and her son until they finally returned to the Orkneys. The Indians thought Isabel was a shaman too."

"That's a bit odd," said John. "I didn't think the Hudson's Bay Company contracted with women to work, certainly not in the nineteenth century. The British traders had no British women, generally speaking. Except for the governor or the officer-in-charge of the coastal factory or post, chastity was the law of the land. The governor could have a local Indian for a bedfellow. She and possibly her family then became permanent residents of the post. Mind you, other officers were permitted to entertain a lady in their apartments, mixed-blood ladies perhaps and aboriginals, but never overnight. Servants were expected not to get involved in liaisons. But the best laid plans of mice and men ..... there was a lot of venereal disease among the servants. Mind you, in such cases the patient was required to pay a month's wages to the surgeon. But I digress."

"The truth is," I pointed out slowly, "that Isabel Gunn went to the Hudson's Bay disguised as a man."

John looked astounded. "You're kidding," he said finally.

I was glad of the interruption because it stopped me from repeating details about her saintly reputation, her magical powers of sex change, and her miraculous conception. On a different note, I continued, "No, that's the truth. She returned to the Orkneys with her son and lies buried somewhere in the town of Kirkwall."

"This is fascinating," murmured John. Then he asked, "Do you mind if I make some enquiries on your behalf?"

"No, no, not at all," I replied quickly. "For months I've been trying to work up enough courage to ask you to do just that. We have a picture of her in London, and very little else. But I know my father would love to hear more. So would I."

John Gage had a friend from college who worked in the Hudson's Bay archives in Winnipeg. Fired with excitement, he promised to send him a note. But he was even more enthusiastic and determined about the need to rejoice in my new-found connection with the Cree.

Pettigrew returned with two coffees, and even put down at the center of the table a box of Tim Hortons donuts, These smelled really fresh.

"So, what was the point of the video?" he asked. "Is that the way you feel about white Canadians?'

"Of course, not," I replied. "The video was on loan from a college professor, a white Canadian at that."

"Hm," he said, and lapsed into silence.

Pettigrew let me return to my apartment that afternoon. He almost seemed friendly as he shook my hand. "We might call you again, he said," as a parting shot.

Alone in my bed that night, I found myself once more on the cliffs overlooking the wretched ship. The mist didn't roll over or burn away. Instead, I found myself standing still in what seemed like the centre of a storm. The mist twisted and turned around me, covering me with brushstrokes of brightness and shadows. Flocks of birds soared above my head, wheeling and tumbling in the wind, crying without a pause. I stood still in the middle of it all, wondering where I was, where I would be. I could feel the tautness in my face, my throat was dry. What would I be doing if I were in Montreal, in London, in Stromness? It was as if my thoughts were raking the furrows in my brain, searching for something, something irretrievably lost. Suddenly, I began to feel troubled by the words from a once-familiar poem that I simply couldn't remember. But I had to remember. My mother loved the poem so, and I had often read it aloud for her. How could I forget?

All I could remember was a few words, a tiny fragment to go by:

". . . . . the gale then wafts me from thee, dear shore!"

How odd! The gale, from thee, dear shore. There were times when the words suggested a sense of terror in the face of mysterious, unfathomable forces; at other times they had filled me with joy as I broke free from invisible chains that confined me to stifling moments at work which held no purpose, no meaning, and where it was always dark. Was I finally standing along the path that would set me free? Even as I was happy at having taken charge of my life, I felt a numbing fear as I contemplated the parting that seemed near. Was this what I was setting out for when I parked my car at the bottom of the hill? Was it the end the ghostly figure in the patchwork cape was leading me to? Why was she tormenting me? Why was she set on punishing me? I had done nothing to her. I had done nothing to reject her memory and all that she stood for, even in my most terrible moments. May be, that was it. I had done . . . . . nothing.

My mind continued to reach out for the poem, for the words that seemed beyond my entreaties. I imagined the forgotten words would have precisely mirrored my mood and the sea's, even though the wind was suddenly quieter as was the sea. But where did the words, where did the lines, begin? Where did they end? I felt annoyed and frustrated by my forgetfulness. I had loved the poem once. Now it was lost in some obscure corner of my mind, restless haunt to faces that called out to me in my dreams and vanished upon my waking. A dull pain began to creep through my heart. Then it flashed through my mind and I remembered, just a little. Perhaps the next lines were:

"It rustles, and whistles — I'll never see thee more!"

Perhaps they were, perhaps they weren't. The words 'never' and 'more' deepened my distracted, troubled mood. Other words floated through my mind — 'nevermore', 'forlorn'. I felt a kinship with the words. They allowed my thoughts to digress briefly. I felt a faint smile light up my lips as I asked myself, pushing the kinship of words a little further, "Do I wake or sleep?" But the earlier lines of the poem eluded me still.

I looked up from my thoughts and discovered that the figure I had been following all this while had disappeared. It was as if the vision had returned to the mist from where it had come. As I stood to rest at the top of the hill, the kaleidoscope of faces, their soft murmurs pieced together in a strange chorus of farewells and welcomes, played peek-a-boo in my head. I looked down at the waters below and found myself immersed under the waves, spellbound by the play of pale, shimmering light and shadows I remembered from my snorkelling days in Scapa Flow and the more recent and terrible experience at James Bay. There was something special about the silent ships lying at the bottom of Scapa Flow, and the ghostly figures trimmed with seaweed and sudden groans and whispers that have haunted me relentlessly. They were the stuff of my childhood dreams and the unspeakable nightmares of later years.

I was no stranger to ships lost at sea. I had lived close to the water most of my life, had seen many rusting hulls. At other times, I might have looked quite dispassionately at the broken ship that lay in the waters below. But this one was different. It evoked a touch of sentiment, because I now knew its every secret, its every nook and corner. The almost invisible wreck belonged to the *Braer*[1], trapped in the congealing amber of a deadly brew of oil and water. It seemed only

---

[1] Early morning on Tuesday 5 January 1993, Lerwick (Shetlands Island) coastguard were advised that the tanker, the *Braer*, en route from Bergen in Norway to Quebec in Canada, laden with 85,000 tonnes of Norwegian Gullfaks crude oil, had lost engine power but was in no immediate danger. Her estimated position then was 10 miles (19 km) south of Sumburgh Head and she was drifting in predominantly southwesterly winds of force 10-11. Then the ship broke apart.

the night before when she was lashed by adders of the deep, riveted to the rocks, pounded by waves, and made to pay with her blood of black gold. Now the ship lay as still as the morning, and the land, the sea, and the air wrapped it, and me, in a floating, dream-like state which made me afraid to breathe, in case a breath blew the dream away.

What would it be like for the barnacled hull a year from now, ten years from now, a hundred thousand years later? Would it be a refuge for fish and a mansion for those lost at sea? Would I perhaps be one of its inhabitants, peering from time to time, unseen, into the eyes of curious divers and hungry predators? There lay the ship, like a dying bear in a leg-hold trap, jammed into a deadly bed of rocks hidden by the tide, a shattered mass of metal waiting for the next wave, the next storm, to tear it apart into little pieces that would someday crumble into sand and oblivion.

The wreck of the tanker lay three hundred feet below the edge of the cliff. I had of course seen it many times before. Today, my interest in the broken ship held undertones of nostalgia and regret. I breathed deeply and glanced at the lighthouse to my left, blinking and flashing its beacon intermittently.

I stood at the edge of the bluff and considered the stones and pebbles scattered along the cliff-lined shore. The occasional wave, slightly stronger than the others, brushed over them with a grey froth and swirled ahead to lift a lazy tongue and lick the salt off the jagged cliff walls, then retreating with a prolonged sigh. I looked at the pebbles and saw myself growing smaller and smaller until I was very small, as common as the rest of them. It felt like a slow metamorphosis of sorts, and I felt good about it. I had after all never harboured any illusions about myself.

From my vantage on top of the hill, I now imagined myself to be one with the pebbles until it occurred to me that I was perhaps even more insignificant, definitely more inconsequential, and no more than a pinprick in the seamless fabric of land and sea stretching in front of me, woven and unravelled continually by a hundred Penelopes—with some help from God—waiting for the improbable end to Ulysses's and Man's eternal voyage.

As for my affinity with ships, they had always flitted through my dreams like butterflies ever since I was a child. I loved ships that challenged the whims of wind and water, but now I could feel a new kinship with the soon to be forgotten cusp of the doomed bow that jutted delicately and unobtrusively at high tide over the waters off the southern tip of the Shetlands. Once a mammoth sprawling ship. Now next to nothing. Is that where I would be? Is that what I would be?

A sudden surge of loneliness came back to me. Where had the song gone? Where had the misty vision disappeared? Even the birds appeared to have quietened down and returned to their craggy aerie. And then I saw a solitary bird in the sky, where earlier I had seen thousands. One single bird flapping its wings against the backdrop of a vast universe spread all around. There was such an air of desperation surrounding the bird that tears rose in my eyes. It seemed to be going nowhere, it seemed to have nowhere to go. The power, the grace, the grandeur, the fury of thousands of birds clamouring in the air, was that simply make-believe, an illusion, a part of the dream?

The information arrived before the party. One evening, John buzzed unexpectedly on the intercom and walked into my apartment, triumphantly waving a sheaf of papers in his hand. Throwing the papers down on the dining table, he said, "Charlie, my boy, she was quite a woman!"

I was beside myself with excitement. She was real, after all, I thought as I read the archival excerpts one by one. As John and I pieced the story together, the Hudson's Bay ship, *The Prince of Wales*, under Captain Henry Hanwell, a very experienced seaman, set sail from Stromness on June 29, 1806, carrying fresh provisions and a complement of men recruited by David Geddes, the Company's agent in the Orkneys. Listed among the passengers were a John Scarth from the Parish of Firth and a John Fubbister from the Parish of St. Andrews near Kirkwall. They were both headed for Albany Factory in James Bay under three-year contracts. Scarth, clearly an old and experienced hand, was to be paid 32 pounds a year; Fubbister, a more modest beginner's wages of 8 pounds a year.

The Prince of Wales dropped anchor at Moose Factory in late August. Travelling by shallop to Albany, Fubbister and Scarth arrived at their destination on August 27. Early in September, John Hodgson, the Chief at Albany, sent a party of three including Fubbister and Scarth up the Albany River to Henley House with trade goods and other provisions. The following summer, Scarth and Fubbister's team made several trips up and down the Albany River carrying provisions and furs. Later that year, Fubbister went with one of the brigades to the post at Pembina which was in charge of a certain Hugh Haney.

On the morning of December 29, 1807, one of Mr. Haney's Orkney recruits, feeling rather unwell, asked to be allowed to remain briefly in the house of another Hudson's Bay officer, Alexander Henry. From Mr. Haney's diary came priceless nuggets of this astounding story: 'I was surprised at the fellow's demand; however, I told him to sit down and warm himself. I returned to my own room, where I had not been long before he sent one of my people, requesting the favour of speaking with me. Accordingly I stepped down to him, and was much surprised to find him extended on the hearth, uttering dreadful lamentations; he stretched out his hand toward me, and in piteous tones begged to me to be kind to a poor, helpless, abandoned wretch, who was not of the sex I had supposed, but an unfortunate Orkney girl, pregnant, and actually in childbirth. In saying this, she opened her jacket, and displayed a pair of beautiful, round, white breasts; she further informed me of the circumstances that had brought her into this state. The man who had debauched her in the Orkneys, two years ago, was wintering at Grandes Fourches, an outpost on the Red River. In about an hour she was safely delivered of a fine boy, and that same day she was conveyed home in my cariole, where she soon recovered.'

Other documents revealed other details. The first direct mention of Isabel Gunn was in the List of Men's Accounts at Albany Fort in the year 1808. Company records suggested that John Scarth was stationed in

Martin Falls at this time. William Harper, a schoolmaster recruited to teach in Albany, wrote on September 5, 1808, to his patron the Lord of Skaill, William Watt of Breckness: 'I have to inform your Honr. that we have got an Orkney woman here, she came out for the sake of a Sweetheart, but as it happened he had agreed for East Main and she for Albany. She has been inland 1,500 Miles & has had a Child to one of the men that was in Company with her, & was never known to be a Woman till the very hour she was Delivered, & then she went to a Canadian house that was near by, & asked the Master for a private room, which he granted, & in a few minutes he was alarmed at hearing the cry of a young Child. She is now at the Factory & her Child, & her chief employment Is washing for all hands, which indeed she is no Witch at, as I think, as she has been washing for me. The Governor intends to make her a nurse for the Scholars, as she seems not inclined to go home & I believe he feels more for her misfortune than she is sensible of doing herself.'

A final piece of information: 'Isabella Gun and her Son embarked on *The Prince of Wales* from Albany on September 20, 1809, Captain Henry Hanwell bringing his ship into Stromness Harbour on October 29, 1809.'

I felt compelled to cover my face with both hands and sit in silence. John Gage threw his hands over his head in an expression of his amazement. "I don't know which of the two diaries is more believable," he said. "I have a feeling both may be guilty of serious embellishments."

"Why write 'the man who debauched her in the Orkneys two years ago'?" I finally asked. John Gage said nothing.

Later that evening, I told John about an article in the *Orcadian*, the Stromness newspaper, which suggested that one David Spence was the father of the boy. The papers from Winnipeg did point to a David Spence who was on a trip with Fubbister and died on the way to Pembina. I remembered the poet Mackay Brown quoting from the 'ballad' which described how John Scarth, summoned to see his cousin, set down a purse of coins beside her bed and left. Apparently, Isabel never saw him again. "Cousin?" I asked incredulously. "Who's one to believe?"

"It's interesting, though not surprising," said John, "that the Company records say nothing about the native woman you mentioned."

I remained silent. Gradually, the earlier exuberance wore off. I felt exhausted, and still troubled. Over the next few days, I sensed a gradual change come over me. Deep inside, some bonds began to loosen, some unknown instincts began to make their presence felt. The image of Isabel Gunn, so delicately shaped and protected by the family, seemed to have suffered some change in the course of a single evening. I couldn't make up my mind whether I was glad or disappointed, because of a nagging doubt which wouldn't go away. I felt I had failed to grasp the truth.

It was with these mixed emotions that I faced the prospect of a Christmas party to celebrate my Cree 'connection'. John Gage's boundless enthusiasm and the charm and energy of his students made it so that I didn't have to lift a finger. Some of the students had already gone home, so that there were no more than a dozen left in and around Montreal. These, their friends, and one professor were expected to gather in my apartment.

I was surprised John hadn't come with his partner. He explained, "Oh! it's not going too well." With that, he turned his attention to other things.

I was half hoping I might see Rosie again. But I suppressed a strong desire to ask anyone whether she was coming or not. Finally, Rosie showed up. She was among the last to come. I felt a charge of youthful joy as I opened the door to her. But my earlier sense of insecurity returned as soon as I saw Larry walk in behind her.

Everyone was having a good time. There was lots to eat and drink. The circle of lights outside, stretching all the way to the Cartier Bridge, left the guests breathless. Except for John, everyone else was a first-time visitor to the apartment. None of the students could ever imagine climbing the economic ladder that permitted someone like me to afford all this. From time to time, they would open the large windows overlooking the pier and Rue de la Commune below and blow kisses at the tourists and the elegant party-goers who still strolled around, in spite of the cold. One of the students asked, "Why is it that others must desire some of the nicest things one acquires?"

As usual, Larry was equal to the occasion. Loudly, he replied, "We natives are supposed to be above it all — no desires, no acquisitions, even the residential schools weren't supposed to change that." Then, turning to me, he added, "But we know why Charlie really came to Chisasibi. He wanted to make sure these marvellous lights would never go out, that the source of all this power was well insured, and that the Cree weren't a credible risk to Quebec's prosperity."

"Stop ragging on your host," said John Gage, and started his own explanation. "Charlie is here," he began, stopping to look at me, perhaps seeking some encouragement to go on, "because he actually has strong Cree connections." John's face broke into a warm smile, while I felt alarmed, and confused.

The initial stunned silence was broken by a round of shouts and applause and a demand from everyone for more details. John gave them an outline without elaborating on the circumstances surrounding the birth of my great grandfather. Then he invited me to tell everyone in my own words about Kechechowieh.

I forced myself to speak. "I haven't really found the connection yet," I said, "except that a Cree woman named Kechechowieh apparently took great care of my great great-grandmother and her son when my great-grandfather was born. She was with them in Albany Fort, and later in Eastmain or Fort George. I wish I could tell you more, but it all happened nearly two hundred years ago."

One of the students from James Bay said, "If anyone can help you track her down, it's got to be Rosie's father."

Everyone turned to look at Rosie. Suddenly the centre of everyone's gaze, she blushed violently. "Sure, she said, "I'll be glad to ask Louis."

I hadn't paid much attention to Rosie all evening, after that initial encounter at the door. Dressed simply in blue, she looked absolutely stunning, filling me with a curious sense of reckless abandon I had rarely experienced before. Ah! but what's the use, I thought.

But wine works wonders. Later in the evening, I suddenly found Larry standing alone near the window, thoughtful, staring outside. "How come you're not looking after your girl-friend?" I asked him half seriously.

"Look after who?" asked Larry, startled.

"Rosie."

"Rosie?" Larry yelled loudly. Laughing, he turned from the window and planted his can of ginger ale firmly on the dinner table. "Hey Rosie," he shouted across the room, "come here, quickly. Quick."

Larry continued to shake with laughter as Rosie walked over.

"Hey, listen everybody," he cried, picking Rosie easily off the ground in both arms. "Charlie thinks Rosie is my girl-friend."

Everyone roared with laughter. I felt my head drooping in shame and embarrassment. I looked around desperately for a place to hide myself. This wasn't the way I had intended to get my facts straightened. In the end, I joined in the laughter. What else could I do? It was as if divine grace had quickly shown me a way out.

"How was I to know?" I asked. "I just thought it odd that Rosie sitting by herself and Larry lecturing on electricity like a philosopher."

"Rosie is everybody's sister, including mine," said Larry, as he let her down.

Equally embarrassed, Rosie quickly walked over to me. "Please don't take any notice of him," she said, sounding apologetic. "Larry is such a ham sometimes. "

I think I muttered something incoherent and just shook my head. Moments later, after Rosie had gone back to her chair, Larry said to me, "I'm sorry, I didn't mean to embarrass you. It seemed so funny because no one would've asked me that. I'm getting married next month."

I grasped Larry's hand in mine. "How wonderful," I said. "Congratulations."

Larry smiled and said, "Thanks." Then he turned and looked thoughtfully at Rosie. She too was looking at us from across the room. "Everybody wants Rosie," said Larry, under his breath, "but no one can have her."

"It's okay," I said. Then, catching sight of his glass of soda, I asked, "Why don't you have a glass of wine, Larry?" Adding, lamely, "Good for the heart."

With a wave of his hand, Larry replied, "Can't take it any more. I've had my fill of booze, drugs, you name it. But not any more. I was on the verge of killing myself. Now I want to live."

We are not so different from one another after all. I was amazed how my own thoughts mimicked some of Larry's. Who could tell who was mimicking me this very moment?

I was trapped in my dream. Pity, it wasn't an untroubled dream. My heart ached to see the visions that had ruled my life, longed for one more brush with the apparition of Isabel Gunn, for just one glimpse of my mother's face. What did they want of me this time around?

My thoughts were riddled with a babble of many voices, real voices, voiced by voices other than my own, strange voices Louis Bearskin, the ever-tormented Cree Indian, had taught me to pluck out of the air. Only a short while ago, before I stepped out of my car, I was more certain of my own voice, my own thoughts. I had proposed to die, and dying, I imagined myself being transported to another life, one immediately beyond and infinitely more full of hope than the present I was preparing to abandon. There were moments when I even felt a certain excitement at the thought of death. It was the other voices that were sowing confusion in my mind. The Cree was still playing tricks with me. The last real Indian. Or was he? What was the hypnotic quality that always seemed to lace the Indian's voice?

On the day we found Pierre's body, I ran into Louis Bearskin in the evening and told him of our discovery. As we stood on a barren headland and contemplated the icy horizon where, he would have me believe, Captain Henry Hudson still lurked in a boat with his doomed companions, still searching for the westward passage they never found, Louis simply said: "The absurdity of certain deaths is a secret between man and his God."

As I thrust my mind, with a child-like curiosity rather than the hardened detachment of the fortune-teller, towards the gaping hole of time that lay ahead — Isabel and my mother would probably have called it eternity — I realized what little difference I would make one way or the other, dead or alive. And yet, it pained me to recognize that, alive, I had not made the slightest difference, that being alive, I could make little difference to anything but myself. No, I could not accept this even if it were the truth . No. No. No. No. Walls of refusal on every side enclosing my own little sphere of refusal in the centre. Surely, there had to be some virtue in saying yes to someone — for at least a flicker of hope, if not lasting satisfaction. Such were my thoughts, as I gave in to the temptation to clutch at this solitary straw of redemption. It was my only hope of believing that I at least was perhaps not — as I have heard people say — a problem which needed to be solved. And, until this moment, what a terrible solution I had willed my problem.

I think I've tried hard to remain a decent human being. Except for the occasional bout of madness and rage, I believe I have succeeded reasonably well. Now, if only I could be certain of leaving behind a corner of the world where children did not cry from endless hunger, where it was forbidden to build palaces until not one person ever froze to death on wintry sidewalks. Of course, I realized I was being foolish and sentimental. It would be like scooping up a bucketful of sand from the beach; come the next wave, and it was as if not a speck of sand had moved in a million years. How many bucketfuls of sand would it take to make a difference? I wonder. A passing thought, for I was swiftly mocked by an unknown voice for my vain presumptuousness. Ah! those voices.

They all seemed to be crowding into my mind in my final hours, all the people I had ever known, ever met. Family and friend, saint and sinner, the wise and the hypocrite, each jostling the other to be heard, to be seen. Each drew me into their secret world for a brief tryst, releasing me with a burden of pain and sadness which grew heavier with every encounter. I closed my eyes in an attempt to shut out the pictures that formed and vanished like flashing dolphins on the still mirror-like surface of the sea in front of me. There was Rosie. Her eyes were like black pearls studded with a single tiny diamond. Perhaps she was really the last Indian, after all. And my mother, she clutched a book of poems by her heart. Malcolm Gunn, my father, pored over a burning map without once lifting his eyes to me. And, seemingly without any reason, there appeared Pegleg Sam—whom I had last seen in another recent dream—who had had his leg chopped off in Chicoutimi to save it from gangrene, idly tapping a pipe against his stump and smiling spitefully in my direction. And the sea became red, the sky was full of smoke, and the wind carried the screams of those falling, falling endlessly as my mother had led me to believe, through the black hole of eternity.

But where was Isabel Gunn, whose song had drawn me to the ruined crofter's cottage, whose will o' the wisp image I had followed to the edge of the cliff?

I could draw little comfort from the vaguely luminous pageant passing before my eyes. I wasn't sure if I myself wasn't a captive, an unsuspecting prisoner, and felt a pang of remorse at the easy escape I had planned for myself. I had caught myself cheating. Was I making a fool of myself? The voices taunted me, mocked me. Rarely had I experienced thoughts so intense and troublesome. But then, wasn't this what they would call my moment of truth? For I was ready to die. Sadly, the excitement, the sense of adventure, had vanished. Now I was beginning to feel afraid. Now it seemed I had lost my nerve.

Slowly, I turned my back to the sea and was amazed at the miles of crofting land that rolled up and down and disappeared into the horizon to the north and west. As I looked away from the perilous edges which fell abruptly into the sea, my thoughts moved from the void in which I would have no part to play back to a past where hundreds of men and women had toiled to reclaim a naked desolation back from nature. Through rain and storm, death and birth, they had fashioned for the earth a green coat, lovingly patched and stitched together over hundreds of years. My death promised to be a pitiful rejection of everything they had done. Would I turn my back on all this? Could I?

Suddenly I found my courage and my voice once more. "Enough," I cried, from the edge of Sumburgh Head. I know my voice was harsh and fearful. I know I uttered a sound that was laced with terror and sorrow and it resounded as far away as Garths Ness and Fitful Head. I hope no one heard me in my moment of shame. Five hundred kittiwakes sprang out of their clifftop nests and soared in alarm over the Atlantic. Five hundred kittiwakes silenced the flutter of their wings and froze against the sky, as the mist shimmered to the ground like a silken dress and the vision appeared once more on the cliff. And her song of lament rose and fell in the wind once more. As the sound of her voice died away, I slowly found some of my normal composure. The sea had been changing colours by the minute. Now it finally settled before my eyes like a sheet of beaten silver, occasionally pierced by burnished skails closer to the shore. A great sense of relief swept through me.

A soft, rising wind wove delicate patterns through my hair. Its touch brought me back to the present. But my life was spread out like a map across the face of the sea. There I saw two unequal stretches of my life, each begging to be understood. On one side was a period of thirty years ending with the death of my parents, my father's shortly before last Christmas. On the other, a mere six months of life with Rosie which had left me full of grief, bitter, and unfulfilled. I had drifted naively, unquestioningly, through these and other salients, some reflecting the drudgery of living, others the drudgery of work, until I found myself on the edge of this cliff in the Shetlands. I was finally face to face with some questions that would no longer accept cheap, evasive replies. On Sumburgh Head, it was as if I had been caught in a roost off the giant headlands where windborn waves crash into tidal currents like a meeting of two angry beasts. There was nowhere for me to turn. On Sumburgh Head, I came face to face with myself. I realized there was nowhere for me to turn but to myself. All my romantic notions of being one, spiritually, with Isabel Gunn and my mother had suddenly vanished into thin air. I still had a little left to do. Perhaps it would've been simpler for me to say goodbye if only I could be certain of meeting Rosie at the end of the road. But walls had sprung up between us in life — walls thought to be impregnable by many caught like me on one side or the other. How could I be certain that death dissolved such walls as surely as walls of skin and bone that shape the human body?

I had been so naive in the past. On this day, I was a somewhat different man from the day back in nineteen eighty eight, for instance, when I read a newspaper column about my great-great-grandmother. I had never seen her, of course. But she had been a constant presence in my life as she had been in my father's, and maybe my father's father too. Everyone spoke of her in hushed tones, invoking her name before making important decisions, seeking her intercession in improbable undertakings. Yet, she had caused me much pain, torn my soul apart time and again. Why, I do not know. It will forever remain a mystery.

"Look at you," Sven said to me. "What's come upon you?"

Sven had seen through me, my six-foot frame, and what my mother described to her friends as my lanky, boyish features, and my shock of light-brown hair tumbling irrepressibly over my forehead. I had overheard her words many years ago, and it amused me to think how others noticed details that one glossed over, ignoring those that one felt important.

I wouldn't have thought I looked troubled. I saw the same face in the mirror that I had seen for years. No changes, no lines, no blemishes. I doubt if anyone suspected anything at work, where I had been swept from one success to the other during these four years — a scholar among marine underwriters, a darling of shipowners, in the words of others. But deep inside, there had always been this growing harvest of dissatisfaction, distraction, and uncertainty.

The night before my fateful walk to Sumburgh Head, nobody would have guessed that I might be in need of help. During the night, I was one with a crowd of hundreds in Lerwick that watched an army of flaming torches come down the hill, like slowly moving streams of molten rock. The men, happily drunk and polite, at peace with one another, held up the torches high above their heads and marched to the rhythm of songs that were at first unintelligible to me from a distance. The air of mystery and quaintness deepened further when the marchers came in front of the row of houses bordering a dishevelled bowling green. The houses began to look haunted and forbidding in the eerie glow, seemingly abandoned by their inhabitants. In the middle of the two rows of torch bearers, a serpent-headed galley moved slowly, lusty make-believe Viking warriors and a young, bespectacled boy on deck. *Up-Helly-Aa*, the annual festival of the Shetlands, had begun.

I was not alone. My companion, Sven, had known me from my first place of work with a Norwegian company on London's Fenchurch Street. We had been good friends ever since. Huddled inside our substantial parkas, we watched in silence as sections of the marchers passed us with rousing choruses of Scottish and English songs. I tried to join in the singing, but the night was cold and my teeth began to chatter.

"Let's go for a drink, Charlie," suggested Sven. "Six years in Hong Kong and I can't seem to take this cold any more. My Norwegian bones are clattering like windows in a storm." As usual. Sven's invitation came with an expected admonition — not from Sven, but from a voice within which some might have considered my conscience, but which I knew to be the ever-prodding myth and memory of Isabel Gunn. How many drinks would you consider proper this time, Charlie Gunn? asked the voice.

The voice had spooked me repeatedly during the ten days we had spent in Lerwick enduring interminable meetings of various insurance companies arguing over the fate of the hull and cargo of the *Braer*. It had turned out to be a messy affair with accusations and innuendos flying across the table. I would have to admit that it was this stern, uncompromising voice within that had unfailingly made it easy for me to assume difficult positions, to say no. You're not going to turn agin your own folk, Charlie Gunn, are you? the voice taunted me.

The islanders hated us, the insurance reps, almost as much as they despised the reporters and the TV crews. But I felt good about my difficult role — goaded by the voice — to the point where many executives questioned whose side I was on, whether my loyalties lay with the industry or the scumbag claimants.

But I had seen the *Braer* crack open, seen birds soaked in oil wash ashore on the beaches, seen crofters' fields drenched with slime. In the end, I had heeded the voice in my head, not the interests of my bosses, and I felt good about it. Still, my heroism wasn't without its price. I realized how unpalatable all the media attention and the bickering over money was to the Shetlanders, and my sense of brotherhood with them bred an inevitable sense of despair about the confused state of my mind. The islanders worried that visitors would stay away from the Shetlands, and I worried over whether I shouldn't walk away from it all — my profession, my job, and the daily skirmishes with my conscience which the pervasive presence of Isabel Gunn constantly provoked in my mind.

Sven and I suffered through the meetings, endless 'happy hours' in pubs during which we were pushing away brown-paper envelopes thrust in our way by shipowners' agents. We stayed back an extra two days simply for *Up-Helly-Aa*. I said to Sven, "We can't go. The best is yet to come." No sooner had I said the words, I felt that, for me, the best could only be a mystical union with a spirit I loved, another I worshipped, and a third I feared. Even as I puzzled over a role for my father, Malcolm Gunn, in this ideal scheme of things, it never occurred to me that such an union might be unlikely or impossible.

It was bitterly cold that night in January. We walked around a little, then jumped up and down for a while to stay warm. It helped to have the bandstand almost next to where we stood, though it made conversation difficult. The nearness of the blazing torches did provide a little warmth against the wind, and the pretty Shetland faces glowing like gold held at least a promise of more.

As the torches passed by, it looked as if Halloween trick-or-treaters and sombre monks, black robes and whites, had all come to party with Viking warriors, trolls, and denizens of Disney World. History was rudely ripped out of familiar textbooks and transformed, time wrenched out of its moorings, but nobody seemed to mind.

It wasn't long before the galley, now in front of the columns of marchers, was wheeled into a field behind us. The rushing marchers, burning torches held aloft, then poured into the field, coiling round and round the galley in ever-tightening circles. Soon the field was a sea of flames. A hushed silence fell upon the crowd, and the amplifiers jacked up the sound from the band.

Then began the torching of the galley. Starting with the innermost circles, they hurled the burning torches into the galley like so many sizzling match-sticks. The flames danced wildly in the wind, dissolving their hissing sounds into the crowd's collective sigh as the galley burst into flames, lighting up the menacing face of her dragon prow. Fed by more and more torches heaved into the hold, the flames shot higher into the sky, and higher still. As the last of all the burning torches, some eight hundred or so, ended up in the galley, the crowd moved in, some for photographs; others like Sven and me, to warm our freezing bodies.

How cold must the waters seem to a drowning sailor? How many shipwrecks littered the gentle coast? How quickly they are forgotten. As the fires lit up the galley, I thought to myself that that's what the owners ought to be doing to their ships, instead of sending out leaky, dilapidated tubs liable to crack like egg shells in the first big storm out of port.

They have no shame, I thought. Manning them with Filipinos and Bangladeshis who can barely read and write. Poor buggers sailing to watery graves, when all they wanted to sail for was a little money to send home. Should I walk away from it all, wash my hands clean of the contagion?

And to think we propped them up, year after year, turning a blind eye to their endless thieveries, I thought again. De-registered by Lloyds, re-registered in Pireaus; de-registered in Japan, re-registered in Liberia. Secret deals aided and enforced by brown envelopes. "I wonder how much we could've cashed in on these last few days if we had wanted to," I asked.

"A lot," said Sven, nodding his head wisely, ruefully.

The flames roared awhile and soon the mast began to tilt at a crazy angle. As the mast fell, the *Vagsoy's* back seemed to split apart, showering sparks into the night. The dragon prow was the last to go. It could have been a sudden gust of wind or the serpent's last breath, but the sparks suddenly scattered like a swarm of fireflies and disappeared in the sky. The spectacle of the fireworks bursting fitfully over our heads paled against the glowing embers spiralling into the blue of the night.

Sven appeared bored. "So what's there to do now," he asked, "but to eat, dance, and get progressively drunk?"

"I thought this was a legendary Norse ritual," I replied. "How come you don't seem too excited?"

"Ritual, my foot! It's a tourist trap. Too bad they save it for the winter. Dreadful marketing."

"I suppose my friend, John Gage, could come up with some learned theories about how it all started. He's pretty smart and holds a splendid job at the university," I said, as we started to walk in the direction of Queen's Hotel.

On the way, we ran into some recent acquaintances who, instead of pouring scorn over us, for a change invited us warmly into their private celebrations. Sven and I were glad to get indoors and knock down some quick drinks. We met other friends as well, people we had gotten to know at the hotel. Over the next couple of hours we sang endlessly and out of tune, watched performances—whose brilliance was greatly magnified through the alcoholic haze—by the Achy Breaky Heart, the Sultans of Swing, and the Pink Rabbits, all punctuated by more and more drinks. Most memorable of all, we learnt the secrets of a Pictish wedding, a quickie affair if ever there was one, worthy of revival—so we thought—in our own times.

"Well, what do you think?" I asked, as the cold wind whipped into our faces one more time.

"The Vikings had better things to do than march up and down Main Street burning their galleys," replied Sven. "They had a more than casual interest in chopping off heads and limbs, lining their stomachs with food and carrying off women, rather than in parading like idiots."

Back in the hotel, we entered the bar and proceeded to warm our innards with more Scottish fire-water. But the sickness stayed with me, spreading silently through my body like a cancer. While we mingled with more drunken revellers, my mood turned sombre at the most unexpected moments, my attention flew out the window during the most animated conversations. What I saw reflected in the ocean off Sumburgh Head the following day was as much a reflection of my own sickness as of the sickness of others which I had tried to ward off all my life at the mysterious urging of Isabel Gunn.

She would never leave me alone.

While it is far from humanly possible for me or anyone else to know when a sickness actually begins to stir in the body or soul, I probably have to admit that I became aware of my illness one morning four years ago. I remember the day very well. From that time onwards, it was downhill all the way. Or so it seemed to me from the edge of Sumburgh Head.

That day, four years ago . . . . . well, it had snowed in Montreal the night before. This was unusual for late October. But, as part of my confused view of the world, I was reluctantly beginning to admit — only to myself, mind you — that strange things were happening to the weather. One could no longer be sure of climatic patterns. Still, it was a beautiful morning. In the clear sunlight, the streets looked freshly scrubbed and the sprawling promenade of Rue de la Commune immaculate. But for a solitary horse-drawn carriage clip-clopping over the cobblestones with an unhurried pace, looking for business, there was hardly any traffic to disturb the peace.

Strangely though, I felt heavy and depressed. Nothing seemed right — my home, my place of work, nobility of purpose, the hockey games in the Forum, the prospect of love. These imaginary strands — for they lacked anything more than casual substance in my life—somehow twisted themselves around me like a heavy rope which I found incapable of breaking out of, perhaps because it was also invisible. As I looked out through the window of my Jardin d'Youville apartment, even the spectacular sweep of the Jacques Cartier Bridge astride the brown Molson's Brewery plant failed to stir me. The glistening dome of the Marche Bonsecoeur, the jagged ridges of the once-and-futuristic Habitat apartment block across the river, the towering ugliness of the Red Roses grain elevators, nothing seemed important enough to seize my attention this morning. Along the pier, directly across from the apartment, four ships lay tethered side by side. Their names—*Ferber*, *Winnipeg*, *Rimouski*, *Ralph Misener*—may not have aroused my curiosity, but their ports of registration would normally have warranted a second look. Not today. I felt dispirited, deeply troubled by something close to a moral dilemma over the insurance of ships flying flags of convenience. This challenged the idea of some sort of nobility of purpose which I relied on to lend meaning to my chosen career. Some of my distress also sprang from a principle my mother had tried to drill into me—when faced with an evil and the lesser of two evils, choose neither. Naturally, my parents traced this moral principle, as most such others, to my great-great-grandmother, Isabel Gunn. Given the circumstances of my upbringing, my reaction this morning was hardly strange and unusual. I felt a little lost.

It took the *Orcadian*—a gift subscription from my father—a week or two to reach Montreal from the time it was published and mailed from Kirkwall in the

Orkney Islands. Sometimes it took another week or so before I got round to reading it. Now that I had finished reading my favourite column by George Mackay Brown, I found myself overcome by a strange mix of emotions. To me, George was the image of the archetypal poet—a headful of dishevelled hair, eyes full of kindness, sadness and humour, and a magical grasp of the simplicity of all life. It was this last quality that endeared him most of all to me. On this day, George had written about my great-great-grandmother, after having read a poem called "The Ballad of Isabel Gunn" that someone had sent him from Canada. He expressed surprise over never having heard anything about the woman, a fellow Orcadian, though of an earlier age. Having gone to work for the Hudson's Bay Company in Canada in the early eighteen hundreds, Isabel Gunn had returned to Stromness from James Bay, according to the ballad, begging for food and shelter "from Stronsay to Hoy" and wintering in a broken Dounby mill. I knew Stronsay and Hoy and Dounby quite well, for I had spent much of my early years in Stromness. George hoped there were more residents there in her days than I could remember from mine, or it would've been pretty dismal living off charity.

As I looked up from the fourth or fifth reading of the column, something on the promenade did attract my attention finally. It was a man wrapped in a brown overcoat, a red muffler coiled round his neck, shuffling slowly from one trash-can to the other. I walked over to the window to catch a better view of the man as he dragged his feet over the snow, exposing a trail of green grass between one bin and the other, stopping only to pick up the occasional can or cigarette butt, finally disappearing behind the concrete solidity of a distant bridge. But did he really, or did he undergo a sudden transformation? For, the very next moment, walking back towards me from under the bridge, I saw a slender woman, a beautiful woman who looked just like the picture in my parents' present home in Bow, London. A radiant glow surrounded her, lighting up the snow with starlight. Right away, I knew it was Isabel Gunn. I felt nervous because she looked so real, so close, and yet so ethereal. I feared she was there to watch over my wandering, disjointed mind, to take charge of my life, to haunt me more insistently perhaps.

Could it be that George Mackay Brown was writing about someone other than my great-great-grandmother who had died, according to the poet's notes, in Kirkwall in 1861? Saint or bag-lady, what was she? If it was that important to me, I realized it would be a simple matter to go up to George and ask him, perhaps on my next holiday in the Orkneys. Although I had never spoken to him, I knew where he lived round the corner from Login's Well, at the junction of Alfred Street and South End. Everyone in Stromness knew the poet, everyone said hello to him as he went on his walks. It would be a good excuse to start a conversation with a famous writer. But George said in his column he knew no more. With whatever information I had, perhaps it would've made more sense to go and talk to my dad instead.

Guided by a pilot, an enormous cruise ship, scrubbed white and gleaming, silently inched into view from the east as it drew towards the pier. My thoughts jerked me back to reality as all the ships—the passenger liner whose name I couldn't quite read and the cargo vessels whose names I could—suddenly zoomed back into focus. It would be another hour or so before the ship manoeuvred itself into position beside the pier. On a better day, I would've dropped my reading or whatever to watch the ship move into position, inch by measured inch. After all, it was the nearness of the ships that had brought me to this apartment in the first place, leaving behind a comfortable house in a more traditional area, Westmount, and a neighbour's beautiful daughter whom I watched obsessively from my bedroom window. She had always seemed well beyond my reach, more so now that I had moved. I never saw her again; she was just a lovely face that crossed my memory without warning and without reason. But, on certain magical nights, when the lights of Montreal shone not only in the sky but also tumbled into the Saint Lawrence in a startling reflection, I forgot all about her. On such nights, I was certain I could open my windows, reach out, and touch the ships as I used to as a child, every time I came near the St. Ola, tied to the pier in Stromness. I guess it would've been silly to do the same in Montreal; too bad, I never tried.

My family moved to London when I was eight, and even though I still saw plenty of ships, I could never recapture the thrill of touching the boats in Hamnavoe.

I walked away from the window with a heavy heart. I had work to do. I and my president were to meet an environmental group hounding the insurance industry to go "green"—to withhold protection to 'risks', objects or operations, which threatened the environment. I knew it would be as hopeless an exercise as the earlier meetings. On the way to my office in Sherbrooke, I kept thinking of the apparition near the bridge and remembered my father telling me, on more than one occasion, "My great-grandmother was a saint; I can sense her presence everywhere. Someday I must tell you about her."

But he never did. So I never got around to hearing the complete story. True, from time to time I heard how she had been abused by Hudson's Bay traders in Canada's frozen north. I heard stories of her healing powers, the gentleness of her touch, her fierce spirit. All this, but never the complete story. For some reason, I couldn't remember ever having visited her grave in Kirkwall, which, I was told, lay on the grounds of Saint Magnus Cathedral. In spite of never having seen Isabel Gunn's final resting place, sainthood was something I had come face to face with in my mother. She was gone now, and I have never quite found anyone who could replace the special void she left in my heart.

And now this disturbing piece of revelation from the poet Mackay Brown—it was an added, troubling burden. Some poets have such a knack for the simple, unbearable truth.

I grew up in a working class neighbourhood in the East End of London. Our home was dominated by maps. So much so, that I was often bothered by my school geography lessons. The maps and globes I worked with in class looked strange, different from some of the precious scrolls my father went into raptures over at home and in the store where he worked in Long Acre. The universe an oval? The world shaped like an egg?

"It's the same old world," explained my father slowly and reassuringly. "Just looks different with age."

But this was far from satisfactory. I questioned my father for details, on our walks through the cheerless

Dockyards and the Isle of Dogs, and during our frequent visits to the British Museum. These excursions held as much romance for me as they did for my dad. Pointing to a boat tied up at St. Katharine's Pier, I asked my father one day, "How could that Captain ever sail to Rupert's Land if he had one of your funny old maps?"

I'll never forget how happy Malcolm Gunn looked as I asked the question. "Ah!" he said, "when you speak of Rupert's Land you speak of a time when the seas were the only highways through which men really cared to travel. They called the men sea wolves, and they could sniff out lands where no one had been before. The explorers were a fierce breed." A far-away look crept into Malcolm Gunn's eyes. He grew pensive and then added, "When you live on a little sliver of land like England, the horizon calls you all the time, leaning towards you, reaching out to you. Mysterious lands, mysterious people. Only when you reach the shores does the land unlock it secrets. So one had to go. One had to conquer. One had to unlock the mystery. For most Orcadians, life is a fine balance between love for the Orkneys and the yearning for distant lands."

In looking back, it seems I could have stayed in one place forever. I remember the Orcadian horizon, gentle as my mother's embrace. When the morning sun shone on Cairston or on the round of Ward Hill giving glory to the valley of Rackwick on Hoy, I often found myself mesmerized by their quiet assertion of permanence. It was especially so in winter after a light sprinkling of snow. Then the weathered brown of Rackwick, stark and devoid of trees, stood out and curved up to the east and west like two perfect alabaster breasts, then sloped away into green fields of numberless hues where time often stood as still as the sheep looking up from their grazing. In summer, the wet canvas of the horizon roared with pastel shades soft as the heather moorlands of Hoy, wild with the tulips and daffodils brought back to life by Spring.

"I will take you to the Map Room today," Malcolm Gunn said to me in suspenseful tones, as we walked up the British Museum steps. At the time, it seemed we marched up and down the entire museum to get to the Map Room. Eventually, much to my amazement, my father pressed a buzzer, and an uniformed security guard with a great sense of drama opened a locked door. Shivering with excitement, I entered a world that was to challenge many of the certainties of my own world for years to come.

Since then, I had visited the room on many occasions, often without my father, and more recently on business, to check on ancient place names referred to in marine litigation cases that represented equally ancient precedents for today.

"Since you have been reading the *Odyssey* of late," said Malcolm Gunn in a quiet voice, "let me begin with this one." The librarian placed a massive folio on the table in front of us and moved away. My father carefully turned the heavy pages until he found what he wanted. He said to me, "You've heard of Aeolus, the god and father of the winds. Here are four wind-blowers seated on Aeolus's bags that Homer wrote about."

At each of the four corners of the map, the wind-blowers sat on bags that looked like cannons, holding trumpets in one hand and squeezing the wind out of the bags with the other. The winds were supposed to tell people in what direction the map was headed. The north wind was the head of a cross old man who looked very unhappy. There blew a gale-force wind out of his bag's mouth. But the west wind had the face of a cherub and a gentle wisp curled out of his bag. From the south wind's bag dripped water, frogs and other creatures. The east wind was a winged young man blowing with puffed cheeks. Adam and Eve stood hiding their nakedness at the top, with an amused snake looking on. This was Paradise, way out in the east. In the centre of the map was Jerusalem. "This here is a map a thousand years old, Malcolm Gunn reminded me. "Looks more like a picture, but it's a map all right."

The map was divided into three parts by a T-shaped partition, a T within an O which divided the enclosed space into a half and two quarters. The top of the map was east and in this half piece there was Asia. The lower left quarter was Europe; the lower right, Africa. My father explained to me how the three pieces of the earth were those given to the three sons of Noah—Shem, Japheth, and Ham.

As we sat side by side on the bus taking us home along the Roman Road, I was puzzled and somewhat subdued. I remember asking, "How come there's no Paradise in the maps we study at school? Where's Adam and Eve disappeared to?"

Malcolm Gunn looked out of the double-decker's window for a while. "Remember what happened to Odysseus?" he asked. "Aeolus gave him a fair wind to send him away, but he also gave him a sealed bag with all the bad winds."

I interrupted him excitedly. "I think I know what happened," I said eagerly in an attempt to please my dad. "The fair wind helped the ship, but the sailors got curious to know what was in the sealed bag. They opened the bag and then there was trouble."

Malcolm Gunn was delighted with my answer. I suppose all the hours he had spent reading to me, all the hours he had spent reading with me, all the stories, all the history, all the little details about honesty, fairness, and truth, the icon we had made of Isabel Gunn, all seemed to come together in moments like these. "You're right," he said, "some day we'll find Paradise again, and Adam and Eve too. Somewhere, but not just yet."

One evening soon afterwards, Malcolm Gunn brought home a slim roll of reprints which he carefully unwrapped on the dining table after dinner. "Ah! Solinus, Solinus," he exclaimed, "the geography teacher's nightmare." He carefully untied the final knot holding together a thin piece of ribbon. Wonder of wonders! My father held in front of my eyes maps, the like of which I had never seen before.

"It was the writings of a man named Solinus that helped put the pictures on these maps," he said. "Solinus knew little about maps, but he could tell a great story." With wide-eyed wonder, I heard how Solinus told of people in southern Italy who made sacrifices to their gods by dancing bare-feet over beds of hot coal. Also in Italy were pythons that grew fat and long drinking milk from the cows in the pasture. There were dolphins in the Black Sea that leaped clear over the mainsails of passing ships. There were pictures of horse-footed men and men with ears so long they used them for a blanket at night. The Niger River was so hot it boiled constantly, hotter than any fire. In Libya there lived a terrible cockatrice, a beast that crept along the ground like a crocodile on his front legs while its hindquarters lay suspended aloft by two wings. His bite and his breath were both fatal to man, and only weasels could kill him. In Africa, there were men without any heads at all, whose eyes and mouths were on their chests. And in India, thanks to Solinus, there were people with eight toes on each foot, and others with dogs' heads and claws instead of fingers, who would bark but couldn't talk. Others had only one leg but a foot so large it could be used for a brolly when it rained or when the sun grew too hot.

At this point, my mother drew me into her arms and covered me with kisses. "Should be ashamed of yourself," she scolded my father, half in jest. "Stuffing his little head with such rubbish."

Malcolm Gunn never told me about them, but my own curiosity led me to ancient writers who were perhaps explorers in their own right. They expressed bizarre fantasies about women's breasts. One spoke of long breasts on which women would lie down and go to sleep. Another of purses sold on the Cape of Good Hope, made from breasts of Hottentot women. Another claimed to have seen, in Ireland's northern parts, women giving suck to babies behind their backs by throwing their breasts over their shoulders. Perhaps it was best that I came across these stories at an age when I was beginning to feel a biological need to explore the female anatomy, thought I, or it might have caused me serious hangups in later life. Nevertheless, the stories did succeed in eroding some of the physical fascination stirring in my mind about this time. It so happened that these stories were classified and shunned as erotica by the Gunn household, and that was another problem. Our family had to be good. We had to be different from our relatives where the men drank too much and women had too many babies out of wedlock. We needed to be grateful to God for preserving us from the dim-witted imbeciles He had inflicted on other families.

About the time of my remarkable literary discoveries on the subject of breasts, I had also been subjected to Sunday meditations in a family circle where biblical strictures habitually got confused with words Isabel Gunn may or may not have said. There was therefore no question of discussing subjects which seemed to come anywhere close to challenging, say, *Galatians 5*: 'Walk by the Spirit, and do not gratify the desires of the flesh; for the desires of the flesh are against the Spirit, and the desires of the Spirit are against the flesh.' Yes, it seems Isabel had uttered words precisely to the same effect, words embroidered in red and blue and framed over our London hearth.

On other nights Malcolm Gunn read Robbie Burns to me, and my mother loved every moment of it. She worshipped the music in my father's voice. Over time, so did I, as I hoped desperately to please my mother with a voice as resonant as my father's.

I remember going to the Map Room one more time with Malcolm Gunn. It was my fourteenth birthday and my mother said she'd be baking all morning. I'll never forget what my father said to me that day. His words were, "The mapmaker gives substance to God's world. If he thinks God has departed from His world, he doesn't show Him any more." On my fourteenth birthday, I wasn't quite sure what my father was trying to say. Later, I thought I understood.

Inside the Map Room, he said to me, "You asked me once about Rupert's Land and how ships ever got there and came back. Your great-great-grandmother, Isabel Gunn, went there. Take a look at some of the maps the captains of her age might have used. Look carefully, try to remember what you see, and when you get home you'll discover how odd it all appears today."

It was a different map, less fantastic than the first maps my father had shown me in the Museum. But the pictures were no less spellbinding. There were pictures of hunters, on the shore and in kayaks, attacking whales with harpoons; pictures of Indians paddling away in birch-bark canoes, pictures of seals, and fish, and puffins. So the animals and birds lived there too, I thought, even though I was somewhat surprised I didn't find the Orkneys on the map. The very fact the puffins and seals were there made me imagine it wouldn't be so unfamiliar after all. Later, at the bottom of the map, right of centre, I found S'chetland I., and almost immediately another connection, however tenuous, was made. When I found Cary's I. on the western edge of the map, with the notation "Hudson wintered", the connection grew stronger. Suddenly, Login's Well—where the ships of the Hudson's Bay Company watered—and Haven, some of the casual landmarks of my early years when we lived off John Street in Stromness became real, bustling with childhood friends, peopled with ghosts.

Login's Well, wells gone dry filling ships that sailed away, wells covered over by towns going dry as the children run away to distant lands. There were times when I felt guilty at having left Stromness for good, and I remembered what Malcolm Gunn had said about a fine balance in which every element is still and every emotion at peace. I wondered what it was that upset the balance for some. Something must have upset the balance for Isabel Gunn as well, or why would she have gone to Rupert's Land?

Malcolm Gunn's finger stopped at a curious name at the southern end of James Bay—Moose Fort. Tapping on the spot with his finger, he said, "Isabel Gunn, she was here." His voice choked with sudden emotion, and he stopped.

A few months later, when Malcolm Gunn returned home from work with a copy of a three hundred year old announcement, I seemed to know right away what I wanted to do in life. It was an August, 1678, advertisement from a London map seller:

> **Atlas Minimus: or a Book of Geography, shewing all the Empires, Monarchies, Kingdoms, Regions, Dominions, Principalities and Countreys in the whole World; With the proper division of each Countrey Comprised in a Pocket Volume, being a Compleat Epitome of Geography; Collected by John Seller the Kings Hydrographer, and are sold at his Shop in Popes-head Alley in Cornhill, London.**

Malcolm Gunn gave it to me.

The whole world, that's what I wanted within my reach, with or without God or Paradise. The maps we had at home were different all right, but that didn't deter me from my resolve.

Pettigrew did send for me a few days later.

"Tell me about your growing up," he asked, as we settled down in our chairs.

I thought for a long time.

I dreamed my way through school. I often skipped classes to sit in the shadow of a toolshed in a corner of the school grounds. From there it was possible to gaze at the sea and imagine wondrous ships, strange people, and dazzling wealth moving from one edge of the earth to another. I was often punished for my absences. It meant I had to stay back in school after class and read a passage or two. I usually completed the task while sitting next to my favourite toolshed. From Stromness to high school in London was a disaster. The decrepit school, the grimy surroundings, the seedy housing projects nearby made the Thames Magistrates Court appear interesting and inviting. Many of my fellow students would end up there on some pretext or the other. I preferred to spend much of my time poking around an old church graveyard a short distance away until I had memorized the names of every person buried under the crumbling, greenish gravestones.

I finished school and apprenticed with a Norwegian insurance company in London. It did not quite bring the world within my reach, but as a marine underwriter looking at — in Malcolm Gunn's words — the earliest highways that knit the continents together, it just about did. I lived with my parents in Bow and led a lonely, uneventful life. For a while I went out with Elaine, a girl from Bethnal Green I had met outside Aldwych Station, where she stood at the entrance every Thursday and gave out to passers by copies of a rag called *Lloyd's List Insurance Day*. She earned a pittance as a part-time vendor. But, at the time, the paper provided a logical connection between our lives. Our entertainment consisted largely of after-work bus rides through central London, marvelling at the splendid offices and brilliant homes around Knightsbridge and Mayfair, wondering if I would ever live in one of them.

One January, I took some days off work and drove Elaine up through snow and sleet as far north as Edinburgh, where I donned a splendid kilt and escorted her to a Robbie Burns dinner in the city. A little drunk, I had frivolously explained to a persistent American tourist that the haggis was a bird with four legs, two shorter than the others.

And the traveller from Nevada or somewhere asked, " Which ones are shorter, the front or back legs?"

I explained, "The ones on the left, so the bird can run in circles."

Everyone laughed and thought I was very funny. Then a woman from Poughkeepsie—I can never forget Poughkeepsie—curious to know what men wore under their kilts, asked me if she could take a peek.

"Sure," I replied, drunk and nonchalant.

Unfortunately, when the unsuspecting woman lifted my tartan and shrieked in horror, it proved to be the end of my friendship with Elaine. Scotsman or not, she thought mine was totally inappropriate behaviour, and childish too. She scoffed at my lame explanation. Forgetting one's underwear, hah!

Somehow, I believed Elaine's rejection was just a pretext. As I had discovered during our bus rides, all she wanted was to settle down with me in a flat in Bethnal Green. But I was far from ready. I was still reaching out for the world. Besides, like my parents, I seemed to be inheriting the family penchant for the saintly, and Elaine still had a long way to go to fit the bill. As I looked into the future a few years down the road, I became increasingly uneasy about the prospect of sharing it with Elaine. For a while, I felt somewhat remorseful thinking my mother would be hurt if she found out what had happened in Edinburgh. It did seem stupid in retrospect, and a trifle disrespectful to the memory of the great poet. Besides Robbie Burns, my mother liked Elaine, and was naturally disappointed. But she said nothing.

Work came easily to me, as did success, modest increments by which it is measured by millions who work in drab, cheerless offices. My real break came when I was offered the chief marine underwriter's position by a prestigious—meaning old and somewhat stuffy—company in Montreal. I was twenty six and I felt elated.

I had spent nearly four years in Canada by the time I read Mackay Brown's column on Isabel Gunn. During this time, I had prospered—as my parents knew I would with the blessings of Isabel Gunn—bringing home rich profits for my employers and valuable bonuses for myself. The president and vice presidents liked me at work, invited me to their dinners and cocktails, and introduced me to the crust of Montreal's English establishment as an Orcadian seeking to emulate my Hudson's Bay ancestors in Canada.

When I told my father about these friendly gibes, Malcolm Gunn reminded me, "You're in good company, and they should know it. Verrazano was an Italian in French service, Estevan Gomez was a Portuguese in Spanish service. Nothing wrong for an Scotsman to be working in Canada."

The first time I met John Gage, a jovial college professor from the Native and Northern Programme, he asked me, "What're you doing here? You Orcadians had a ball for two hundred years all the way from Churchill to Richmond. Did you know that British officers and servants could live with native women right till the time their contracts with the Hudson's Bay Company expired and they went home? And these liaisons were seen as marriages. How marvellous! How enlightened! How convenient! Go north. That's where you'll be in your elements, not in this silly, provincial city. Your roots lie there."

We had met in a bar I had grown fond of visiting after work. As was my custom, I had washed down quite a few drinks with my sandwiches before John Gage's exhortation. It therefore seemed perfectly natural for me to reply with a poem:

> Then, first an' foremost, thro' the kail,
>   Their stocks maun a' be sought once;
> They steek their een, an' grope an' wale
>   For muckle anes, an' straught anes.

It was a Halloween custom, I explained, for people to go out, hand in hand, eyes shut, and pull out the first cabbage or colewort they came upon. Big or little, straight or crooked, the plants foretold the size and shape of their future mate, husband or wife.

John Gage hadn't expected me to be looking for roots in such a literal sense. "Ah," he said, "I like that. I must use this magic to check out my own perennial emotional entanglements. I fall in love all the time, mostly with my students. Surely, I can't always be wrong."

My mother wanted me to fall in love too. That seemed to be her dying wish. It was her illness that gave me the leave, a respite I wanted, to fly to London and find out more about Isabel Gunn. Who was she? What was she really like?

My mother's sickness happened just before Christmas that year. I came to London, held my mother's hand in mine, but never got around to asking my father what I had wanted to. It didn't seem to be important, especially as my beautiful mother, still resplendent in her golden hair, lay dying. She had never uttered a harsh word, never spoken ill of anyone, never looked at another man, never in her life appeared angry or despondent. Was it possible, was it real, I asked myself? Or was it the spirit of Isabel Gunn that had descended upon her, transforming her, making her so pure?

"Read to me, Charlie," she said. "Read me Tam O' Shanter." And I did.

"You too have such a beautiful voice, Charlie," she said. "Never lose it." A bunch of red roses in a tear-shaped porcelain vase spread their dark sweetness in the air. My mother paused to take a deep breath, closed her eyes, and added softly, "It'll be such a shame."

I held her hand and murmured to myself:

> "And hast thou crost that unknown river, Life's dreary bound?
> Like thee, where shall I find another, the world around?"

Malcolm Gunn was standing next to me and probably heard me. The tears flowed freely down his cheeks.

Mary Gunn finally faded away on Christmas day. She had whispered a wish that she might be buried in the little village in northern Scotland where she had grown up. It must have been a passing thought, one among the hundreds that must blow like leaves in autumn before the final moment when time stands still and eternity begins. Malcolm Gunn, now retired from Stanfords, hardly had the kind of money needed for such a funeral. But what he had was an uncompromising love for his wife and he was determined to bury her in the north.

For the second time that December, I flew to London and then boarded a plane for Inverness. It was still dark when the train pulled out of Inverness station. Gradually, the countryside began to appear as an outline drawn against the winter sky, dark and motionless over parted lips through which a pale sun, gathering itself from the ocean floor, stroked the day into a leisured awakening. And flocks of sheep, clustered near dykes like balls of cotton candy, dappled with blue, red, and yellow coloured markings, broke away into little puffs flying across the meadows as the train clattered by.

It was a simple funeral in a tiny graveyard bounded on one side by a crumbling flagstone wall, on the other by a stream still trickling away under its icy edges, still exposing a wonderland of colours etched on the pebbles below. They looked exquisite. I instinctively picked up a stone, wondering how many million years it had taken to create art so painstaking and rare. But then the water dried as I held the stone in my hand, and the art withered before my eyes. It was with a touch of regret that I dropped the stone in the water. We left Forsinard that same afternoon.

After the funeral, I felt glad and at peace. But there was a lost, frightened look in my father's eyes. It remained with Malcolm Gunn even as we unwound ourselves in our modest living room in London.

"Dad," I said, "I'm quite wealthy. So you must let me pay for the funeral."

Malcolm Gunn remained silent. He looked just as scared as before. After supper that night, he sat staring at one of the walls of the living room. Suddenly he started, "We'll have to find a place for Mary's picture. I think I know the spot I want."

I quickly looked around the walls, making a note of the space where Malcolm Gunn wanted his wife's picture. There were pictures, plates and dried flowers all around us, and I had no previous recollection of the empty space which seemed suddenly to have materialized from nowhere. I set my eyes on the familiar picture of a slender woman on the wall behind my father's head. It was a faded picture of an ageing face, touched in sepia tones. Soon Isabel Gunn's picture would be facing my mother's. I found the thought strangely disquieting and I wasn't sure why. I tried to put my mind at ease by telling myself I needed to find out more about Isabel Gunn. Perhaps I needed to know where she was buried. But I was not asking any questions that night.

I was determined to see my father a little less despondent before I returned to Montreal. So I suggested we take a bus and go for a walk near the Isle of Dogs. The air was crisp, the sunlight strong and clear. As we boarded the bus near Mile End Station, I couldn't help noticing how lovely London looked in the sun. "One tends to forget," I reminded my father.

Malcolm Gunn smiled and nodded at the fruits and vegetables glistening in the sun as the vendors stacked them on tables or stalls out in the open. Old ladies beamed with happiness as they walked their dogs. Old men puffed on their cigarettes at street crossings, continued to puff while the traffic lights changed to green and they decided not to cross. Young mothers pushed prams and stopped in front of store windows to check sale prices.

The Docklands was in the grip of frenzied activity. Still unfinished, Canary Wharf was beginning to glow with the splendour of a new age palace. All around us were towers, some with scaffolding rattling gently in the breeze, others shooting phosphorescent and golden sparks at the touch of the welder's torch. Stupendous cranes drew arcs across the cloudless sky, opening and closing their jagged jaws like prehistoric monsters. Water, awakened in their beds as trucks lumbered by, lapped against the marble parapets.

"To think," murmured Malcolm Gunn, "that a hundred, two, or three hundred years ago, ships would be piloted down this way and let loose at Gravesend in search of new worlds. Past St. Katharine's Dock, a last prayerful view of St. Katharine's Church and the spires of St. Katharine's Hospital as London disappeared from view around the Isle of Dogs. A prayer for the soul of some nameless pirate as he mounted the gallows at Execution Dock. Past commons and marshes, the Parish of Stepney, Hamlet of Mile End, Bethnal Green."

"It's the same world, isn't it?" I asked.

"As fashions change, so does the world," replied my father softly.

I had to block off all other sounds as I strained to catch my father's words. I heard, I understood, and nodded to my father. As we walked past Island Gardens, I turned towards my father. I must finally tell him, I thought. So I said, "I came across George Mackay Brown's column in the *Orcadian* a few weeks ago. He wrote about Isabel Gunn, about how she returned to the Orkneys and died a pauper. I'm very curious. I suppose you don't get the paper any more."

"No. But what did it say?"

"Not much more than I know already," I replied.

Malcolm Gunn stared hard into the distance. "You may find it hard to believe this," he started, "but she did have the power to change her appearance. She could be a man if she wanted to. I suppose some would have called her a witch. But that she wasn't. I'm told the Indians worshipped her. When the Hudson's Bay Company, still following orders given by Jeffrey Amherst forty years earlier, unloaded for the Indians sheets on which smallpox patients had slept and died, Isabel draped the sheets over her own body one by one. The general's intentions were to infect and exterminate the Indians. But not one Indian died of smallpox at Rupert House where this happened. True, she gave birth to a son, my great grandfather, but to her dying day she swore she had never been with a man. That's what my grandparents told me, and I believe them."

I looked at my father in utter disbelief. "Surely you don't believe that any more?" I asked.

"It's not for me to believe or disbelieve," replied Malcolm Gunn. "But there were those in Kirkwall and Stromness who remembered stories about her. Where surgeons failed, she cured the sick with her potions. She brought back to life many whose souls had withered away through sorrow and sadness. No wonder she's buried outside the grandest of all cathedrals, St. Magnus. I'm sorry I've never taken you to her grave." My father paused and looked up at the sky. He continued, "Why should I, when I carry her in my heart? Besides, there's a family belief that she wanted it that way. No visits. No flowers."

I kept looking at my father incredulously. Finally I said, "But she died a pauper, begging for food from Stronsay to Hoy, wintering in a ramshackle Dounby mill. What does that tell you about her?"

My father's voice was wistful. "Maybe she died a pauper," he said, "but she had gathered enough riches in heaven to free a thousand lost souls."

I decided I didn't wish to carry on the discussion any further. I remained silent. We kept walking a long time. It was my father who broke the silence. "We are not clever people," he said, "not very smart. That's why I married your mother, and why my father married mine. Because they were good people, honest, the salt of the earth, satisfied with little, asking nothing for themselves." Fresh tears rose in Malcolm Gunn's eyes.

After he had regained his composure, he continued, "There was an Indian woman. I don't remember her name. My father said her descendants called her a shaman. They thought the same of Isabel Gunn. The woman cared for Isabel Gunn and her son. Times were different even if the world was the same. I believe Isabel came face to face with God. But God doesn't live in Rupert's Land anymore. There lies the difference."

A faint smile played over Malcolm Gunn's lips and I felt happy to see it. Suddenly, I remembered the apparition in old Montreal and my thoughts flew into confusion once more.

Back home, Malcolm Gunn went hurriedly to a bureau where he kept his papers in one corner of the living room. He opened and closed several drawers until he found what he was looking for. An old photo album. He lifted the back cover carefully and pulled out a discoloured sheet of letter paper. "Ah! I have the name," he said, "Ke-che-cho-wieh." He spelt it out for me, letter by letter.

Later that night, before we said good-night to each other, Malcolm Gunn turned to me and asked, "Why is it important to you, Charlie?"

"What?" I asked, startled.

"Why do you want to know about Isabel Gunn?"

I let the thoughts form slowly in my mind. "I don't know, Dad," I answered. "It's hard to explain. Seems she casts a shadow across everything I do, my relationships with men, with women. I look for words from them which I don't hear. I want them to act a particular way and they don't. There are times I think of her as a saint who lived in a wild, unfettered world. At other times I think of her as wild as the wilderness she went to. She drives me to desperation sometimes because I don't know who she is, don't know what she wants. Yet, she is somewhere very close, all the time."

Malcolm Gunn sipped his port wine in silence. Eventually, he said, "Don't know what to tell you, Charlie. I suppose you think I'm crazy, an old fool. And have been all my life."

I was confused all right. I loved the old man too much to imagine he was crazy. But it did seem rather unsettling to be sitting in London's East End towards the end of the twentieth century, the world in turmoil and the IRA blowing up the city, and talk of miracles. And yet, we were far from religious in a conventional sense. Malcolm Gunn once told me how much he loved God and that's why he was an atheist. He wanted, he said, to be like God, who simply had to be an atheist. There was no other way out for God.

"Perhaps I should tell you something else, Dad," I said. "About the time that I read the story in the *Orcadian*, a strange thing happened. I was looking out of my window one morning, watching the progress of an old trash picker below, when I thought I saw somebody in the distance. Somebody who looked very much like the person in the picture above your head. It was as if the trash-picker had transformed himself. The entire experience lasted a brief moment and I am sure it was nothing. Plain nonsense. But I wasn't so sure then." I looked at my father for a response and then returned to stare at the darkness framed by the window whose shades no one had drawn that night, now that my mother was gone. Then I returned to my father and asked, "Where do we find maps that can chart us through such experiences?"

"I don't know where you can find them," said Malcolm Gunn, "but I know it's not nonsense. Tomorrow you'll be gone and I'm certain I'll feel and see another presence around me all the time. It won't be nonsense. I'll want it that way. I want your mother's presence around me, as we both wanted Isabel's around both of us. If I'm lucky I could have them around me every moment of the day." There was a fresh burst of energy in his voice as he continued, "But why only here, in this little room? I'll be holding hands with her on Brinkie's Brae. When the sun sets over the Ring of Brodgar and the raindrops come whipping from the west, I'll know its her presence dissolving around me, drawing me into the Ring. And while she is with me against the wind on the towering red headlands of Sneuk Head at Rackwick, under the screaming, whirling delirium of the birds overhead, maybe I'll finally know what the waves below have been trying to tell us through the ages. I'm certain they have a language all their own. And you'll laugh at me, Charlie, and I'll laugh at myself. But the pain I feel tonight will be gone. There'll be no more pain."

As we fell silent, I could feel London becoming silent as well. The city had curled itself up and gone to sleep. But that was hardly the case, as I knew full well. If only I held my ear to my pillow, I was certain I would hear the city's restlessness. Old men crawling into unwelcome doorsteps for rest and warmth. Screaming voices in one night stands in cheap, loveless hotel rooms. Sad saxophones, unmindful of time, wailing notes of blue through empty passages in Holborn or King's Cross Station. How I loved the city and its people! It pained me to think of leaving London the next day.

If there was an emptiness that awaited me in Montreal, I was not quite sure where or when I would begin to feel it. I didn't need too much to fill my days, my life. After all, I was far from ambitious. I wasn't troubled by greed. Not troubled by greed? Not quite. A sense of the greed of others was beginning to bother me—maybe it was the nature of the business I was in.

Certainly not bothered by the absence of a woman in my life. My mother's hand brushed against my hair, and her lips brushed mine. Soon the pillow was wet with my warm tears. In my heart, I knew my mother was gone forever. Still, I believed it would always be possible to remember. But how could I be certain? Much could be forgotten, should be forgotten. But there was always a tiny speck of gold, and it would be a shame to lose that. Like my father, I too gradually grew certain she would always be around.

One day I decided to tell John Gage what I had found out about the insurance shenanigans around James Bay. I confessed to him how upset I was about how little I knew about the land and the people, and John said I was ready for lesson number four.

"You don't have to drown in self-pity, Charlie, to prove your point," he told me. As always, John was very perceptive. "Ten thousand dumb caribou did that six years ago," he continued. "They lost their way and drowned in an altered Caniapiscau River. It was like turning day into night, suddenly and without warning—a river that was flowing from east to west was made to flow from west to east. Once familiar trails transformed in a flash into death traps. Poor caribou, they didn't have a clue. Smart animals, eh? Nothing changes." John Gage looked pensively outside the window, his fingers drumming staccato notes on the table. After a while, he said, "But drowning's such a mystical passage from life into death, like re-entry into a mother's womb."

I thought about the dead caribou, thousands of bloated carcasses careening down the rapids. I remained silent.

If John Gage was interested in educating me about aboriginals, Pierre seemed equally determined to give me, as he put it, the real scoop on James Bay. From time to time, he brought me impressive and colourful literature from Hydro Quebec. In the pictures, the rivers glistened like emeralds, the mountains were serene, and the woodlands lush and inviting.

In March of that year, the Mohawks of Kanesatake set up a blockade to stop the expansion of a nine-hole golf course onto an old Mohawk burial ground.

"Shameful," said John Gage. "I'll have to take you to Oka soon one day," he told me. "But don't let my attitudes fool you. There are as many English-speaking Canadians who'd love to see the aboriginals disappear as there are French-speaking ones who feel the same way."

But before we had a chance to travel to Oka, Pierre came up with another trip to Northern Quebec. We could've easily flown all the way to Fort George, but Pierre thought it would be more interesting to see how the province of Quebec was transforming the north. So we arranged to pick up a rental car and drive up from Val d'Or.

In the lounge bar of the Val d'Or Hotel a few nights later, I decided it was time I got to speak to some real, live aboriginals. A few quick drinks was all I needed to screw up enough courage. My chance came when a young man, his hair pulled back in a braid, walked up and stood next to me at the bar, two young women hanging from each shoulder. He turned his head and looked curiously and defiantly at me. His strangely piercing eyes seemed to say: "So I'll stand here next to you, white man. See what you can do about it."

I tried to remain unfazed. "I'm Charlie," I said, extending my hand.

"I'm Dale."

"And this is Pierre," I added.

"Hello, Pierre."

"Hello, Dale."

"And these are my friends," said Dale, laughing, looking from one woman to the other in a very disinterested way. Adding, "Whose names I seem to have forgotten."

We drank together for a long time, and finally I asked Dale if he and his friends would care to join us at a table for supper. Pierre looked rather flustered at this invitation, but then there was little he could do to prevent it. Dale and his friends accepted.

"So what do you think about Oka?" I asked at one point, trying to appear as casual and matter-of-fact as possible, turning my question to Dale.

Oka was more than three hundred miles away, but I imagined the distance — between Indian brother and Indian brother — wouldn't probably stand in the path of solidarity in Dale's mind.

Dale replied, sounding equally casual, "Oka, nice town, nice cheese. Dumb mayor, the big cheese of Oka. Who cares about Oka, man?"

I didn't pursue the matter any further. A short while later, Dale returned to the subject on his own. "The white man claims," he said, "that God gave him the land to work on — to plant, to harvest, and yes, to play golf. All I can say is that the white man's God must be a real estate developer."

Pierre bristled visibly at Dale's words. I merely smiled and said nothing. At the end of the meal, when the two women went off to the washroom, I let my curiosity get the better of me. The women had laughed a lot but said practically nothing at the table. "So what do your friends do in Val d'Or?" I asked.

"I couldn't care less what they do for a living," answered Dale with an euphoric smile. "What I care about is what they do to me."

As we said our goodbyes, Dale apologized to both Pierre and to me. "I'm sorry," he said, "had too much coke this afternoon." Then, returning from the door and grabbing hold of my hand one more time, he said, "They tell me coke helps focus your intellect and sharpens your personality. But what happens if you're an asshole to begin with?" With that, without waiting for an answer, he turned away and walked slowly out of the room.

Pierre shook his head with displeasure. "They're barbarians and they know it," he said. "Deep in their hearts they'd rather be like you and me. Stupid pride and crafty politicians prevent them from admitting it."

"It wasn't such a bad evening, Pierre," I said, trying to mollify him.

In the morning, we had our customary donuts at the Donut Shop opposite the motel. Afterwards, we stopped to buy gas in Matagami for there wouldn't be another gas station for two hundred miles.

Utterly desolate, the beauty of the land took my breath away. The freshness, the fragility of the scene, quickly wiped away all my jaded expectations. I had travelled a short distance along this very road once before. This time, the experience turned more and more intense and compelling the further we travelled north from Matagami and Val d'Or.

"All this is land God has given the people of Quebec," said Pierre, his voice quivering with pride.

The road wound lazily through a vast, undulating expanse. How many million years had it been this way, home to unseen spirits, I wondered. There were no signs of animate life. Only occasionally did we see a Telebec or Hydro Quebec van or truck, emerging like a speck in the distance and passing us like a speeding arrow.

"There are immense possibilities locked around these forests," continued Pierre. "Tourism. Hunting. Will the Cree ever be able to develop it on their own? Never."

But behind the curtain of trees bordering the highway, I was able to pick up telltale signs I hadn't noticed before. Like missing forests. The more north we travelled, the more I began to notice vast fields of moist earth churned up like fresh battlegrounds. Stripped and naked, the odd limb left behind from trees long dispatched to the lumber and plywood mills lay kneaded into the earth like the bones of soldiers killed in battle.

The power was real enough. Power lines that would stretch, as Pierre explained it, twelve hundred miles from Radisson to Boston. Mile after mile after endless mile, the giant transmission towers stood over the horizon like dancers linking hands. Closer to the highway, the wooden poles carrying the power locally sat like buried crosses on the side of the road, each casual cross a memorial to wars that will not end and unknown soldiers who will not cease to die in the quest for power.

From time to time, flocks of little birds scattered like dry husk in the wind. There seemed fewer and fewer resting places for them. The powerlines were clearly *verboten*, and the trees were vanishing fast.

Perhaps Pierre could read my mind. He seemed more subdued, less talkative about the subject of energy as time passed. Near Poste Nemiscau, rows of slender, dead trees sat upon the hillside like a grey mist, uncertain like refugees, with nowhere to go. Too large to simply disappear, too useless to be carted off to the mills. Copper-coloured sand lay exposed to the wind where the topsoil had been scraped or washed away, spelling a not too distant end for a handful of doomed bushes cowering with their heads bowed in dread and submission.

There were unexpected stretches of purple sage. Close by, bordering the highway, were the faces of lakes, some small, others vast, still frozen in the month of May. But the Eastmain River, which must've been massive—I could tell from the breadth of its dry bed— now slept like a squalid lizard, taped, defanged, its back studded with stained boulders, puckered, dead, devoid of all charm. The Telebec communications towers popped their clusters of pods over what remained of the forest. They looked like sci-fi eyes and ears spying for signs of life.

We filled up gas in the middle of nowhere at Km 381. One gas pump, one pump operator, who made us wait a half hour with a sign on his door which said 'Back in 15 minutes'. The shadows began to lengthen as the sun slipped lower and lower to the west. Now the land became even more bare. No more dead trees, just a scattering of freshly planted saplings, sadly unpromising. Gouged out and blown up into clods, the land looked exhausted. In the gathering darkness, it crawled quietly over to the horizon and just lay there like a sick animal. Only the towering dancers raised their heads to the sky, their hands linked together as before.

Except for a grouse which smashed itself against the wheels, we saw no game. But Pierre assured me it was there. And I did notice the odd hunter's shack patched together with blue and orange plastic insulation sheets.

The moon came up about the time we reached the vast jungle of towers and high-voltage lines clustered in the Radisson sub-station. Under a pale sky, stars nested between the drooping cables like eggs trapped inside a maze of tubes.

The Auberge Radisson was a comfortable hotel. But where were the aboriginals? I wondered, until Pierre explained they lived in a village called Chisasibi sixty miles away. Relaxing in the lounge later that evening, we saw a video of the final leg of the voyage of the *Odeyak* as it reached New York's Central Park on Earth Day the previous month. Half a canoe and half a kayak, the *Odeyak* apparently represented the solidarity of the Cree and Inuit nations against the Great Whale Hydro electric Project, planned to start only a hundred miles or so north of Radisson. From the shouts of derision that rose from the audience in that darkened lounge, it was obvious the Cree and Inuit either weren't there or were fast asleep. The New Yorkers glee and enthusiasm failed to spill over from the screen into the room where we sat.

Pierre completed his discussions with Hydro Quebec on a matter of salvage the following day, and we prepared to leave. We were still struggling over the earlier million dollar claim. As matters stood, it was decided Pierre would take an engineer and examine the hold where the cargo had been stowed the next time the ship came to Montreal, which was going to be soon. But, with a long weekend coming up, I wanted to stay on. Rather than let Pierre drive the four hundred miles to Val d'Or all by himself, I decided to drop him off at the airport that very afternoon.

Back at the hotel, it seemed to me rather odd that I should actually wish to spend a long weekend at such a dull and dreary spot. I had a sudden urge to try and discover places I might somehow associate with Isabel Gunn. I quickly dismissed the thought for what it was, truly wild. I was far from ready for such an undertaking at this time.

The few guests at the hotel were either suppliers or contractors connected with Hydro Quebec. I met a middle-aged lawyer from Montreal who said he worked for the Cree Band Council. His elegant assistant, also from Montreal, seemed to be the only woman staying at the hotel. In fact, I was surprised that I hadn't seen more than three or four white women while there were scores of men. The lawyer, who introduced himself as Phillipe Rochard, discouraged me from driving to Chisasibi on my own. "It'll be a waste of time," he assured me. "But you're welcome to come along with me," he added, though not with excessive enthusiasm. This was after we had exchanged cards and he had carefully read mine.

So I spent all of Saturday and the better part of Sunday morning exploring the low hills and lakes near the hotel. The weather remained sunny, though cool, and I enjoyed myself immensely. Late Sunday morning, I was beginning to feel desperate. I needed someone to talk to, someone other than the two teenagers working the hotel reception desk. My head was still reeling from a visit to the bowels of the La Grande 2 power plant which Pierre had arranged for me before he left. A final attempt, as it were, to convince me of the limitless promises of the great project.

It was mind-boggling, a totally out-of-this-world experience. The LG2 dam was two miles long and the height of a fifty-three storey building. I was driven down a two-lane tunnel that went down four hundred feet into what was described as the largest underground generation plant in the world. Sixteen penstocks led to sixteen humming turbines sitting below a gleaming machine room a quarter mile long. The pent-up waters of the reservoir crashed through each penstock, twenty feet wide, and dropped four hundred and fifty feet to roar past the turbines with a force of four million tons per second. The guide kept piling detail on detail, number on number. Each of the sixteen turbines had a six-hundred ton rotor screaming at one hundred thirty three revolutions per second.

There was a hint of art as well. It must have occurred to someone that this was too blatant a homage to technology. So, inside the machine room, they had installed 'Marie Quebec', a semi-abstract statue commemorating the labour of fifty five thousand workers.

The guide saved the most fearful experience for the last. A visit to the floor below the rotors seemed a descent into hell. The noise was enough to make my head want to explode. My feet began to buckle under the terrifying vibrations. When I reached out to the concrete walls for support, the walls appeared to bounce out of my touch from the force passing through them.

Back in the open, I looked at the blue sky, and the world looked beautiful. I felt the wind crawling over the lake without the slightest hint of a ripple, felt the wind on my face, and I was glad to be alive. But then I caught sight of the towering cranes, the giant yellow earth movers, the steel skeletons waiting to be moulded in concrete, the huge discarded spools of cables scattered along the lakeshore along with other debris, and my spirit sank in despair. The mood stayed with me all the way to the hotel lounge.

Later, as I looked around me in the hotel, I saw a Cree of immense size and, as far as he could make out, of equally immense strength. Larry Snowboy was sitting at the next table, idly turning an empty Coke can in his hands, staring at the blue smoke hovering under the dark ceiling.

"We had an interesting video here last night," I said, trying desperately to ignite some human conversation. "The 'Voyage of the *Odeyak*."

"Yes, answered Larry somewhat laconically, I was on the *Odeyak* myself. Came home only last week. Then, moving his chair so as to face me, he asked, "And what brings you to this part of the world?"

I was pleasantly surprised by the directness of the question. Even the lawyer hadn't bothered to ask me what I was doing in Radisson. I was unprepared for my reply. "Well, you've got to let me think," I said, "as I'm not sure I have the answer worked out."

Larry laughed. "That's a funny answer," he said.

"I have an interest in maps," I started, "and I think I came here to find out how the landscape has changed from the maps I knew when I was younger." I paused to look at Larry to see if he didn't think me mad. "But you know what," I told him, "I didn't remember to bring my old maps with me. Now that's not funny. It's positively stupid. Now I'm stuck inside this hotel."

"Ah!" said Larry, "then there maybe something else that brought you here."

"I don't know," I replied. I explained to Larry how I thought I might have liked to see Chisasibi but that a lawyer staying at the hotel had discouraged me from visiting on my own.

"Ah, Rochard," said Larry with a knowing smile. "A lawyer. You mean you guys in the big city still trust lawyers?" he asked. "We don't."

He said he was about to leave anyway. Since I had a car, he suggested I follow his beat-up station wagon. "Three hundred thousand kilometres, and the odometer's stopped," he declared proudly.

"GM technology triumphs at last," I chimed in.

After nearly an hour's driving, Larry stopped his wagon at what seemed like a barrier manned by two young natives. There was a coffee-coloured van with the markings of the Cree Band Council parked perpendicular to the road. A blue sedan had already stopped at the barrier. Larry came to a halt behind this car, and I braked behind him. Larry walked over and said to me, "We don't allow any booze beyond this point. Come out and take a look."

He led me to the front of the blue sedan from the trunk of which one of the Cree men was hauling out one six-pack of beer after another. Molson, Labatt's, good Canadian stuff. Two native men and two women sat quietly in the car, stone-faced, showing no emotion whatsoever. They obviously knew what the rules were. The men shut the trunk, took one more look near the feet of the passengers, and waved the car on without another word.

"This is my friend, Charlie," said Larry, introducing me to the two. "Take a good look in his car if you want to."

"It's okay," said one of them, as he and his companion went to work on the beer hauled out of the blue sedan earlier. They proceeded to pull out each can from the six-pack plastic collars. Quickly, they lined up the cans side by side on a rocky ledge nearby. Then, one of the men pulled out a baseball bat from the van and systematically struck a hefty blow to each can, dispatching each with its ruptured contents into the wilderness beyond.

"Here, let me take a few shots," said Larry, grabbing the bat in his massive hands. Right away, I got a sense of his strength.

"How was that?" asked Larry, turning to his friends after a dozen booming hits or so.

"Pretty good," said one, approvingly.

"You get better every day, Larry," added the other, as we said goodbye and moved on.

A little further down the road, we passed the sprawling camp at the La Grande 1 construction site. A security van was coming out of the gate. It stopped to let us pass, and the guard at the wheel threw an enquiring, unfriendly glance at us. Larry promptly responded by giving him the finger as we passed by.

Larry circled around Chisasibi without actually stopping and then headed on to a gravel road ending at a rocky point. "I thought you'd like this better," he said, pointing to the sandy bluffs of Fort George, the former island home of most Chisasibi residents.

We took a leisurely walk along the water's edge and Larry pointed out James Bay in the distance, its scattering of ice floes still shining white against a cold grey sea.

I could feel a shiver of thrill go through me at the mention of James Bay. It was as if I was a child once again. I stood staring into the distance for a long time. There seemed something subterranean calling out to me, drawing me to the bay.

We walked away from the water and I remember facing rolling woodlands of black spruce and larch stretching for miles. In places, the sparse spruce stood apart from one another in a sea of lichen and muskeg stirred with pastel shades of grey and orange. As we walked, we planted our footsteps over soft moss, so soft, so unresisting, that it felt as if the footprints would remain for a hundred years. Suddenly, to the east, the giant towers of Hydro Quebec loomed into view. They appeared to sway over the land as the wind gathered force and rocked the strands of powerlines strung like garlands under a passionless sky. Holding his forefinger out like the barrel of a pistol, Larry pointed to them and said, "We'll have to bring those towers down one by one."

Larry next showed me a clearing in the distance where the rotting poles of a teepee stood like a wasted skeleton from the past. "I prayed and fasted in that teepee many years ago," he said. "I was a young boy then, and I was looking for my spirit helper. I was all alone. I promised to stand and face the sun all day and to turn with the sun. By late afternoon I could stand no more. I fell asleep over a caribou skull my father had left for me. Sure enough, the caribou spirit came to me that night. I stayed there three more days, forcing myself into many acts of stubbornness. All kinds of different spirit powers came to see me each night. They left me with some of their powers and many of their songs. That's how I got my power, that's how I know many songs." Larry turned his face to the horizon and appeared reflective. "Pretty nearly every night now I sing some of those songs. Before that I used to hear my father singing all the time, and I couldn't figure him out. He sang when he mended the nets. Sang when he shaved. Now I know why. Said he was giving thanks for the act of shaving his beard, and he truly was."

As we came close to Chisasibi on the drive back, Larry suddenly stopped by the side of the road. He walked over to my car and said, "I want you to meet one of our elders. He's quite a character."

Old Bill Pepabano still set his decoys on the shallow lagoons ringed by muskeg as he waited for the geese in Spring and early in the Fall, sprinkling his hair with hay and grass to blend better with his surroundings and, half-heartedly, almost despairingly, dabbling his fingers in the water from time to time to mimic the sound of feeding waterfowl. Those days when he felt particularly bored he would wander off from the water's edge only to return with handfuls of slender spruce staves. In between sounds to attract the phantom geese, he would lash these staves to wire hoops stowed away in the innards of his vast parka, shining with grease stains. These were the beaver funnel traps which he had almost always used in the days of his father, and more recently on rare occasions when he set out to trap beaver. On this day, Larry and I came upon Bill making these beaver traps with single-minded concentration.

Larry introduced me to him. The old man looked up, smiled and nodded at me, and went back to his work. I cleared my throat, as I usually find myself doing before speaking to strangers. "Looks very interesting," I said. The old man didn't even seem to hear me.

Just then, a young woman emerged from the trees on the other side of the road. As I saw her, I actually thought my heart had stopped pumping blood, that my lungs had become paralysed, leaving me breathless. She was the most exquisite creature I had ever seen, and the unexpectedness of it all sent me reeling. Fair and slender, her dark hair streaming behind her under a beaded hairpin, a perfectly oval face with lips as edible as ripe melons, she was the archetypal Indian princess as far as I was concerned.

Larry looked up and asked, "Hello, Rosie, what're you doing here?"

"I brought Bill some lunch," she said. "Usually try to do it when I'm home. He'd rather starve than give up on the geese." Then she turned to the old man with a puzzled expression on her face. "What're you up to, Bill?" she asked.

Bill Pepabano was hungry. He quickly dipped his potato fries in the gravy and explained to us how he would clear a break in a beaver dam and place the conical trap in the water pouring through the gap. The larger end easily allowed the passage of the beaver, but the smaller end was only large enough for the beaver's head. The smaller end pointed downstream. As the beaver came to check out the break in the dam it would swim right into the funnel. There was no backing out. The springy sticks of the staves extended beyond the last hoop at the small end and caught the beaver at the base of the skull. Soon the beaver drowned.

"How come I've never seen these before?" asked Rosie, shaking her head.

Was she shaking her head in dismay? Dismayed by cruelty? I couldn't tell.

Bill replied, "That's because we don't trap beavers hardly any more. It's not worth it. Your father gave up trapping beavers before you were born."

Bill finished his lunch and we took leave of him. But not before Rosie had emphatically announced she would never trade places with a beaver with one of Bill's traps around.

Larry called out to Rosie and offered her a ride. She promptly hopped into his wagon. I followed, but my heart ached for wanting to speak to Rosie. I felt like a fool for not having introduced myself to her. I had lost my voice. My throat had become dry on seeing her. When Larry stopped his car to let Rosie off, I made up my mind and walked briskly over to them.

The moment Larry saw me he said, "I'm sorry, Charlie, I forgot to introduce you to Rosie."

"Hello, Rosie." For once, I didn't have to clear my throat.

"Hello."

There was an uneasy silence until I broke it saying, "I guess I should head back to Radisson. It's been a wonderful day and I'm really, really grateful to you, Larry."

Larry showed his genial self again. "Hey, man, you don't have to be so formal and stuffy," he said.

I felt myself turning hot and red behind the ears.

"I'd like to offer you some goose for dinner," said Larry, "but you'll probably eat much better at the hotel."

"I'd love to stay," I said, "but I'm afraid I've taken up a lot of your day." Again, having said it, I could have kicked myself for sounding so pompous. "But let me give you a card," I said, hurriedly. I offered one to Rosie as well, who showed only the slightest curiosity as she read my name and stuck the card under her watch band. I told them, somewhat lamely, "If you should ever come to Montreal, please give me a call. And I really mean it."

"Come to Montreal?" asked Larry incredulously. "Rosie and I both go to school in Montreal."

"Where?" I asked, in total disbelief.

"McGill," they both replied together.

"McGill," I repeated. "Do you know John Gage?" I asked.

"Man," replied Larry, "everyone knows John Gage. He directs the training programme we're both in."

Malcolm Gunn lived on, a solitary man propped up by beliefs and visions that had haunted his family from one generation to the other. If his eyes drifted from the hollow gaze of someone past caring, if his careless beard and ill-fitting clothes gave him the appearance of a street person, it was because my mother was no longer there to carry the burden of those beliefs with him. From the moment I had broached the subject of the truth about Isabel Gunn, my father had grown more and more alarmed at my scepticism. I think in my letters to my father I began to strike him as a somewhat changed person, stronger, perhaps more worldly-wise. In retrospect, it seemed true that in the ten months since my mother's death, I felt and expressed less and less pain in my letters. I remember the tenth month because it was something of a watershed in my life. Suddenly, I began to believe in myself.

As the year passed, the single event of my mother's death and her funeral—like the childhood image of a solitary boat that I always remembered tied up against the vast expanse of the sea beyond the Point of Ness in Stromness—seemed to be the only precious memory that stood out over the accumulated drudgery of the past months. I couldn't remember ever seeing anyone row the boat out to sea, nor could I imagine anyone but myself ever renewing the flowers on my mother's grave. I found it amusing that I, like others, circumscribed life in neat little packages of years, months and days. I was amused because it seemed to give life something of the precision of a finely crafted watch, or better still a marine insurance policy, every word steeped in history, shaped by legal battles pitting the craftiest lawyers against each other, by wrecks at sea and lives and fortunes rotting on the ocean floor. In fact, I had often thought of life as an insurance policy against oblivion, the premium being the energy one was prepared to put into it—each moment, each event, a thing of permanence nothing could change. At the time, I had thought nothing of the insight. Today, it seems positively profound.

Perhaps nineteen eighty nine wasn't as stark and uneventful after all. In Montreal, people fought over the English language—or the French language if they were French—but did not, fortunately, kill each other in battle. Elsewhere, politicians fumed at public meetings over matters of monumental significance, and they too survived. Was French culture being held hostage by the ordinary English-speaking Joe? Should French-speaking women produce more children in a spirit of patriotism, in answer to the calls of Church and State? I watched some of these debates from the warmth of Woody's Pub on Bishop Street where legislative bills numbering 101 or 178 were hacked, minced, or flushed down along with gallons of Molson's or Labatt's beer. Then there were times when the intellectuals in the bar mused over the fate of the Indians—poor buggers who they feared would be made still poorer by smart-assed Indian lawyers. Once, a strikingly handsome Indian actually walked into the pub even as Indians were being discussed at my table. Everyone fell silent and stared at the newcomer. I felt very embarrassed. Then the man left as suddenly as he had come, and the table broke into a strange, nervous laughter. Soon every table was laughing. These evening distractions, occasional at best, often ambivalent, gave me a chance to get together not only with friends from the insurance business but also with clever university people like John Gage. One day, I teasingly said to John, "You guys are really smart people; you want to send the savages back to the Stone Age, pretending that's what they want, when all you want is their land." Some of the people at my table might have taken offence at the remark, but it seemed to endear me to John Gage. He showed more warmth towards me after that.

Later that fall, one evening when I was feeling particularly mellow, I decided to tell John about Isabel Gunn. "My father insists my great-great-grandmother was a saint," I said. Almost immediately, I was overcome by a feeling of guilt. Still, I pressed on. "She could change her shape from that of a woman to a man. She even gave birth to my great grandfather without ever having known a man," I said.

A vast grin flashed across John Gage's face. I found his response unsettling and annoying. "What're you laughing about?" I asked John. I felt upset, mostly with myself for having opened my mouth. "My father believes it," I said.

"But do you?" asked John.

I shrugged and reached for my beer. But the professor came at me once again. "You're such a fake, Charlie," he said, smiling into his glass. I remained silent, focusing my attention on the rainbow of colours spilling from the bottles stacked behind the bartender.

Moments later, John Gage looked up and turned an accusing gaze at me. "Charlie," he said, "you're prepared to believe all this rot, and yet you pretend the aboriginals are ready for modern civilization. So many among us believe we're dragging them screaming and kicking into the twenty first century. Why should they drive cars, have flush toilets? Why should they profit from oil under their lands? Isn't that how you really feel too, like millions of others in this country?"

"Let's drop it," I said. "I'm sorry I brought up the subject in the first place.

The matter would have rested there, except that John Gage swore he would educate me about aboriginals. "You mean Indians?" I asked, weakly trying to get even with him.

"No, aboriginals," replied John. "That's lesson one."

On another occasion, John promised he was also determined to educate me about women. "It's not that I have anything against women," I protested. "It's just that my family has a history of involvement with saintly women. Got to keep up the family tradition."

"Maybe we'll find you a saint then," remarked John. "But we'll get you started all right."

Even as we laughed and joked about saints and how hopeless I felt about women, my own life began to tilt out of balance. This had nothing to do with women, considering John hadn't found me my saint as yet. Rather, it had something to do with my attitude towards work. During the previous year I had been promoted to vice president of the marine insurance division within my company. My job now came with many more frills and trimmings. But I couldn't get rid of the uneasy feeling that these rewards had come my way because I had somehow schemed for them, through my behaviour, my habits, my tastes, my compliance. I didn't think there was anything morally wrong, but at times I did feel like a mercenary. I looked back at my family and my childhood and realized how far I had drifted from our simple, unadorned lives. I remembered the visitors to the house, the doors always open, in Stromness, people dropping in whenever they wished to. Uncle Billy with his passion for shipwrecks along the coast, forever clipping pages from newspapers and magazines. Mary Scott, the pharmacist's wife, gushingly curious — to the point of being nosey — about other peoples' lives, yet so gentle, considerate, and generous to all.

Maybe we did keep the doors locked when we lived in Bow, London. I don't quite remember. But that didn't seem to stop Mr. Templeton, the librarian from Stepney, who loved his drop of port but claimed he was only coming to help me with my home-work. And Jenny who would always walk with me to school, whom I kissed once in the alley only to be slapped for my impudence, and whom I never kissed afterwards though she swore she would never slap me again.

With my father's passion for maps and my own love of the sea, it was perhaps inevitable that I would be drawn to a job such as mine. "You should've been a sailor," said my company president, complimenting me on my eye for maritime detail and my knowledge of European and American coastlines. The president had added, in jest, "One way or the other, you'd have driven many insurance companies out of business.

I liked the compliments. What I felt uncomfortable about were the compromises I thought I was making in order to deserve them. The pub was something of a confessional. "Look at the river," I complained to John Gage and my drinking buddies one night in Woody's. "My company must insure billions of dollars worth of ships and cargo going up and down the St. Lawrence, not to mention factories and smelters along the banks, and the water's filthier than a sewer."

John Gage said, "I'm no Greenpeace activist, but I do think your industry could play a part in helping clean the environment, the rivers, the oceans, the air."

"How?" I asked.

John explained, "Simply by not insuring the worst offenders, or charging them such high premiums that they cry uncle."

"That's so simplistic," I retorted, "typical of you fellows in the ivory tower. Don't you know there's always another company willing to charge a little less and take the business away?"

"Yes, but for how long?" asked John. "Sooner or later the claims will come home to roost. You guys can band together over my car insurance, and you mean to say you can't do that over noxious cargo or rotting hulls? Surely the industry can do something if it seriously wants to."

I had heard it all before. So I could shake my head in resignation. "To think that I paid good money to live next to the river," I said.

John wasted no time rubbing salt into the wound. "I suppose you know you've lost some money already with real estate prices as they are," he reminded me.

"Ah! I protested. "You guys sure live in a fool's paradise. Who do I claim against for a filthy river? Besides, it's not the river or the foul Montreal air that's driving prices down, but the political shit over the French language and the Holy Grail of sovereignty."

"When the shit hits the fan, Charlie, it covers everything—real estate, the river, Macdonald's. Nothing will escape."

I couldn't help laughing. "You've such a wonderful way with words," I told John.

It seemed our neighbours had been listening in. From the table next to us, an anonymous voice commented, "Distinct society is such a crock." At which point, everyone fell silent. Nobody laughed, perhaps unwilling to take the chance of offending the odd Francophone lurking in the shadows.

After a while, John Gage said to me, sounding more serious than before, "Look at the Mohawks, the Cree, the Inuit. Who cares a damn for their distinctness? They practically own most of Quebec's land anyway. And all Mr. Parizeau can do is slap his guts and mutter 'Jolly good' and 'By Jove'. What hypocrites." John looked me straight in the eye and added, as we got up to leave Woody's, "That's lesson number two."

Lesson number three seemed to take on a life of its own, with John having nothing to do with it for a start. It began with a million dollar consignment of electronic gear from France, destined for the Hydro Quebec project in La Grande in northern Quebec. My insurance company found a real mess on its hands when a large trailer carrying the equipment overturned on a desolate road north of Val d'Or. I decided to fly to Val d'Or with the loss adjuster, Pierre Tremblay.

I had gotten to know Pierre quite well over the years, having met him hundreds of times in the course of my work. But travel with Pierre was a different matter. It demanded a certain patience, a certain nearness of less than matching tastes and behaviour which wouldn't necessarily be required at work.

"You've never been to Val d'Or, right?" asked Pierre. "Well, have I got a treat for you. It's a seedy old place, but there's a lot of action really, if you know what I mean." Pierre winked at me and I laughed, not knowing how else to respond.

I had of course no illusions about the nature of the action, but I was still caught by surprise. The motel we checked into after a short drive from the airport was clean and quiet, in keeping with the lifeless character of Main Street. There was the usual clutch of stores one found anywhere. We had beer and pizza at a restaurant across the street a short distance away. Pierre patted the pretty waitress' bum and made a half-hearted pass at her, without any success. She smiled at us but, turning to serve a native family seated at the next table, went through a sudden transformation. She screwed up her pretty face into a scowl, her voice became rude, and her air one of impatience. I looked at her in surprise and, turning to Pierre for an explanation, heard him mutter under his breath, "Scum, the town's full of them."

We finished our meal in silence. Afterwards, Pierre drove me to a hotel in the centre of town.

Bright and spacious, the lobby of the hotel was a sharp contrast from the drab exterior. I was pleasantly surprised to see groups of Indians in business suits, braids and all, chatting among themselves. As we entered the lounge, I asked Pierre, "These don't look so scruffy, do they?"

"No," replied Pierre, "these guys think they've made it. Just a matter of time before it gets to their head."

Aboriginals, not Indians, I reminded myself. I was amazed how invisible they seemed in Montreal. Or, if visible, they slipped inevitably into stereotypes of drunks and thieves, waiting for handouts near liquor stores, hanging around underground stations. True, I had occasionally seen business types in the lobby of the Queen Elizabeth or the Sheraton, in office buildings, or that strange apparition in Woody's one evening, but somehow the scruffy types displaced all other images.

In between drinks, Pierre left the table to proposition an ageing but attractive woman seated at the bar. Here, there were younger Indians too, men and women, smoking and drinking, laughing and talking very loudly. There was an unmistakable air of defiance about them. White folk didn't look at them, pretending they weren't even there. The Indians seemed to know this and were determined to make their presence felt. As we finished our drinks, Pierre asked, "Don't get me wrong, but do you need a woman?" He sounded perfectly casual and matter-of-fact. So was I, as I politely declined.

"I'm going to drop you off at the motel," said Pierre, "if you don't mind." On the way out, we passed a Surete du Quebec officer walking towards the lounge. "Bon soir," he exchanged greetings with Pierre as they passed. "He'll keep the bastards in place," murmured Pierre.

Light snow was falling on Val d'Or. As they scattered aimlessly in the light outside my window, the snowflakes calmed me down, occasionally forming and re-forming themselves like flocks of geese, or changing directions like a flailing whip, without warning but with unmatched grace. From time to time the snowflakes even formed the faces of people I remembered — odd, unaccountable faces that seemed to turn up from nowhere. An irate boat-owner in Fenchurch Street whose boat had capsized and who felt he was being swindled by his insurers. The odd secretary in my London and Sherbrooke Street offices who always seemed to have other men in their lives, and no room for me. And Pierre. I had nothing against people like Pierre, felt no hostility towards them. But I had some strong feelings, even a secret dread, against the idea of one-night stands, however occasional and perfunctory, however casually forgotten. Because that's when you're getting ready to kill yourself, an inner voice told me; that's when you die a little, every time, and it gets nearer every night.

I was reminded that, lately, there had been times when I felt that I too was drifting, much like the whirling snow outside. And yet, it was not supposed to be this way. Malcolm Gunn, echoing the sentiments of the masters of the Hudson's Bay Company, had told me that the boys from the Orkneys were the best. The Company was well and truly wary of the swaggering, drunken lads from London.

So where had I changed? The city, perhaps it was the city. From Ness's Point, on the right day with the right sunlight, one could feast one's eyes upon bands of emerald, each slightly different in shade from the other, the last band mounting into the sky, melding with the blue. Yes, it was exquisite in the Orkneys. London, on the other hand, was often something of a festering sore. It needn't have been, but there was Brixton and Notting Hill, and decay and destitution masquerading as hope. But why was Charlie Gunn so concerned? Why was he disturbed? After all, men were supposed to be busy with the business of putting bread on the table. And women, as he had been led to believe, with the business of babies. There was probably an obvious connection between the two. Maybe I was missing the connection, maybe that's where the problem was.

Sometimes I wished I was as educated and wise as John Gage, if only to help me work through some of these questions that seemed so intractable, so beyond my intellect. Sure, I was John's equal in many ways, probably lived better, certainly had a more fashionable address with rock stars and politicians as neighbours. Come to think of it, my training as an insurance man never really prepared me for London's exploding turbulence, or Montreal's simmering irritations. In London, I chose to hate the IRA, the Labour party, Khaddafy, and homosexuals with equal passion. In Montreal, I had chosen to ignore the problem of language, of aboriginals and gays in the same way. What a fine recipe for mental peace, thought I, Charlie Gunn.

One day, I confided to John, "I wish I had a Ph.D. like you." I'm sure John detected a note of envy and regret in my voice.

"You're crazy," he replied, trying to demystify my sense of awe over his academic achievements. "It's not all that it's cracked up to be. I may seem a happy, contented man to others, but that's nothing to do with academics. It's only a job. I could've been just as happy selling snake-oil.

I am sure Pierre thought of me as very smart in insurance matters and very stupid in others.

The damaged consignment and the overturned truck were still sitting in a gully by the time Pierre and I arrived. It seemed a straight forward claim until I happened to notice some older stains at the bottom of the crates. To my experienced eyes, these looked suspiciously like salt-water stains. Both Pierre and the Hydro Quebec representative thought that was impossible since the consignment had landed in Montreal under a clean bill of lading and transferred onto the truck without a fuss. I was not prepared to back off and wanted Pierre to send the wood for analysis.

When Pierre finally had the crate opened in his presence, they found rust on the lower parts of some of the machinery. Clearly, the rust hadn't formed following the road accident in which the crate had fallen on its side. The conclusive evidence of sea-water stains and old rust set in motion a claim against the ship for sea-water damage. As was to be expected, the ship denied all liability. But I was far from satisfied.

Another day, shortly after my trip with Pierre, I brought to work a large map of North America my father had given me as a gift. It was not an antique map by any means, simply a very detailed mid-twentieth century map. I told Pierre, who had stopped by to discuss the claim assessment with me, "I can't believe this. The place has changed so much. Since the hydro project started, this new land covered by water looks half the size of Lake Ontario."

Pierre corrected me, "The new reservoirs cover four and a half thousand square miles.

I had to laugh as I put the map away. "The old map's useless," I said. "You'd drown if you had to rely on it."

Pierre thought I had got the spirit all wrong. He protested, "But it is our Premier's vision. It's the greatest hydro project in the world, will cost over fifty billion dollars, and cover a hundred and thirty five thousand square miles before it's finished. It'll free Quebec from the oppression of Toronto's Bay Street bullies once and for all," he announced proudly. Then, looking up in response to my silence, he added, uncertain as to whether I had been upset, "Hope you don't misunderstand me."

I allowed time for the statistics to sink in. Pierre looked at me anxiously. I was English-speaking after all. Finally, I had to tell him, "Of course I don't, Pierre, but how come this has gone on for so long? All this planning. All this manpower."

Pierre smiled. "Times change," he replied, somewhat enigmatically.

I remembered then. That's what my father used to say: "Maps change but the earth remains the same." Not in this case, surely, I thought.

Pierre shrugged his shoulders. "It's a good project," he said, "run by good people."

"Next time you go up north to Val d'Or or beyond, will you take me along, Pierre?" I asked.

Pierre grinned. "Business or pleasure?" he asked.

"Strictly business," I reminded him, with mock seriousness.

That was my life, in a somewhat haphazard if precise package of a somewhat desultory year. In a sad, uneventful sort of way, nineteen eighty nine came and went, and I was nowhere close to falling in love.

Pettigrew had gone to sleep in his chair.

Montreal winters can be long and hard.

But Spring came early that year. For the first time in my life, if somewhat belatedly, I sensed I was feeling real passion, though still undefined, for a woman. The invisible spell of Isabel Gunn hadn't loosened its bonds sufficiently to allow me to express, let alone recognize with certainty, the feeling in terms of sexual passion. Never a very reflective person, I felt no different walking past the sex shops on Saint Catherine's Street and wondered if my physiological development had been arrested in some curious way. But whenever I saw Rosie, it was different. In fact, it felt excruciatingly different. I began to wonder if much of what I had read, much of what I had seen, hadn't twisted reality out of shape. Rosie was exciting. Rosie was scary.

I think I had invited Rosie out to dinner on three occasions, and she had accepted happily, each time. The first time, we went out with Larry, John Gage and his soon to be estranged girl-friend. The evening was doomed to failure from the start. John's girl-friend didn't like the menu, didn't take part in the conversation, and spent most of the evening either in the washroom or on the phone.

The next time, it was just the three of us, Rosie, Larry, and I. It was a lot of fun, with Larry recounting—for my benefit—some of the white man's most horrific perceptions of the aboriginal male. "We're not supposed to be studs like some of the other inferior races," said Larry, "but useless, worse than animals." The statement lies engraved in my memory.

The third time it was just Rosie and I at an elegant place on St. Denis. Still, nothing happened, sexually speaking. Somewhere in the back of my mind there was a notion—and I was secretly ashamed of it—that native women would jump into bed at the drop of a hat, or at least a drop of alcohol. Rosie loved her wine, but she was unyielding in every other respect. And, in a world where such things seemed quite irrelevant, I imagined I still had a grain of delicacy which simply froze me at the thought of coming on too strong towards her.

Our mutual concern for Barry gave us, unexpectedly, something in common. It came up during the first dinner when I happened to ask John how Barry was getting along. I found out that he was withdrawing himself from others more and more, had no job still, and was probably not doing any painting or sculpting at all. Larry thought he might agree to go to a centre near Edmonton where they were using sweat-lodges and other spiritual means to fight native alcoholism. The question was money. Larry was going to see if the Chisasibi Band Council—to which Barry really had no claim—might somehow be persuaded to come up with the travel costs to send him to Edmonton.

I was willing to come up with the money right away. Rosie looked at me with surprise when I made the offer. I think, from that moment onwards she began to see me in a different light, or so I thought, although I had no intention of trying to appear generous. There was a change in her from that moment. She appeared more thoughtful, more gentle, towards me.

Larry didn't think it would work. Barry probably wouldn't go if he got the slightest hint that the money was private. John Gage agreed.

About this time, an exhibition came to the city — "The West as America: Reinterpreting Images of the Frontier". The exhibition had generated a lot of heat in the U.S. and I thought it would give us an excuse to get together with Barry once more. Rosie said she would get in touch with him.

Barry came, but we had to go and fetch him from Oka. Someone had slashed all his four tires in his own driveway, and he had no money to buy new ones. Of course, he never had insurance. In spite of all the trouble we went to, and Barry's genuine pleasure at having been asked, the evening proved disturbing to us all. The causes of this discomfort seemed different for each one of us.

I felt angry as I read the catalogue against the backdrop of heroic paintings of the American west. "I'm not that familiar with American history," I said, "but surely the people who wrote this are perverting history." I didn't know any one of the painters, but I was certainly not prepared for what I found. I finally said to them, "Look at this drivel."

I read from the catalogue.

Images from Christopher Columbus to Kit Carson show the discovery and settlement of the West as a heroic undertaking. A more recent approach argues that these images are carefully staged fiction, constructed from both supposition and fact. Their role was to justify the hardship and conflict of nation-building. Western scenes extolled progress, but rarely noted damaging social and environmental change. Looking beneath the surface of these images gives us a better understanding of why national problems created during the West-ward expansion affect us today.

I looked up and was surprised at not hearing a response either from Barry or Rosie. Both smiled politely, nodded, and turned their attention to the exhibits ahead. I was taken aback by this reaction. I would've thought we were all on the same wave-length. Perhaps I was wrong. Was it possible there'd be people who would disagree over the meaning of the great European Cathedrals, perhaps even Saint Magnus Cathedral? These doubts soon subsided. I put the catalogue away from my mind and joined the pleasant, curious crowd that shuffled along the carpeted aisles of the gallery. I stopped with a large group of visitors in front of "Carson's Men", a striking painting of Kit Carson and two companions on horseback, majestic against the sky, relishing almost a sacred, spiritual experience out of the conquest of the West. Now what was wrong with that? I wondered, but this time I stopped short of asking either Rosie or Barry.

Rosie was silent, but Barry was beginning to look distressed. In any case, he had looked very poorly when we picked him up in Oka. So I asked him politely if he was feeling all right.

"I can't seem to understand these people," said Barry. "They seem to be enjoying this all so uncritically. But this is a travesty of art. It makes a complete mockery of the truth of what happened to the aboriginals in North America. I don't care if it's the American West or the Canadian North. So some white soldiers got butchered. Don't tell me the Indians didn't get paid back in kind." Barry looked as if he was in considerable pain.

People were staring hard at us, and I began to show my embarrassment. Somewhat lamely, I said, "Yes, I think that's the point the catalogue is trying to make."

I started to walk away discreetly from "Carson's Men", but Barry caught up with me. He continued, "Everyone knows the details left behind by Hearne on his voyage to the Coppermine River when two natives cruelly speared to death a young girl even as she entwined her arms around his legs begging for mercy. Or of the starving Indian woman who dug up one of her own relatives, buried some time, and fed on the putrefied body for several days. So what does it prove? That it's okay to obliterate the aboriginal way of life? From there, the next step to wiping them out completely is so easy and natural."

I wasn't ready to agree with Barry, but wasn't prepared to argue with him in public either. I actually liked the young Mohawk and was trying, in my own mind, to understand, if not accept, the Mohawk's point of view.

Rosie was now standing in front of a painting which seemed to be attracting a lot of attention. But the longer she stood, the angrier she seemed to get. I noticed this as I was walking up, and felt curious enough to work my way to the front where I could get an unobstructed view. I recognized the picture as one the newspapers had devoted a lot of space to. "The Captive" was based on the capture of seventeen-year old Lorinda Bewley by Five Crows, the Cayuse chief, in 1847. The painting shows Lorinda lying on the ground, in the light, with the Indian chief sitting cross-legged, observing the sleeping or unconscious woman from the shadows. There's blood on her wrist, and any fool could surmise that she had been sexually attacked by Five Crows and that he seemed to be contemplating the next attack on the young white woman. Again, I thought, an interesting painting, but what's the big deal? I stepped out of the line of viewers to take another quick look at the catalogue. It said the painting, as much as the event itself, was a key element in the transformation from the noble Red Man to the murderous savage within a single generation. I looked up just in time to see Rosie turning away and head slowly for the exit. Barry seemed also on his way out with her.

I had reserved a table for dinner at the nearby Four Seasons Hotel, so it made sense for all of us to head in that direction. But it seemed all conversation had dried up between us. Once we were seated, I tried to break the ice. "Having read bits and pieces of the catalogue," I said, "I can see the point the exhibition is trying to make. But do you have to read a book to understand art?" I looked straight at Barry, for it seemed logical to first seek his views, as a practising artist, on the subject.

"I'm not a very learned person," said Barry, "but I think it's important to understand the impulse that gives rise to art. There may be many impulses working together. When I work on a piece of stone, there's a strong desire to create something that is related to the Mohawk experience. There may be some anger, some regret, some nostalgia. What we saw today is propaganda, pure and simple. Being such, it is biased, misleading, and untrue. I didn't have any money to buy a catalogue to check if my understanding is correct." Barry left no doubt that he resented it all.

"It is," I felt compelled to reply. Then, somewhat firmly, I added, "I want you to have this catalogue because I am going to get two more tomorrow, one for Rosie and one for me." Turning to her, I asked, "Rosie, how come you haven't said a word since we sat down?"

Rosie smiled sadly. "I was thinking of a strange irony," she said. "Some artists get paid to create what their patrons would like them to. Others like Barry create what they—as artists—want to, and never get anyone to pay for it."

Barry smiled back and said, "Thanks, Rosie, you don't have to rub it into me. Don't remind me I'm an artist *sans* reputation."

After this brief exchange, the atmosphere around the table lightened up a bit. I had tried to make my peace with Barry, and I refused to give up easily. I said, "I want both your help in understanding why art can't be appreciated without some stupid scholar's commentary." I shook and thrust the catalogue towards them for emphasis. The candle on the table flickered wildly, causing the flowers in the vase to cast wild shadows on a basket of bread and rolls.

Barry stopped himself from reaching out for one of the rolls. "I don't think you need someone else's commentary," he said.

Rosie jumped in. "I didn't read the catalogue either. But I was especially mad with 'The Captive' because I'm sure there are as many cases of white men jumping native women as the other way around. Not only are you demeaning the aboriginal male, but also creating a paranoia which'll lead to hatred and contempt for such males and eventually mushroom into hard-core racism."

Barry was relishing the bread. Somewhat thoughtfully he said, "I doubt if art, or any expression, can be separated from its background, its context. If you did that, it would easily create a totally false impression."

I turned to the catalogue, read silently for a few moments and then spoke to the others. "Well, it does say here that several of the artists we saw today were paid handsomely by railroad companies to glorify and romanticize their commercial objectives. Others were openly racist and hostile to non Anglo-Saxon immigrants coming to America. What do you think of that?" I asked.

"That's the point," answered Barry. "These artists did what they had to. A twentieth century Columbus wouldn't succeed, wouldn't even be a hero, because we'd kill him first before talking. I wouldn't, but someone else would, I'm sure. I think our ancestors knew the white man would come, so they weren't surprised. They had heard of a white man who had carried Chief Donnacona to the land of the dead. The white man wanted the secrets of the Kingdom of the Saguenay because they lusted after its gold and diamonds. Our ancestors knew what they were after."

In a somewhat different vein, Rosie recalled stories she had heard that many native people had no idea other lands lay beyond the ocean, an area they supposed to be a part of the supernatural. Micmacs, for instance, believed that the first European ships they saw were floating islands. Some thought that the sails of such ships were white clouds and the discharge of guns, thunder and lightning. Many welcomed the missionary in the white robe because they imagined him to be White Rabbit Manbeing, a great supernatural power.

The dinner came back to life finally. Conversation moved to the food, to the mussels, the steak, the creme broulee. "This is the best meal I've had," said Barry. "Now I'll allow myself the supreme luxury of a cognac."

We had already gone through two excellent bottles of wine and Rosie looked with alarm at me over what she imagined would be the final price tag for the night.

Barry caught us exchanging glances. "I know what you're thinking," he said. "That I'm drinking too much. But I'm drinking only to fight my anger, to feel a sense of peace that disappears the moment I wake up. The evening and this glorious liquid — the white man's greatest gift to the Indian — brings that peace back to me. We're all dead to start with; but for alcohol the North American Indian wouldn't even be considered animate. This way, at least we move and twitch. Show some signs of life."

"You're being too kind to the white man," I said, trying to lighten Barry's mood.

"Barry, we'll have to get you home," said Rosie, "or one of us will get a ticket for drunken driving. If we don't stop now, poor Charlie will have to take out a loan."

"Isn't that what his company does, give loans?" asked Barry. Then he slapped his forehead with his fingers. "What am I saying? It's insurance you're in, not banking. You guys just give the money away." Ha, ha, ha, laughed Barry mockingly.

I joined Barry in his laughter.

We waited for Barry to finish his first cognac, and then his second. "Art is fine," mused Barry, "until it gets blown away by disorder and confusion. Mussorgsky had it dead right in 'Pictures at an exhibition'."

Rosie and I looked at each other, trying to figure out what exactly Barry was talking about. We all agreed it would've been nice if John Gage had come to the exhibition too. I confided to them that he was probably having some personal problems. I also added I wouldn't have said it if I hadn't drunk so much wine. Rosie agreed, saying that John had appeared somewhat distracted of late.

As we wore out the evening, I felt increasingly drawn towards two specific problems. One was the problem of Rosie. I was finding it impossible to keep my eyes off her. The other was Barry's comment on the question of art and its context. It seemed so simple as to be almost ingenuous. Yet, it made such a lot of sense. But wouldn't this yoking together make hardened sceptics of us all, I thought. The prospect of a world peopled entirely by highly intelligent adults — each reading between the lines, each person's understanding sinking below surface appearances to seize the inner reality — seemed somewhat daunting. Perhaps quite boring too. What place would there be in such a society for simple folk, for people who heard ancestral voices, for people trusting and childlike. For Rosie, for instance, I imagined, as I looked once more at her. She caught me looking at her, stared back at me, then dropped her eyes in obvious embarrassment. I eventually gave up trying to pursue this line of thought much further. Still, I could see Barry had a point with the pictures at the exhibition. The context gave them life, gave viewers a pretext to love or hate them.

"It's the lights that make Montreal so beautiful," said Rosie, as we pulled out of the underground parking and into Sherbrooke. It looked such a happy city and yet there was so much sadness around. Rosie looked sideways at Barry sitting in the rear and felt troubled by the change she had seen come over him. He looked defeated, she later explained to me. Not the kind of defeat some thought the Mohawks may or may not have suffered. The Warriors were all out on bail anyway. But a kind of defeat that has to do with oneself, where one no longer finds the strength to carry on. She felt the more deeply because she liked Barry very much. The Stone Carver with the heart of gold, they called him, until the name Gandhi came up and people forgot the other. Rosie loved his carvings, his paintings, and might have secretly loved him a little too. But the connection never happened.

"The context?" I asked with a sly smile.

"Yes," she agreed.

"That's where the Premier has always had an office," said Barry sleepily from the backseat, pointing to an office tower—an 'edifice' as they called it in Montreal—on Rene Levesque Boulevard. "That's where he sits and plans the destruction of the Iroquois nation and of each of the First Nations he can lay his hands on. And some of our chiefs seem only too keen to help him out." Barry's voice drifted away.

It was a pleasure driving on the expressways at that hour. We drove in silence for a long time. Barry woke up and said, "I might help him out too." Then he started humming an odd tune.

"And what does that mean, you helping the Premier?" asked Rosie.

"Oh! I don't know," replied Barry, breaking off his humming and drifting into silence once more.

And this was the way we travelled all the way to Oka. The town was deserted. The houses wrapped themselves in the shadow of the ancient pines and seemed to be as much at peace as the ancestral graves that had been spared for the time being. The shadows remained impenetrable, inseparable one from the other, with the moonlight splashing on the crests of little waves in the lake. The boats, especially the white ones moored along the water's edge, looked ghostly and phosphorescent in the light. I saw Rosie looking at this scene with such a sense of wonder that I couldn't help but slow down until the car too was crawling like a ghost, noiselessly.

Rosie put up her hand slightly in a gesture which I took to mean 'please stop'. Slowly, I moved off the road onto a pebbled patch and came to a halt.

"Wonderful," said Barry, whose house was only a stone's throw away from the spot. "I can get down here and walk across."

Barry opened his door and stepped outside. Rosie and I did the same. The light wind that brushed across the lake was the same wind that was rustling through the pine needles and making the trees creak and groan. We stood there for a long time, breathing in the night air and the smell of pine. Barry filled his lungs with a deep breath and said it felt as fragrant as a first kiss, made him feel so good to be alive. He lit a cigarette and offered me one. I am not a regular smoker, but I accepted it anyway, and so did Rosie.

Barry kissed Rosie. "Good bye, little sister," he said, somewhat unsteadily. He turned to me and held me in a strong embrace. "You're a good man, Charlie Brown," he said. We laughed, and our laughter rippled across the lake and disappeared, it seemed, into the very heart of the continent, a heart still full of secrets and wonder to folks like Rosie and Barry. We had talked about this once before, and I had argued that there were no secrets this side of death. That night, I said nothing.

On the way back to Montreal, Rosie admitted that she seemed to know very little about me except where

I lived, some notion of what my job was, the kinds of places I liked to eat at—expensive ones—and a less than vague notion of how much I might be earning. I corrected her by reminding her of my possible Cree connection.

"Oh, yes," she remembered. Then she said, "But that's hardly positive. It might point to alcoholism, irresponsibility, and low intelligence, living but not being alive—as Barry put it."

I asked her, "When are you going to find out about the true nature of this connection?" I thought you were going to find out from your father about Kechechowieh."

Rosie apologized for having neglected the matter, promising to attend to it come summer. I couldn't help telling her that I too knew very little about her. "I could say the same about you," I said, "since every time we've met we've discussed art, politics, the environment, the white man's injustice, and little else."

I think Rosie figured she could tell me about herself, as one usually does, choosing little details that surface in the mind at the time of the telling. She would tell me where she was born, what she remembered of Fort George as a child, where she went to school, about her beautiful mother whom the Spirits called away, about how she worshipped Louis and missed her brother Matthew who killed himself at sixteen. She would tell me about her job with the Cree School Board, and how much she valued the training she was getting at McGill. She probably shouldn't have said anything about her hopes and fears for her own people, because that would again get into politics, but she did. In conclusion, she said, "I don't know what more I can tell you that will make you any the wiser."

The car had come to a halt in front of her apartment building on Maisonneuve. "I don't want to be wiser," I remember blurting out. "I just want you to love me as I love you."

Rosie sat in silence, staring ahead of her through the windshield. Moved by my awkwardness, she told me later she imagined she should be flattered. Instead, she said she began to feel a numbness come over her. "It's not as easy as you think, Charlie, for either of us," she said. "You've been to James Bay once or twice and perhaps you've grown to like the place. But you really don't know anything about us, or about me."

I thought I ought to say something. I could point to a long-standing friendship with John Gage who identified himself so closely with Rosie and her people. I thought I was beginning to see some of their political problems from their point of view. I was almost convinced that their social problems were not of their making. Most important of all, I felt certain that it wasn't a romantic world that Rosie and Larry and the others were nostalgic about, one they were secretly hoping to revive. No, like everyone else we were all trying to come to terms with a harsh world, the present, one that seemed harsher every day even to me. As I quickly noted these points to try and tell her what I knew, I laughed inwardly at how feeble it all sounded. The words remained unspoken.

"I'm glad you didn't drive up to your apartment and invite me up," she told me. "I'm really grateful for that. In gratitude, I will invite you up for a cup of coffee. Nescafe Instant. Nothing more fancy than that."

By then, I had gotten over my confusion following my impulsive declaration of love. I laughed at Rosie's invitation. "Beggars can't be choosers," I reminded her.

"Prime Minister John A. Macdonald," she shot back. "I know my history." Then she pointed to a poster plastered on one of the pillars of Concordia University. It read: "No Means No".

I couldn't disguise my amusement. "You're a stickler for detail and emphasis, aren't you?" I asked.

Rosie was stepping out of the car, when a black sedan, its stereo belching bass notes into the night, suddenly rounded the corner and missed hitting her by inches. The car screeched to a halt about twenty feet from us. Two heads popped out of the driver's side. "Too bad we didn't kill the bitch," yelled one of them. "Shit," yelled the other, "now we must fight her for a fuck." Then the car sped away towards the Forum.

"Asshole," I cried after them, seething. "Vermin," I muttered to myself, feeling relieved that they hadn't hurt Rosie. "Now I know why we have posters like that in Montreal," I said.

"Happens all the time," said Rosie. "When they can't run you down, they shoot you in the classroom."

While we finished our coffee, Rosie invited me to come up to Chisasibi for the pow-wow in August. She sounded very excited about it. This was going to be only the second time they had had a pow-wow on the island within her memory. The first one was only the year before. That first year, she didn't know any of the dances because no one had taught her. Her mother, who should probably have done the teaching, had herself never been allowed by the nuns to learn the dances. Rosie remembered every word her mother told her about how they took her away with her brothers, Rosie's uncles, to a school in North Bay.

The day Rosie's grandmother walked her three children to the doors of the Indian Residential School, she began to understand the extent of the black-robe's power and influence. Grandmother was pushed back out of the door almost immediately by a nun who asked her not to get too emotional about farewells. Alone for the first time, Rosie's mother sobbed and cried while the nun listed the rules of the school and the punishments for disobeying them. Then she was herded away unceremoniously, powdered with DDT to kill lice, and showered with scalding hot water which made her scream in pain. At night, off to bed with orders to always sleep facing right, hands folded in a praying position under the head. She grew up with prayers and knew nothing of the dances that bound her people to their ancestors and their land. Rosie said, "It's not so much the land belonging to us, as us being a part of the land."

Like a child being told a story, I listened with rapt attention as Rosie told of her mother's endless rounds of prayers — prayers before shower, before meals, before classes, prayer circles before bed, prayers on their knees. As if this was not enough, there were threats of eternal damnation, threats of visits by Satan himself and other desperate souls languishing in purgatory. As she grew older, Rosie's mother graduated to the big girls' dorm on one side of which lay the Sister Superior's private chambers. Hardly anyone escaped entering these quarters, there to be laid across a wooden horse and whipped by Sister Superior on their bare buttocks till they could choke their screams no longer.

And there were nights the girls clung to each other for protection at the sound of footsteps that regularly crept up the fire escape, followed by whispers, moans, and muffled cries of pain. Nobody believed Rosie's mother or her brother if they ever talked about these experiences, which they would tell to anyone prepared to listen. By the time her mother came out of school she knew only of a God prepared to exact revenge for every transgression. There seemed little mercy anywhere, let alone from God's own chosen people in the Department of Indian Affairs.

I could see Rosie was in pain, but there were no tears in her eyes. I kept hoping she would tell me something of her own experiences. There was a risk I might cause her more pain, so I did not press her. Instead, I reached out and covered her hand with mine.

She didn't look up. "What you told me back there in the car," she said, "please don't say that again." Then she brightened up suddenly. "Charlie," she said, "be sure to come to Chisasibi. Besides the pow-wow, there'll be lots of fishing even though most of it'll probably be tainted. Especially at the First Rapids of the La Grande, perhaps less so on the coast at the Kapsawis River. There should be ducks flying all around, and the berries will start to ripen so the animals can get fat." Then she grew thoughtful again. "One thing we noticed a couple of years ago," she remarked, "was that whenever berry bushes are under the powerlines the berries tend to grow much bigger than usual. Almost three to four times bigger. We plucked them and ate some one summer. Each one of us became violently sick for nearly two days. I don't know if the bears eat them, but we don't any more."

"I've got to visit my father this summer," I told her, "but I'd love to come up for a few days in August."

"Do," said Rosie. "I'd ask you to stay with us but our place is so small we can hardly move sometimes. It was different with our old house on the island. I'm sure Larry can fix you up a place, either in the motel or with someone else."

I was about to get up and leave when she asked me, "Aren't you going to ask me over to Arcadia someday?"

"Arcadia?" I repeated, surprised.

"Isn't that where you come from?"

I tried to explain patiently. "Rosie," I said, you may have heard I'm an Orcadian. But I don't come from Arcadia. It means I come from the Orkneys."

"Where's that?"

"North of Scotland." Then, teasing her, I said, "So much for the geography teacher from James Bay."

"I'm not a geography teacher," protested Rosie. "But wherever it is -"

Just then, the phone rang, cutting her off in mid-sentence. It was Barry's father, calling to find out if Barry was going to be spending the night in Montreal.

Rosie's face turned pale. She took the receiver from me and explained to the old man that we had dropped him off near the beach at Oka. "It was such a beautiful night he said he'd walk back from there. Maybe he decided to drop in on some Warrior friends."

The police found Barry's body floating in the waters of the lake the next morning. He had a mask tied around his face. Barry's father kept looking at the masked face and murmured to himself, "We must all wear masks, all the time, for they'll always be blind to our real selves." Then, his eyes filling with tears, the father turned to me and said, "The worst pain you can inflict is on the mind and the heart. For that, there is no healing, no forgiveness."

Later, on the back seat of my car, I found the catalogue which Barry had forgotten to take with him the previous night.

For a few days I stopped going to Woody's pub. I was angry with myself, disappointed with John Gage. All this added up to my decision not to attend Barry's funeral. John Gage called me over the phone to find out what was the matter, and was obviously taken aback by my coldness and what he described, in his always well-chosen words, as a profound gloom in my voice. John asked me, "Do you suppose you could've saved Barry if you had bought some of his paintings, or that I could've added another day to his life by offering him money?"

I stared in silence at the sunlit sky framed by my window. "No," I said, "but he may've been able to buy a new set of wheels to replace his slashed tires." John didn't say anything in reply, and I said to myself, angrily: "You are a snake-oil seller, after all."

A strange mix of emotions seized me and made me restless and deeply unhappy. There was anger, of course, but a sense of guilt as well, even a touch of self-disgust. My bitterness increased with each day. I wanted to share my anger with someone, but I couldn't. At work, I caught myself becoming short with others, sending out sloppy work, careless calculations and projections. Since I couldn't bring myself to go out drinking with John and my other friends, I found I had more and more time to spend alone in my apartment. Here, I could cocoon myself in self-pity.

On those lonely evenings in my elegant apartment, standing behind the spotless windows overlooking the ships tied up at the pier, I felt John had inflicted another blow upon me. In tearing away the carefully woven cover of sanctity and secrecy that lay around Isabel Gunn, he seemed to have set me precariously free in some respects. He had put me in peril. I remembered the Sunday prayers in our living room at home where I was encouraged to meditate on the woman whom I knew only as a picture on the wall. I grew up thinking she could make anything possible. As a child I prayed to her for things that seemed desirable but somehow beyond my grasp. A woollen cardigan I had seen behind a store window in Kirkwall. A sound thrashing for the class bully who had roughed me up for supposedly being a teacher's pet. A beautiful pencil box I had seen in someone else's possession. I made fewer and fewer demands of Isabel Gunn as I grew older. But she remained a presence in my life, a kind of moral safe harbour to which you escaped from the storms and uncertainties plaguing others, as long as you played by the rules. And the rules said that one could be less human, but more God-like. Now, with a single stroke of his scholarly wand, John Gage had breached the harbour walls. Much that was denied to me before, seemed suddenly very accessible to Charlie Gunn. But how did it help? I felt lonelier than ever, more empty than before. Now the mystery of desire seemed less so, less unspeakable, but how was I to find satisfaction? John wasn't able to tell me that.

A big freighter, rusty black with a white hull, churned upstream leaving a great splash behind. Ships too had begun to seem irrelevant. This one held no more than passing interest for me, now that my superiors at work quite pointedly wanted me to cool my obsession with old and hazardous ships.

I wished I could speak to Rosie, but she had taken a break from her programme at McGill and gone back to teach at Chisasibi. She had missed me at the funeral and called me the very next day. Rosie said she understood my feelings, but didn't ask to see me before she left Montreal. She still hoped she would see me later in the summer though. I told her I hoped so too.

Sitting under Isabel Gunn's picture in London in May of that year, I wondered why I hadn't reminded Rosie one more time to find out something about Kechechowieh from her father. Perhaps it was just as well, now that she was just another picture on the wall, shorn of much of her mystery — seemingly vulnerable, to me at least, if not to Malcolm Gunn.

Should I tell my father what I had found out? After all, wasn't that what scholars were supposed to do — disseminate new knowledge? Again, to what purpose? Short of exacting some sort of revenge on my father — for some imaginary wrong having to do with vague moral strictures — I saw nothing to be gained by passing on the archival information to Malcolm Gunn. The men who might have helped debase her in my father's eyes were real enough. But, then, they were always real, weren't they? John Gage might think he had set me off on the road to the truth, but the process now appeared to have come full circle for me. I wondered what it was that really motivated John to shatter my illusions.

Was he really in love with the Cree as he made it out in public? Could it be that it was no more than a posture, just somebody trying to do a job—as effectively as possible—that somebody had to do. Where would John be if his college never had a programme to help the aboriginals? Could it be that John was, in reality, just another liberal intellectual masquerading as a lover of natives when all he really cared about was, once again, the land—a place to escape to, a place to forget the urban filth, a place for pleasant family vacations, gorging on smoked salmon and cheese, bagels, baguettes and wine, and Sudan be damned?

Then there was the problem with Barry. In the final analysis, Barry was surely wrong. Why would those who thought differently necessarily be wrong? What sacrilege could possibly have resulted from the larger golf-course at Oka? For every cairn found in Westness, thousands must be lost to the sea or to man. I failed to see how the question of disrespect for the dead could be linked to the extension of the greens and fairways. The truth was that I found it difficult to understand Canadians. I had certainly come to a point when Oka had once again become incomprehensible to me. But I warned myself to be careful to hide my thoughts from Rosie.

Of course, I had no doubt in my mind Barry was right to have opposed violence. And he was wrong to have taken up arms beside Lasagna, the masked Mohawk Warrior who was made out to be a drug-running terrorist one day and a Vietnam War veteran from the U.S. the next. And Barry's death? Perhaps he did what had to be done. Perhaps John Gage was partly right. Yet, sitting below Isabel Gunn's portrait on the wall, I couldn't hide my momentary surprise over how

I had suddenly devalued Barry's life, and perhaps all human life. Malcolm Gunn would probably be shocked to see this transformation in his son. Still, there had been recent occasions when I had felt my sensibilities squirming in the company of John Gage and his Cree friends as they reflected upon the so-called wrongs inflicted on the natives. Why should I have felt apologetic? After all, it was a problem that the French and the English had to come to terms with now that the crafty aboriginal, Elijah Harper, had so cleverly scuttled the quintessential snake-oil salesman's potion, the Meech Lake Accord, that was to have placed all Canadians, especially the French and the English-speaking, snugly in the same bed. Forget the aboriginals.

I began to experience a sense of relief as the image of Isabel Gunn shrank in reverence to no more than what I owed to any ordinary mortal. What did it all mean? What changes could I now expect in myself and in my attitudes?

All the aboriginals wanted was money. Away in London, I was slowly becoming convinced of that. The golf course was a pretext. Hydro Quebec was another pretext. The shores of the bay were still studded with forests of pine, poplar and juniper. The tide still rippled in and out of the white pebbled beaches. Maybe there was some truth to the theory that the native is more prone to alcoholism than others. How were my ancestors supposed to know that?

So, even as my father and I prepared for another summer visit to the Orkneys, I was compensating myself for the loss of Isabel Gunn with a new sense of the glory and value of the British Empire. Of itself, this game of changing sensibilities made little sense. For, oddly enough, I could still detect in myself a continuing susceptibility to tradition and conformity. My newfound self-confidence began to revive a jaded sense of pride in my own career, because it once again seemed so inextricably connected to the making of the Empire. And this is where it all began, I thought, as the *Ola* sailed past Rora Head and I caught a brief glimpse of the Old Man of Hoy raising its wind-battered, weathered head over a shroud of mist. They were liberators, the fearless explorers who pieced together the earth on their maps, little by little, patched and stitched like a quilt, bringing light where there was once darkness, truth where superstition reigned supreme. If I didn't understand Canadians, I also felt sorry for my own countrymen who were helping turn the Empire inside out. Still, in the remoteness of Hoy, in the wild dunes of Eday, one could forget the unwelcome metamorphosis of London, the filth and the aliens.

My troubles were far from over though. There were lovers on the deck whose loving antics brought home the need to try and fit Rosie into the new equation of my awareness. In the next few days, Rosie would prove to be a recurring and bothersome intrusion in my thoughts.

But nothing seemed to change in Stromness. That was something to be thankful for, I thought. Malcolm Gunn agreed. Boom towns, cities that grew and grew, always made distances longer. The station moved further and further away, the pier, the post office, the school, the doctor's surgery, the butcher — it just keeps taking longer and longer to get to them. Perhaps it now took others longer than it had taken me to get to school, the old Academy, which was a pity. Other than that, everything was still the same. There was also a slight drizzle, which too was familiar.

As soon as we stepped off the ferry, we saw a man we remembered seeing always. "Damper weather here," said the bearded man in greeting, his frayed captain's cap pulled low over his brow, as he crossed the road from the opposite direction.

"Aye," replied Malcolm Gunn, nodding, wiping the rain off his face with a paper tissue he had saved from the boat. I remembered seeing the man every summer we had visited the island. I didn't know his name, but that was all right. We spent the night in the Ferry Inn, watched the fishing boats cast away at dawn, and left the next morning for Hoy, where we had rented a cottage for the week.

It was wild. The rain came down in sheets when we stepped off the ferry at Lyness. None of it seemed to matter. I thought I had never seen my father so happy. Malcolm Gunn looked approvingly at the back seat of the car where we had two bottles of excellent scotch, several bottles of wine, and plenty of food, and assured me we would be well taken care of. We had nothing to fear from the cold winds and the pouring rain, now hissing as they drilled into the rocks. It seemed we would have the island all to ourselves. The screaming elements often keep the masses away from Hoy.

There were two other guests in the house in Rackwick where we were staying. The two, a couple, could not have chosen a better place for their honeymoon, I thought. Rackwick is one of the most exquisite valleys in the world when it presents itself dressed in bright sunlight. Then its green crofts stand out most vividly against the surging line of red crags within which the valley rests.

The rain changed its path and its music as the wind changed. But the waves kept up their untiring bass all night and then stopped abruptly the next morning. The honeymooning couple from Edinburgh went walking between the Old Man of Hoy and St. John's Head. My father and I chose a different route and set out for the top of Ward Hill where, all through the previous day, we had seen a ghostly ruin, surrounded by a few sheep, standing in the teeth of the storm.

This was the highest point on the island. In the distance, we could see the couple walking hand in hand towards the headlands. Malcolm Gunn began to sing softly:

> 'Ah, Wi a boanie lass aside you
> Back and fore alang da gaets
> Hits' a pleasure ida Simmer,
> Whin you geng ta ledd da paets.

He hummed and sang and gradually fell silent. The dome of the sky over our heads was a perfect round. One could see unhindered all the way, it seemed, to Creation. Malcolm narrowed his eyes into a squint, trying to pick the faraway outline of Fair Isle. Still searching the distance, he said, "She had to come back. This was where she belonged."

I had to ask, "Who are you talking about, Dad?"

"Isabel Gunn," he replied. "Even when she had James Bay staring her in the face, this is what she must have seen. For the sheep needed to be caad when the men were away. She would know that the men who stood on this hill might have been crofters, but they were fishermen too. From this spot I suppose they could make such sense of tide and waves as we have forgotten. When they went out to sea, it was the women and the dogs that gathered at the cru and rounded the sheep in the scattald beyond the dykes."

As we stood watching the ruins, as Malcolm Gunn reminisced about the past, it seemed the ruins came alive and poured into our eyes images of what they had been in their prime.

As Malcolm spoke, the straw roofs and the stone walls seemed to firm up around two rooms that lay in ruin. One of the floors was of trodden earth; the other, covered with square flag-stones. A fire came to life in the middle of the room, the smoke spiralling up through a hole in the roof, for the framing of which the crofter had hauled in a large supply of wood from wreckage salvaged along the seashore. The only other source of light was the dancing flame of the kollie lamp. It would burn all night, for there was always plenty of fish oil to keep it going. Everyone slept in huge boxes with doors on the side and mattresses filled with straw or chaff.

There was a byre built at one end of the house. The barn was at the back. Every morning, the dung from the byre was hauled out and dumped in the midden in front of the house where it gathered until the voar came round. On dark winter nights, many a careless lover had plumped unexpectedly into the soft mass of byre manure and become the object of ridicule for weeks to come.

Malcolm continued. He imagined that, like the others, the Gunns probably had two milking cattle, two calves, and one or two year-old beasts at different times. They would sell a one year-old each year to provide the money to pay the rent. The sheep roamed free in the hill, each crofter having his own mark to distinguish his sheep from the others. In those days, the mark was usually a slit or a hole cut in the sheep's ears, each mark different from all the others. They might also have had a pony or two, at least a couple of pigs, a score or so of hens and a few geese.

Before the churning, they always collected the milk for two or three days in big earthen jars, brown on the outside, cream on the inside. Malcolm Gunn seemed familiar with many of the rituals, while I knew nothing. For some hours before the start of churning, the jars were made to stand beside the fire. The extra heat made the milk run or turn sour. Then the tall narrow churn was brought out, the milk poured into it, a little hot water added, and churning began. The actual churning was done by hand, by quickly lifting and lowering a plunger attached to a long wooden handle up and down in the churn. After many minutes of non-stop churning, a thick layer of butter formed on top of the milk. Grandmother would lift it out, place it in a muslin bag, and squeeze out as much water as possible. Then the butter was placed in the butter koog and sprinkled with a little salt. When more hot water was added to the liquid remaining in the churn, the contents separated into three. On top was buttermilk, below it was blaand. Right at the bottom lay kirn-milk, a white cheese-like substance.

My father's eloquence brought forth before our eyes new kirn-milk, fresh from the churn and dipped in a smidge of sugar. It was every child's delight. For ages, the blaand had been the yoal men's drink at sea. It must have been a rare sight to see the frail boats go out, always rowed by three men, often lost inside the waves. It was even more exciting to see the boats when the large square sails filled with the breeze and skimmed the roiling seas like birds.

With the coming of voar the cattle were brought out from the byre at the first sign of a green paek and tethered. There was seldom enough food to keep the byre animals properly fed during the winter. Often, by the time voar came around the cattle were hardly able to stand through sheer weakness. Each day the women flit the beasts to fresh bits of grazing. Almost continually, they had to wage war with their hoes on the weeds which threatened to swamp the growing crops. The peats had to be raised and turned to get them properly dry. Then they were taken home, sometimes on the backs of ponies in maeshies, but more often in kishies on the backs of the women. And as they carried the peats and tramped the hill-gaet with their kishies on their backs, their nimble fingers would be busy knitting as they trudged.

Summer rolled on and the hairst approached. Soon the men were home from the sea and the hay crop was cut and dried, then carried home to store in coles in the yard. Potatoes were lifted and stored in pits, covered with straw and soil for protection against the frost and pests. When ripe, the corn was cut laboriously with corn-hooks and tied in sheaves. When dry, it too was carried into the yard and built in screws for the winter. The cattle were taken in to spend the winter in byres. Everything was made as snug as possible to await the coming of the cold weather.

Hairst was the loveliest time of all. Everyone gave thanks with added fervour at the Harvest Thanksgiving services when the hairst was especially good. There would be occasions during the hairst when Isabel would accompany her father to the craigs to pock sillocks. She would see her father chewing limpets to soe into the voe to attract the sillocks. And the trick did work. Sometimes, there were so many of the little fish swimming above the wide open mouth of the pock net that they could fill nearly two buckets with them when the net was lifted out of the water. They would then rush home with the fresh sillocks. Mother would probably put them into the pot right away, with the new season's potatoes, for supper. What a meal it would be, for everyone loved the fresh fish.

Grandfather came home from the herring fishing in September. The barrel of salt herrings he brought would last right through the winter. He also had with him a plentiful supply of salt cod. This was fish caught on handlines by the man on watch while his boat lay at the nets waiting to haul them in.

As for the crops, the main ones were oats and bere, and potatoes the main root crop. Oats were often grown for two years in succession in the same field, followed by potatoes in the third year and bere in the fourth. The fifth year would be a rest year when the field would lie ley or fallow.

Before cultivation could start each year, the food for the land had to be made ready. This meant that the dung from the byre midden had to be carried out in kishies on people's backs and spread on the fields to be dug. But this was not enough. So waar or seaweed had to be carried up from the beaches and also spread to supplement the byre manure. Meanwhile, potatoes would have been cut ready for planting. Only parts of potatoes — the parts with an eye showing — would be used. The rest of the potato was kept for food.

Then they dug the ground and planted the potatoes — the seed sown and the harrow brought out and dragged by hand over the fields to break up the larger soil lumps and to cover the seeds.

Malcolm recalled how his grandfather, when quite young, often had the job of walking in the furrow behind the plough, sheuching the seaweed which had been spread on the field into the furrow with a fork so that the plough covered it with a layer of earth the next time round. Flocks of seagulls, fearless through hunger, followed close behind the plough, ready to pounce on any hapless worm which appeared in the newly turned earth.

Sometimes grandfather would wake up at two on a summer morning to accompany his brother with the two carts to the peat hill several miles away. Though the sun was beginning to rise, the early mornings were chilly, and he sat in a state of cold drowsiness in the front of the cart as his sure-footed mare followed his brother's cart with an unbroken clip-clop of hooves. By six o'clock they were home again with their loads. After an hour's break to rest and feed both horses and boys they were off again for the second load of the day. They needed about sixty loads for a year's fuel.

The men would cast the peats before they went off to the summer fishing. For the next three to four months the work of the croft would fall on the shoulders of the women. Everyone prayed and hoped that nature would be kind and send a good growing season and a quiet hairst.

Only after the crops were safely gathered did they kill the mert. The site of this gory deed was always the barn. Children never failed to be transfixed by the carcass of the cow, hoisted up and hanging from the rafters. First, the hide was removed to provide rivlins for the whole family. Then the cow's insides. There'd be plenty of pudding making using the cow's intestines. The ones Malcolm Gunn liked best had currants in them. When the carcass was cut up, it gave enough meat for the family and the family next door. The chunks of meat were carefully placed in layers in barrels, each layer covered over with coarse salt. Very soon, the salt changed to brine, but the meat kept well in it right through the winter and early spring. Pigs also ended up under the rafters, but the hams were removed inside the cottage where they hung from the ceiling until completely cured.

Isabel probably helped her mother grind some of the meat which was first spiced and then packed tightly into small earthen pots and covered over with a thick layer of molten fat. Sealed in this way, the saucermeat remained fresh at least for a month or two.

In spite of all this industry, winter was a long and dreary time. The barn hummed with activity most every day as women threshed the sheaves with flails to separate the grain from the straw, then winnowed it to remove the chaff, eventually spreading the grain in the kiln to make it hard. This grain was later ground into meal to make the beremeal bannocks and the oatcakes, porridge, sooins, swats and burstane.

It was a time for making kishies and buddies, of winding simmonds to use on the roof thatches or to hold fast the screws and coles in the yard. Any time there was a break in the winter weather, the men put out to sea to try and get a few fresh ollicks or haddocks for a change from the salt meat and salt fish which seemed to be inescapable winter food. It was a time for repairing and renewing the fishing lines. It was a time to do anything for which there would be no time in the spring.

Malcolm was certain that Isabel Gunn, like most other women, took pride in being able to handle the wooden needle filled with net twine and fashion the meshes to fill the holes which had been torn by dogfish and other unwanted creatures during the herring season. Sometimes one of the visitors—perhaps a crew of her father's fishing boat—sat down and joined her at the mending. She listened to her father and the guest exchanging yarns of past fishing adventures. She heard of the night the nets sank to the bottom with the weight of herring, of the time a shark tore through five of the nets, of rescues that brought men back from certain death, and of rescues that failed.

I joined my father in looking with undisguised curiosity at the sheep huddled under the lea wall of a nearby ruin. Therein lay another story, for it was not difficult to imagine how swiftly disaster and tragedy could overwhelm the crofters, most of whom had hardly any money. In fact, they were virtual servants to the laird, who owned the crofter's land, the crofter's house, the crofter's boat. He expected his tenants to do much of his work free of charge. He insisted that all fish landed should be sold to him, and that all the crofter's purchases should be made from him. This meant a system of barter all round, and the crofter-fisherman rarely received any money.

It was apparent one day that a great deal of money could be made from fish. Some lairds encouraged ever greater numbers of fishermen by splitting up the crofts into smaller units and creating ever-greater numbers of crofter-fishermen all tied to them. Then it was discovered that sheep were an even better proposition than fish. But sheep needed room to graze. To get more land for this purpose was simple. In the year 1874, the lairds simply drove away the crofters from their holdings. Their houses were destroyed, and the stones from the walls used to build dykes.

Malcolm Gunn turned and spoke to me in a voice choking with emotion. "That's how my father lost out on this gentle way of life. It was the laird's greed that destroyed my father. We may not have lived in this croft, this sad ruin before us, we may not have lived on Hoy, but somewhere on the mainland my grandfather had a place like this, and a life like the one I've described. I have no doubt Isabel Gunn shared some of this life too."

On the eastern side of Hoy, the tide was going out, leaving bare mudflats below the dykes. On the other side, we could see the couple returning, way out in the distance. They were coming out of a tiny village which, like the eye of the needle, let in the narrow thread of a dirt road and tossed it out again to the westward edge of the island. All that my father had described happened, I know, when the Old Man of Hoy was probably not so old, and the Standing Rocks at Stenness—as legend had it—still moved to the sea from time to time. I imagined the winds whipping up the sea, not into giant waves, but into a crowded picture of hundreds of frail white boats gathering in the spirit of a carnival at sea.

It didn't matter any more that we couldn't find Isabel Gunn's gravestone within the walls of Saint Magnus Cathedral. I was reminded of the hollow echoes of the wind swirling and wailing over Betty Corrigal's lonely grave on the island of Hoy and it didn't matter any more that we couldn't find Isabel Gunn's gravestone. Betty Corrigal waiting for her faithless lover, cradling her child in her womb in the womb of a dark grave miles from any churchyard since none would bury her, miles from human habitation, loved only by the wild wind and the wilder sea each night. So it was with Isabel Gunn, the mystery of anonymity, the majesty of isolation.

Malcolm Gunn had shared with me, giving me of his nostalgia, so much joy through his remembrances that I could'nt bear to think of causing him more pain. Isabel Gunn had once again ceased to be an object of my curiosity.

On the way back to London, we got off at Forsinard to place a bunch of flowers at my mother's grave. The land was green and the creek flowed gently over rocks that shone like precious stones under the sun.

The evening before I was to return to Montreal, Malcolm Gunn came home with a slim parcel under his arms. After dinner, he asked me to open the parcel, a gift for me. Inside, I found a beautiful map, beautifully framed. Chart of the Canadian Arctic and Greenland, Johannes van Keulen, Amsterdam, 1680.

Sipping from his glass of port, Malcolm Gunn reflected over the polar bear hunt drawn into the title, and the trading transactions dealing with trapping and whaling drawn around the scale. "Clever man, Johannes," he said. "They hadn't found the Northwest Passage in his day. But see how sensibly he turns his back on the failures of exploration and emphasizes the exciting commercial possibilities of Rupert's Land."

"It's a beautiful map, Dad. Thank you so much."

"That it is," mused Malcolm Gunn. "But it's all wrong. Baffin Bay is wrong. It was the northern continuation of Davis Strait rather than an extension of Hudson Bay. We had to wait another two hundred years, into this century, to find that it was really the entrance to the Northwest Passage."

I told him, "Wait another hundred years and who knows what changes we might find around there. Rivers tamed, forests uprooted for golf courses, marinas, a new Disneyland."

Malcolm Gunn threw his head back slowly and smiled. I guess he wasn't sure whether I was being sarcastic or not. After a while he asked, "You really like this girl Rosie, don't you?"

"Yes, Dad, it's a new experience for me." I watched his face closely.

"Too bad I may not ever see her," he replied, without looking up.

"Well," I said, and stopped. I looked hard into an uncertain future and was at a loss for words.

"You know, Charlie, the mapping of the region where the Crees live was an extraordinary achievement. Our friend John Seller, the London map maker, had a big hand in it. He made the finest nautical instruments and sea charts of his time. He was especially noted for the hand-crafting and repairing of compasses. He did a lot of business with the Hudson's Bay Company who, you might say, were Canada's first national mapping agency. They encouraged their ships to chart the Hudson Bay coastline and gave many incentives to employees to map inland territories. Most were untrained in the use of instruments for surveying or astronomical observations. Others were probably terrified of the strange, unpredictable wilderness. But there were some who relished the excitement and some from the Grey

Coat and Blue Coat hospitals who obviously knew how to handle the compass, the quadrant, or the sextant. I suppose it was they who really discovered Canada. Through such accidents are empires made, through such perseverance are immigrants shown the way."

We sat in silence for a long time. Finally, Malcolm Gunn said, "I think I need to correct myself. Discovery is a very arrogant way to put it. Nothing was undiscovered to the local inhabitants, to the Cree for instance. So discovery is no more than a claim to prior viewing among Europeans. That's probably all it was, all it took to establish sovereignty."

My father's cynicism surprised me. "That's an interesting thought," I said in response. I was beginning to notice changes in him that I wouldn't have thought possible. And I began to feel sorry for him, sorry that he was aging by the hour, by the minute, through every breath. "Thanks again for that lovely map."

My father's last comment continued to puzzle me for a long time. It seemed to shake loose some of my earlier feelings about the nobility of conquest and discovery, a sentiment which I—in my own odd way—had felt drawn to of late.

I could clearly see Louis too was getting old, starting to live more and more in the past, tired of looking into the future. Rosie once told me he often caught himself dreaming of his grandfather flying across the plains with his band of warriors to keep a promise of help made by one Gabriel Dumont in a letter to another rebellious Louis a hundred years ago. The letter promised five hundred warriors. It fell into the hands of

Hudson's Bay officers, not Louis Riel, and the restless warriors kept circling the plains waiting for the signal of welcome that never came. They were still waiting, fifteen years later, when, in a prairie outpost called Regina, ringed by three hundred Canadian troops armed to the teeth, they hanged Louis Riel until he and his brief fight for freedom were both history. Louis hated these turns in his dreams, where he slipped unwittingly into hating the stale air engulfing the parked trailer in which he lived and railed and cried alone.

If the trailer was tacky and grimy inside, the world outside had at least the appearance of wide open land and waters, desolate at certain times, and teeming at others. Louis kept his trailer parked on a rise overlooking the bay and his memories of the almost deserted island of Fort George less than a stone's throw away. It seemed only yesterday that the space surrounding this slight cliff was in turmoil. Massive Hydro Quebec earthmovers roared past all day long. Explosions tore through the air as engineers blew up the surrounding hills and gouged through rock walls to make way for the new dam and the power station. Now the roads were in place, and the graders gone. But so were the geese and most of the animals.

I watched as Rosie washed her face over a tiny washbasin in one corner of the trailer, changed, and went about adding colour to her eyebrows and lips. She threw her long black hair to one side and fastened a dull paisley scarf, one of her mother's few belongings, around her neck. We imagined her father was probably out on one of his endless, solitary walks, talking to himself. Just as she was putting on her raincoat, Louis returned. She heard his footsteps crackling on the pebbles covering the path leading to the trailer and opened the door to him. He stopped for a moment, startled. It took him a moment to collect his thoughts. Haltingly, he spoke to her, "You look as beautiful as your mother, Rosie. Where are you off to?"

"I have a class I'm walking to with Charlie. Then I'm meeting him in the Community Centre. He has promised to take me out to dinner at Radisson. There's some pie for you and ice cream in the freezer."

"Charlie?" asked Louis, puzzled. He appeared not to have noticed me.

"You're impossible, Dad," cried Rosie. "Charlie's the guy standing right there," she said, pointing in my direction. "The person you met last evening, right here. Remember? Have you forgotten you sat up with him till midnight?"

"Ah, yes! And Kechechowieh. How could I have forgotten?" He looked apologetic, but continued not to notice me. He watched Rosie as she gathered her things together. Then he said, "He's kind of odd and different, isn't he?"

"Dad," cried Rosie, a touch of exasperation in her voice. "He's perfectly, absolutely normal. I think he'd like to spend some time with you, tomorrow or the day after. He's here for the pow-wow, you know." She nodded to me to follow. Then the door clicked shut, and we were gone.

The trailer stood on a lonely stretch outside the village of Chisasibi. We had only to cross a short trail before we came to the new road which went past the skidoo shop, the churches one on opposite sides of the road — like Macdonalds and Burger King, people said — the police station, and straight to the Community Centre and the school. Along the way, we ran into a group of children playing across the road. "Rosie, Rosie," they cried, and began to blush as she looked back and caught their eyes. They knew her well, because most weekends the children gathered around Louis on the steps of his trailer and listened, mouths wide open, to his stories until the sun went down and it was time to go home for supper.

We parted company in front of the school, but I couldn't wait to see Rosie until after the class. I was in her classroom a short time later. "I'm going to ignore you totally until the end of class," she said, trying hard, I think, not to show how happy she was that I had come early.

Ten plump-faced children, some with snort running down their noses, surrounded Rosie. She was about to begin a new story.

"Today, children, I'll tell you the story of 'The Woman and the Dog'." The children clapped delightedly and began to shuffle around for the best seats in the house. With Rosie, they knew you had to be able to see her face as well, not just listen to her words. The expression on her face almost always charged her words with special meaning.

"There was once a woman who lived all alone, without a Man," said Rosie. She looked up, caught my eyes at the back of the room, and smiled shyly. She continued, "There wasn't a man for her to marry, to look after her, or to make a living for her. The poor woman had to live alone and do everything for herself. If she could kill some animal by herself, she found something to eat. Otherwise, life was very difficult for her.

"One evening, she had finished all her work and was sitting alone in the tent, when the tent flap moved and a dog came in. The woman had always hoped a man would come to her, but a dog?"

Rosie looked at the children, smiling, questioning. Some of them clapped their hands with pleasure, in anticipation of what was to come. Others moved closer.

"'I want a man for a husband, says the woman, not a dog.'

'But I am like a man, almost a man,' replies the dog, 'and I can make a living for you.'

"The woman was really surprised. She had never heard a dog talking before. Then she gathered her senses and found the whole situation quite funny. So she teased him. 'If you want to marry me,' she says, 'I guess it's alright.'

"It had been a long time since she had anyone to talk to, so she kept talking with the dog. The dog kept wagging his tail all the time. Soon it was evening, a time when a woman would usually feed her husband. Still thinking it was very funny that this dog thought he was a man, the woman gave the dog some food too.

"When it was time to go to bed, the dog seemed very happy. At this, the woman grew worried that the dog was taking her teasing about marriage quite seriously. She couldn't sleep all night, and began to feel bad over having teased the dog. She knew it was not right to talk to the dog the way she did.

"In the morning, the dog pushed the woman's leg with his foot, to let her know he wanted her to get up and make a fire. She made a fire and a meal, and sat down to eat with him as if he were her husband. As soon as they had finished eating, the dog ran out of the tent. After a while, he returned with two partridges. The woman did not like this at all. She was now sure the dog intended to marry her. Every once in a while that day, the dog came back with another partridge. In the evening, he even brought her a porcupine. The total for the day was several partridges and two porcupines. The woman was really, really worried. She didn't know what was on the dog's mind, but she was sure she didn't want to marry a dog."

Rosie stopped and looked at her children. "Would you?" she asked.

"No-o-o," they answered in unison.

"She wanted to marry a man. Wouldn't you?" asked Rosie.

"Ye-e-es," answered the children, with one voice.

"The woman was worrying all the time now. Again as before, when they went to bed the dog lay down beside her. The woman did not like this way of living at all. She had never known of a woman marrying a dog before. But he was making her living for her, so one day she decided she would marry this dog after all. But she told herself she would not bother with the dog a moment longer if she could ever find a man to marry her.

"The dog was really good to the woman, and went hunting for her all the time. He even killed deer and, just as a man would do, he brought the heart home first. And, just as a wife would do, the woman would tell him that she was going for the meat in the morning. The dog killed everything that a man would, even beaver.

"In another camp somewhere else, a man who was doing some magic found out about this woman who had married a dog. So he went to see the woman. When he entered her tent, she fed him well. He did not ask her where her husband was, but told her instead that he had left his own wife not far from there.

"Then the man who had done the magic put up his tent near the tent where the woman lived. While he sat in his tent, he spoke to his *Mistabeo*, his guiding spirit. 'If a man married this woman,' he says, 'I suppose that the dog that she is living with would do something to him, kill him maybe.' His *Mistabeo* warned him not to sleep in her tent. 'If you sleep in her tent,' says the Mistabeo, 'the dog won't like you talking to that woman.' Then his *Mistabeo* told him the whole story of how the woman came to live with the dog. He told the man about the child she had. It was half dog and half man. When the woman saw how the child looked, she did not want it to live. She wanted to throw it away.

"Some time afterwards, the man with magical powers left his camp. But the story of this woman began to spread. Many people heard the story, and some did not believe it was true. One day, some men decided to go to this woman who lived with her dog-husband to see for themselves how much of the story was true.

"The first time they went to the woman's camp, she was alone. But they had seen the woman's and a dog's tracks outside. The woman fed these men well. Then they left for their homes. Once again, the men returned to the woman's camp. This time they were planning to take the woman away from the dog, but first they wanted to see whether or not the woman would sleep with the dog. The men planned to sleep in the woman's tent. Once more, the woman fed them very well and they waited for the dog to return.

"When the dog came home he brought the woman many partridges. He dropped them where the woman sat. The dog could not seem to sit still, but you could see he was very happy.

"'We're not married,' the men say to her.

"The woman thought to herself, I won't bother with that dog anymore if I can marry one of these men.

"When the dog finally tried to sit beside the woman, she hit him. The dog growled at the men. But each time he tried to come near her, the woman kicked him. She kicked and struck out at him again and again.

"It was bed-time. The woman tells the men, 'This dog does all the hunting here. We have lots to eat.' She didn't think the men had heard the story about her being married to the dog.

"Soon everyone lay down for the night. Again, the dog tried to come close to the woman, to crawl into her blankets. The woman got up and, taking a piece of firewood, she began to beat the dog. After his beating, the dog sat near the doorway, between the woman and the men. The men were afraid of this dog, and watched him closely.

"As soon as the fire went out, the dog tried again to lie with the woman. The woman began to beat him again with a stick. She did not want the dog to come near her again. She wanted to marry one of the men.

"Once more in the night, the men heard the dog whining near the woman. When they woke up in the morning, they saw that the woman had been killed. The dog had run away. The dog had known that the woman wanted to marry one of the men and did not want to bother with him any more. That is why the dog killed the woman.

"The men were sorry that they had not killed the dog before he escaped. Now they were afraid the dog would try to kill them too. Long afterwards, they still watched for the dog, especially at night. They felt really sorry for the woman because they had wanted to marry her."

Rosie finished her story and looked at the class. There was no clapping this time, just silence. She asked them, "Did you like the story?"

"Yes," said some. Yes, nodded others. Standing against the wall, next to some posters of animals and birds, I just kept looking at Rosie, wanting her as I had never wanted a woman before. Like the dog, I imagined.

Over dinner, I asked Rosie, "Do you suppose at their age they believe a lot of this stuff?"

"I hope they do," replied Rosie. "It's better to believe animals are somewhat human — as we do, mind you — than to believe that humans are animals."

I realized there would be times when it might be impossible to keep up with Rosie. This was one such occasion. The restaurant wasn't too crowded. It was too expensive for the general population of Chisasibi. Apart from some obvious visitors in business suits, most of the others were local technicians and engineers, all males. I could see their envious glances in our direction, perhaps trying to figure out what it took a white man to pick up a gorgeous Cree woman like Rosie.

There was a time when the men from the construction camps would drive over to Chisasibi to pick up young girls. All that became a thing of the past when the Band Council set up the barrier on the road to the village, manned by volunteers no less formidable than Larry. I suppose the men in the restaurant were especially surprised because they couldn't seem to connect me with Hydro Quebec in any obvious way. Besides, on this occasion I was not staying at the Auberge.

"Did you have a good visit with your father?" she asked.

"In Arcadia?" I asked, teasing her. "Yes. Like your father, he too is getting quite old. He forgets a lot of things nowadays."

"But he's not as crazy as Louis, I'm sure," said Rosie with a smile.

"Not crazy, but very simple-minded," I replied. "Which I find hard to accept in a person who has lived so long in London, a city which has everything, all kinds of people, the greatest city on earth. Don't know why, but he thinks all men must basically be nice. Why should they be otherwise, when the Bible lays down the clearest guidelines? He believes that people in authority always mean well. He honestly believes his own grandmother to have been a saint."

"So what's wrong with that?" asked Rosie.

"Nothing, except that I have come across some evidence which suggests that she might have been anything but." I paused to carve a corner off my steak. "Maybe I'm wrong. Maybe he's changing." Then, recalling our last visit to the Orkneys, I thought it important to tell Rosie, who was somewhat sceptical at first, that I had tried to be honest and forthright, but not cruel, with my father.

"If you want to find out anything about Kechechowieh," said Rosie, sensing that I might be about to remind her, "perhaps you should sit down with my father tomorrow. During the next two days we'll all be tied up with the pow-wow." She contemplated the rich head of beer in her glass and added, "Unless, of course, you think the information irrelevant now that you have come up with some scientific—no, empirical—facts."

I knew she was having me on. So I thanked her politely for inviting me to the pow-wow. The accommodation

Larry had arranged for me was perfect, much better than the Auberge. But I was sorry to hear Larry was planning not to teach school for a few years. Instead, Larry was going into the bush.

"Oh! he's thrilled to bits," Rosie assured me quickly. "We're very happy for him and his wife too."

When I woke up the next morning, I was greeted with a view of something resembling an enormous Cousteau submersible raising its head over a grimy field of mud littered with cans and bottles, and a solitary shopping cart resting against a scruffy tamarack tree. I had asked Larry about it when I came into the room the first day and was told it was the Sports Centre. I had since gathered that the monstrosity had never been put to use. The doors and windows were all boarded up. Shaped like a huge teepee, the structure stood poised like a sluttish mockery of the enforced union of native structural designs and modern, sophisticated structural materials like steel and concrete. Of course, the Community Centre didn't have much to commend itself either. Groups of youngsters always hung about the dark stairwells and some looked suspiciously spaced out like they were on drugs.

Larry agreed that they had not been wholly successful in banishing booze and drugs from Chisasibi. In fact, he pointed out specific individuals who they knew were dealing in that stuff. "This is one van that drugs bought," said Larry, pointing to a woman speeding in a gleaming red van. He admitted she was pretty smart.

On this day, I saw a side of Louis that I wouldn't have imagined during our first meeting where he had seemed so warm and affable. Louis told me, "You'll have to bear with me today. I'm starting a fast. It's my own way of spiritual regeneration." Standing on the steps of his trailer, pointing outwards with a broad sweep of his hand, he told me, "Look at this wasteland. Not just what they've done, but what we've helped them do. All for a couple of hundred million dollars. I kept telling them, this land's not a place for us to buy and sell. We are its custodians, and it's not for us to give it away. But who would listen to me? And even if they did, who can fight Indian Affairs and their fancy lawyers, always so full of smiles and clever compromises?"

Louis asked me to follow him. He led me slowly in the direction of a grassy knoll secluded behind a cluster of jack-pines. "I see you like Rosie and she likes you," he said. "Five, ten years ago, when I had more strength in these hands, I would never have allowed you near her." I remained silent. Growing somewhat more thoughtful, Louis continued, "As late as the mid-eighties, we would gather here on this knoll most evenings — I and more than twenty or so of the finest men in the Cree nation. Most of them have gone, all of them have changed. The spark has gone from their eyes, their soul. Now they're quite content to take orders from chiefs who are afraid to fight."

As we skirted past the line of trees, I was surprised to come across a large tent covered over with stained, green canvas. Louis laughed and told me how the Hydro Quebec work crews who had been digging and slashing only thirty feet away never noticed the existence of the tent. Holding up a corner of the flap, Louis asked me to step inside.

He lit two candles and the walls came alive with dark, shadowy faces of warriors carrying guns or spears, some hunting, others in warlike poses exhorting others to follow. All were canvas paintings with the colours red, black, and yellow powerfully overshadowing everything else. "Are these yours?" I asked.

Instead of answering me, Louis turned to question me instead. "Do you believe in God?" he asked.

I hesitated for a moment. Finally, I said, "I don't know if I do." A further thought occurred to me, and I added, "I suppose I believe in some sort of power, some life-force."

"Well, then," said Louis, quickly moving three paintings and lifting what looked like a black sheet of cloth behind them, "this was our God."

I found myself staring at a stack of guns ingeniously arranged on a slender wooden rack suspended from one of the poles holding up the tent.

Louis went on, with a touch of secret pride in his voice, "We even have a pile of grenades and two Uzis here. I don't think it's still too late to blow up the dam."

I began to feel nervous, not because I was afraid but because of the unexpectedness of the revelation. For certain, it left me speechless.

"In your churches," he said, "you're looking for perfection personified. Elsewhere, others are looking for leaders, generals, but they all come with feet of clay. Truth is, you can never find God except in your imagination. God exists in man's imagination, and man in God's. Everything is imagination. We imagined we could turn the tide with this stuff — these guns and ammo — but we never gave it a chance. Our collective imagination cowered like a puppy dog."

Louis shook his head slowly, sadly. He pulled down the sheet of cloth, placed the paintings back where they were, blew out the candles, and stepped outside. "I brought you here to show you where you'll find me over the next three days," he said. "I'll be fasting here. I have no interest in the pow-wow. I must communicate with the Spirit and regain my strength before the long journey. You see, out in the open spaces the Spirit is really man's greatest ally. We talk to him all the time, we see him everywhere. He brings us food, sees us through the long nights, shows us the way home."

We walked silently in the gathering twilight back towards the trailer. As we drew near, Louis said, "I know you want to find out about Kechechowieh. Make yourself comfortable while I brew you a cup of tea. Then I will tell you."

Rosie was already back at the trailer, sitting on the steps. She smiled as she saw us, moved a little to let us pass, but didn't say anything.

Rosie didn't seem interested in coming in. So I pretended to read some old magazines while Louis boiled the water.

"Kechechowieh was a great woman," Louis began. "Her father was a chief respected throughout the Cree nation, fearsome in battle, generous and open-handed at other times. Sounds like our chiefs of today, doesn't it?" Louis laughed scornfully and cleared his throat. "You know what changed it for us?" he asked. Ignoring my nod saying I didn't, Louis continued, "The Hudson's Bay Company."

I found him staring hard at me. "When our people came to trade at a post, it became a practice for the factors—the chief officers at the posts—to present the chiefs with several barrels of whisky and many trade items to distribute to their followers. Freebies, as the kids call them today. The Company thought this would drum up more business, and it did. But it also became a matter of some importance to be recognized as a chief by the Company. There was a catch though. The English traders liked peaceful, industrious trappers; they were afraid of, and discouraged, troublesome warriors. There you have it, the precursors of today's chiefs, fearful as pheasants, whiter than whites."

Rosie was still sitting outside. "Dad, tell him more about Kechechowieh," she cried from the steps of the trailer where she was apparently writing her diary. "That's what Charlie wants to hear."

Without any change in the expression on his face, Louis continued, "Kechechowieh was a spirited woman. When she was a young girl she went to work for the Grey Nuns at their hospital in Montreal. Rosie tells me you live where the hospital used to be, but I probably know more than you. Marie Marguerite, the widow who started the Grey Nuns, died in 1771, just two days before Christmas. That night, several people, Kechechowieh included, saw a strong concentration of brightness forming over the General Hospital where the nuns worked. Gradually, the light straightened and took the form of a cross. Meanwhile, inside the hospital, Marguerite's body had been prepared for viewing. She looked very beautiful and very much at peace.

"After seeing Marguerite, one of the persons, a learned man who had seen the light, suggested getting an artist to paint her since she had never sat for a painting during her lifetime. But when the artist came, he found Marguerite's face so distorted, so ugly, that he quickly went away without painting a single stroke.

Next morning, however, Marguerite's face returned once more to its gentle, peaceful beauty.

"Kechechowieh was a witness to all this and knew Marguerite to be a woman with special powers. When Isabel Gunn and her young son were entrusted to Kechechowieh's care thirty six years later, she believed Isabel when she told her she had never slept with a man. Of course, all the Company's servants in Pembina thought she was a whore. Kechechowieh travelled with mother and son when they decided to move to Albany six months later to escape the attentions of the men. The same thing happened in Albany, until Kechechowieh persuaded Isabel to come to Fort George. The interesting point is that she discovered Isabel had been born about the same time that Marguerite had passed away. She had no doubt Isabel was a powerful spirit woman. She did some wonderful things. In our language, she was a saint."

We sat in silence for a long time. I felt deeply moved, extremely uneasy with a burden of conflicting thoughts. "Thank you, thank you very much," I told Louis Bearskin.

When Rosie heard my voice, she stood up where she was sitting and stepped inside the trailer. "Dad," she said, "I'm getting Charlie to take me for a spin in his car."

Louis nodded, he understood.

Once outside, Rosie slipped her hand in mine. We drove around on deserted, winding roads for a long time, happily, aimlessly. Finally, we stopped at a clearing where the road ended. The road sloped down to the water's edge and we could see Fort George directly in front. There was no one around, neither in the boat house to our right, nor among some skidoos gathered for repairs close to where we stood. Rosie said to me, "The boat's on the other side, or I'd have taken you to the island."

"We'll save it for the pow-wow tomorrow," I suggested. Rosie agreed, moved as close as she could to me, and drew my face to hers for a long, interminable kiss. Later, we scrambled over some slippery rocks and stood on high ground from where we could see a little of the mouth of the La Grande River. The dark, shadowy rocks reminded me of the flagstones in the Orkneys and, for a moment, I forgot where I was.

"When I was a kid," said Rosie, pointing to the river, "there'd be solid ice across the river's mouth in the winter."

"Doesn't it happen any more?" I asked.

"No, the waters too warm these days. There's much more water than before, because of the dams. The generators also heat up the water. Why don't you let my dad explain everything to you later?" asked Rosie. For the present, she put her arm around me and shivered in the cold wind.

Somewhere out there in the bay, I could almost picture *The Prince of Wales* getting ready to sail. A young woman steps off the familiar York boat with her son. As she climbs onto the ship, all activity stops around the deck. All you can hear is the rustling of the woman's starched dress. Everything else is silent. Perhaps it was different on the shore. There, it was with a sense of loss that the men looked at the lithe body disappear on board, her golden hair still drawing the sun to her face. The first woman, perhaps the only woman, to sign up as a servant of the Hudson's Bay Company.

"My father's the smartest person I know," said Rosie, looking at me with the innocence of a little girl. "And that includes all my profs in Montreal. If you stay with him you can learn a lot."

"I've found out a lot today, already,' I told her.

Rosie looked up at my face, her own breaking into a smile. "You're not being sarcastic by any chance, are you?" she asked.

I turned and drew her close to me, then silenced her concerns with a kiss. Louis had awakened Isabel Gunn in my mind once more, but her spirit seemed far from constricting now. Suddenly, Rosie became almost a different person in my arms. It had something to do with a mutuality of expectations, of hopes and desires, of sadness and disappointments, of goals achieved and the joy of success, of reaching out to others as much as reaching out to each other. Perhaps this is what love is about, I thought, with a touch of amusement and sentiment. This, rather than never having to say no. I was certain I could touch Louis through Rosie, and understand him, for that had become very important to me. I was equally certain Rosie would be able to touch, through me, Malcolm, and the sweet spirit of my mother and, who knows, the spirit of Isabel Gunn.

Five days after the first one, they fished out another body from the waters. He too had the same neat incision around his neck. This time it was a resident of the Francophone camp, one of the team of mechanics responsible for the maintenance of the giant turbines. This time I was summoned to the Chisasibi police station to speak to the Surete du Quebec investigators who had flown into Fort George the day before. "Can you tell us anything?" asked one of their officers.

No, but you can," I replied. "You," I said with anger and impatience in my voice, "can tell me what's going on with Rosie."

"We're working on her case," both the officers replied in unison, shaking their heads reassuringly.

The sandy bluffs of Fort George, parting the La Grande River into two wide braids, caught a shaft of the morning sun reflected off the waters. What looked dull and ordinary from the shore now shone like burnished gold as we set out in a boat for the island. A happy, chaotic spirit moved restlessly through the air and settled on Fort George.

Dozens of trailers and campers had crossed over to the island during the previous day. They came from Arizona, New Mexico, Alberta, Saskatchewan, British Columbia, Wisconsin and places much nearer. In small campfires burning near their trailers, men and women were busy preparing breakfast. The sizzle of frying bacon and sausages mingled with the sound of rock music from portable radios and filled the fresh morning air with energy and expectation. Children ran around with complete abandon, tripping over one another, throwing things at one another, with not an adult voice raised against them in warning or anger.

On the eastern side of the island a vast tent, or arbour as some called it, had risen overnight and now lay stacked with a pile of chairs. Young men were busy arranging the chairs for the drummers and for those likely to sit and watch the dancers.

Even though this was only the second pow-wow on the island in decades, Rosie couldn't conceal her excitement. The island held fond memories for her and she danced with light, airy footsteps from one group to the other, greeting friends, hugging little children. She seemed incurably childlike herself. I felt a bit lost at first, left out of the spirit of things, until Rosie made up her mind to prod me a little. From then on, if she wasn't introducing me to friends, she was pointing out familiar landmarks to me. It was fun, even though I was having to compete with others for Rosie's attention.

If one turned one's eyes away from the spot where the pow-wow was being held the island looked wild and untended. The grass grew tall in most places. Less than a dozen families now lived year-round on the island, so that many of the wooden houses appeared on the verge of self-destruction. Still, there was a stark, primeval beauty to the island which the sunshine scrubbed and presented with pride to the several hundred folks assembled that morning.

Rosie pointed to a small island that lay to the south. It was called Earthquake Island. Legend had it that a group of Crees were camping on this island one moonlit night when one of the men noticed a large group of strangers paddling in. He told the others what he had seen. Then, fearful that the strangers might not be friendly, he took his pregnant wife to hide with him in the bushes on the other side of the island. With the break of dawn, the strangers rushed the camp and killed everybody. Only the couple hiding in the bushes survived. Later, they described how the footsteps of the charging men sounded like an earthquake. That's how the name came to be.

When Rosie wasn't describing landmarks, she was explaining to me how Cree words often developed to satisfy specific needs of hunters and fishermen. For instance, the side of a body of water facing the sun was called *ashtikakam*; the side facing away, *okikam*. So the side of a hill facing the sun was called *ashtitayawch*, and the side facing away from the sun *okitnayawch*. A bay on a lake is *yetwakami*, but a bay in James Bay was called *washaw*.

"Did you know," she asked him excitedly, "that Cree hunters here killed geese with bows and arrows right up to the First World War? This wasn't because they didn't have guns," she explained, but because they didn't want the birds to smarten up." She still remembered Louis using an old style musket when she was a child. He even filled his own shells, carefully putting together cartridges with pieces of string.

Rosie was a source of endless information. This was where the school house used to be, she pointed out. And the Catholic Church was here—they got over a quarter million dollars in compensation when they had to move from the island. Another spot was where a mixed-blood ran a motel. He did pretty well too from the compensation and then disappeared. Never put up a motel near Chisasibi as he was expected to. Then, with a sigh and an air of finality, she said, "And this is where we used to live."

Rosie pointed to a small, peeling, faded green structure, the doors and windows blown away in the wind. Turning to me, she asked, "Looks terrible, doesn't it? But walk ahead a little, and you'll see the curve of the land ringed by the most beautiful sandy beach. A little narrow perhaps, it used to be freezing cold most of the time. But we loved every minute there."

The wind blew her hair over her eyes. Rosie seemed not to notice as she stood pointing, frozen like her childhood memories. She went on, "I still think we were the last band of the Free Spirits on this island home that's so inhospitable to others, especially your people. This land, hard, bare and forbidding to many, must've held some charm for my grandfather, and his great grandfather, and his. I suppose they could've drifted south to the warmer plains and not all been destroyed. But they stayed on."

Why do some stay on? Why do others leave? I don't know the answer. I told Rosie how I would sit with Malcolm Gunn and trace the voyages of some of the great explorers of the Northwest Passage. Frobisher's battles with the Eskimos and his crew's discovery of pyrite, fool's gold. The weariness of heart, the bitterness, the dissension that overtook men thrown together during cruel, paralysing winters. The Greely expedition. Captain Back and the *Terror*. How Jens Munk came to the mouth of the Churchill River only to have his crew struck down with scurvy during the winter. When summer returned the following year, only Munk and two other survivors sailed back the three and half thousand miles to Copenhagen. Thomas James escaped after a miserable winter, giving only his name to James Bay. But not Henry Hudson. Never saw another summer after his crew set him adrift on the bay with eight men. The Hudson and James Bays had never been too kind to voyagers. Still, upon reflection, I thought the traders hadn't fared too badly, for a while at least.

Rosie interrupted me, her voice full of passion. "That's because they took pains to change the society with cunning and guile," she said. "You bring in whisky, you'll have one kind of society; guns, another kind; energy, oil and electricity, another kind; cable TV, something different still. Accepting change is no big deal. Some of our people rely so much on history that they forget the future is passing us by. A few brave souls like Larry decide to re-live history. The rest are quite happy to shape the present according to the white man's model, according to the white man's wishes. Look, there's our old outhouse lying on its side. Frankly, I don't miss it one bit."

Rosie became silent as she moved to take a closer look at the decaying walls, to kick a few planks of siding. She seemed to have settled into a sombre, reflective mood. "Maybe we'll destroy ourselves," she mused. "I'd prefer to have the blood on our own hands than on anyone else's."

As I listened to her, I began to wonder if I hadn't been too harsh with John Gage after all. Not only had I profited some from his education, he'd also helped me find a companion who made sure I kept up with learning every moment we were together.

"My father's convinced Henry Hudson and his son never perished in the Bay," said Rosie, looking out over the waters.

"What?" I asked, jolted out of my thoughts.

"Louis is convinced they came ashore and left their descendants among us. He has often felt their spirits, which he wouldn't if they hadn't left their blood among our people."

I wasn't quite sure if Rosie was making fun of me. "I'm not," she promised. "You can ask my father."

I couldn't help feeling I was being tested, if somewhat light-heartedly, in more ways than one. My whole way of life, all my education, seemed to be under siege. Yet, on the surface, what was there to make me different from Rosie except physical appearance? There was no reason for me not to believe in the things Rosie believed in. But that could never happen, could it?

My new-found faith in Isabel Gunn was also being tested. My sense of the glory and romance of discovery had certainly suffered a blow from which I doubt it will ever recover. It must be history, I concluded, that marks us as different.

Preparations were now well under way for the pow-wow to begin. We hurried back to the main tent. In the space of time we had been walking around the island, the scene inside the tent had changed dramatically. Some men dressed ordinarily in jeans and parkas had transformed themselves into feathered and tasselled apparitions from a bygone age. Some of the younger women and girls had also undergone a similar metamorphosis. Some were dressed in silk, others in velvet. Everyone looked resplendent in beads and new, colourful moccasins, feathers tucked under their beaded bonnets. Beads in their hair, beaded ear-rings, slender dream-catchers, beaded necklaces and armbands, beaded belts, beaded moccasins.

It occurred to me that in those early days the Hudson's Bay Company had certainly stumbled upon a marvellous medium of trade with the Indians. Beaver skins for beads.

"Beaver skins for guns too," Rosie corrected me, reminding me of how the first Cree received a gun from the Company after he had stacked enough beaver pelts one on top of the other to reach the full height of the gun.

Rosie made me sit down while she excused herself to get changed. I found myself facing two circles of men looking at me with curiosity from time to time. In one, older men sat smoking pipes, passing them around the circle. The second circle was the circle of drummers, all young men among whom Larry was one. They sat there, some looking rather tense, mumbling their lines to make sure they had the songs right, others striking the drum lightly with the drum-sticks for want of anything else to do.

An elderly woman came and sat next to me. As I smiled at her and she smiled back, a puzzled look flashed across her face. After contemplating the sky for a while, she turned to me and said, "It should be a good *mikushaan*, it's such a beautiful day."

I stared back at her and started to laugh. "I can't understand you," I admitted to her.

"I'm sorry," said the woman, "I mistook you for a Cree."

"No such luck. I'm just an ordinary Englishman working for a living in Montreal."

The woman explained, "*Mikushaan* means feast. I hope you'll stay till the evening when there's lots to eat. Till then you can sit with us and watch the others." She pointed to the people sitting around us, and I realized I was sitting in the middle of a group of old women. The woman shrugged her shoulders and said that none of them knew the traditional dances which the Residential

School system strictly forbade them to perform. Sadly, she told me, "Too old to learn now, or I'd be out there on the grass with the others. Our girls danced for the first time last year. They had to have dancers from Saskatchewan and Alberta come and teach them. The only thing we knew and taught our girls was moccasin-making, beadwork, and the tanning of hides."

From where Larry and his friends were seated, the drum now started to reverberate tentatively with the first booming sounds. Dozens of children came running from all sides and began to form a circle around the tent. Big sisters started to rearrange the circle, moving children around according to their height.

Just then, Rosie returned, a different person. I was certain my heart and head would choke while I allowed the fullness of her beauty to sink into my consciousness. What I found most incredible was how young, almost timeless, Rosie looked in her tribal finery. She hardly looked older than sixteen.

Rosie caught sight of the woman sitting next to me and bent down to give her a kiss. "Hello Violet," she said, "this is Charlie. Can I trust him with you?"

"Oh, yes!" replied Violet, breaking into peals of laughter. "I'm too old for him, but I still have my teeth." Rosie left me holding her bag and ran off to join the dancers. "Be careful of Violet," she said in parting.

"These dances were different in my grandmother's days when they were still allowed to dance them," said Violet. "This one used to be called the Moving Slowly Dance. I think it came from the south. A woman of the Mud House People had four adopted children. She made feather bonnets for them and showed them how to dance. She said, 'This dance will be all over and everybody will dance in it.' And so it is. In my grandmother's days, they would make a special feather bonnet which was worn by a woman leader of the dance. A different woman would wear the bonnet for each song."

Violet pointed to the girls standing one behind the other and described how in the earliest pow-wows the dancers stood shoulder to shoulder in a circle and shuffled sideways in a clockwise fashion. The singers stood in the centre of the circle, beating a large double-headed drum.

Now the drummers broke forth in song and the dance began in earnest. At first, the drummers stroked the drum gently, respectfully, for it too had a Spirit. The slow rhythm of the drumbeats gradually began to quicken. The voices wailed a curious chant—a pulsating, high-pitched, almost feminine sound. A little later, the drumbeat and the voices settled down almost to the pace of a loud, hypnotic heart-beat. I thought it was like a mother's heart-beat, jealous and insistent, that hammers out the soul of a child in its mother's womb. The dance went on and on and on.

"In the old days," continued Violet, "I heard a man would cut in for the right to dance with a woman he had chosen. When the song was over and the dancers went back to sit down, he would present her with a gift for the privilege of dancing with her. Women could also cut in next to a man in the same way and later present him with a gift."

In between dances, Rosie came and sat with us and chatted with some of the other women, all of whom she seemed to know, all of whom she kept encouraging, without much success, to get up and dance. Young boys seemed to have taken to the dance quite early. Later in the day, older men felt emboldened to join in as well. Violet looked at me and asked why I wasn't dancing. I shook my head in mock embarrassment and confessed I didn't know the dance.

Violet assured me that the steps were simple and that Rosie could show them to me quite easily. Suddenly, out of the blue, she told me, "Go and ask her. You're going to marry her, aren't you?" I felt the blood rush to my face in a welter of pleasure and embarrassment. I covered my face in both hands. I just shook my head and said nothing.

"Go on, dance," repeated Violet again a few minutes later.

"Not today, perhaps tomorrow," I said, trying to sound as firm as possible without appearing rude to the well-intentioned woman. Violet didn't bother me any more, but I felt certain I had offended her. So, towards the end of the evening I put my hand on hers, thanked her for all the fascinating things she had told me, and promised that I would dance the next day, if it was all right for me to do so.

"Of course, it's all right," replied Violet, kissing me on the cheek. "Eat well before you go."

I drove Rosie home from the water's edge and walked her to the steps of the trailer. It was totally dark, which meant Louis wasn't in, and perhaps hadn't been in all day. She knew he'd probably be in his teepee and I wondered if we ought to go and say hello to him.

"No, let him be tonight," suggested Rosie. "Tomorrow his fast will be over and you might spend some time with him."

I kissed her goodnight and went on my way towards the Community Centre, wondering what it took two persons to open each other to the urgings of passion, and thinking that it was perhaps my own virginity that was standing awkwardly in the way. You see, I loved Rosie more than anything else in the world.

I parked my car in front of the police station, for safety, and was walking back the short distance to my room when Larry drove by in his station wagon.

"How did you like it today?" he asked me.

I said that I couldn't think of anything better, more fascinating.

Larry laughed. "Maybe you have something of a Cree in you, after all," he said. "Maybe you should come with me to the trap-line."

I said I would be game for that too.

The following day began with some of the most exquisite dancing by seasoned dancers from Arizona and New Mexico. A hunter from Wisconsin also held the crowd mesmerized for nearly a half hour with a kind of a Sun-Dance. Before his dance, an elder, a leader amongst his singers, uttered a short prayer, mentioning how and where he had learned the songs he was about to sing. Then the dancer, adorned with eagle feathers, said how he had made a pipe offering of sweetgrass and tobacco to Eagle spirit power, asking Eagle to allow itself to be taken. Over and over he sang:

> The sun helps me to stand,
> The sun helps me to walk.

Rosie sat with me most of the morning. "I'm glad you don't carry a camera," she told me. "I'd be embarrassed."

I didn't miss my camera either, but I did point out to Rosie the number of camcorders that were filming videos all around us. Rosie defended them saying they had to record the events so their children would remember themselves and not forget the beauty and the excitement.

A fresh group of singers sat huddled around their drum under the arbour. The drumbeats came to life, and the jingle dancers came and went, followed by dancers doing the crow-hop. But a solitary hoop dancer stole the show that afternoon. His body draped with golden feathers flecked with black and green, he danced himself to a frenzy as the orange feathers cascading down his head bobbed up and down in a swift and dizzying rhythm.

After all this wild riot of colours, the final round dance seemed tame by comparison. Almost everyone except the oldest men and women joined in. By now, I had begun to feel I was in a different world, perhaps in a different life as well. Rosie had already joined the line of dancers when, unbeknownst to her, I slipped behind her and grasped her hands in mine. She turned round to see who it was, and a look of almost unfathomable pleasure and tenderness flashed across her face. She squeezed my hands and held them that way as the drummers' song rose to a crescendo:

> The sky blesses me,
> The earth blesses me up in the skies;
> I cause to dance the spirit on the earth,
> The people I cause to dance.

Before the evening drew to a close, Rosie and I held hands before the approving gaze of many, while a couple distributed gifts to the elders of the community and to those who had rescued their little daughter from certain death. The previous summer, the little girl had slipped and fallen into the waters of the bay while clambering from one empty boat to the other. When the gift-giving was over, many in the crowd walked over to the couple. They embraced them and rejoiced with them over their good fortune.

Rosie and I joined the others too. The daughter was standing next to her parents, somewhat bewildered by all the attention she was receiving.

I hugged the father and told him, "She's so beautiful."

"Yes," replied the father. "If she hadn't come back to us, she would surely have lived a mermaid in the bay."

"Look, look," cried Rosie, pointing to the sky as we crossed over from the island and stepped out of the boat on the mainland. Other boats were coming ashore too, with people laughing and talking and children shouting to one another. Suddenly, there was a hushed silence as everyone looked up.

Crystalline shafts of emerald rained down from the sky. Straight ahead of us, the Northern Star and this vast shimmering curtain of emerald. On both sides of us, leading up to the stars, a wide border of snowy light that twisted itself into convulsions as the edges of the light folded themselves into towering arches, dissolved, and formed new arches again. It was a good omen, a fitting end to our communion with the Spirit. Men, women, and children, all stood transfixed, reluctant to move away and lose this rare outpouring of jewels from heaven.

By the time we reached Rosie's trailer only the stars and a half-moon remained in the sky. Like the night before, the trailer was again in total darkness. On our way to the teepee where we imagined we would find Louis, we had to pass a high ground which gave a brief glimpse of the bay over a barren headland. As we passed this spot we caught sight of a figure perched precariously on its edge. Rosie stopped and turned. Knowing it to be one of her father's favourite spots, she said, "I think that's him sitting over there."

Louis had seen the light too. But now he appeared not to hear us. He sat there as if in a trance. We stood behind him to one side and waited for him to say something. Instead, he sat there like a statue quarried out of the very stone whose smooth surface shone under him. Finally, Rosie called out, "Dad, we're back."

"Good," answered Louis, "I'm through with my ceremonies too, except for one. Come, I'll show you," he said, addressing me, gathering himself nimbly off the ground.

"It was a wonderful day, Dad," said Rosie. "Charlie loved it too. We were hoping to spend some time with you tonight."

Louis did not answer, just kept on walking briskly towards the knoll. We followed. As soon as we had cleared the first row of trees, we saw a glowing bed of fire on which there was piled a large number of rounded stones.

"What's that, Dad?" asked Rosie excitedly. "You're not planning a sweatbath, are you?"

Louis smiled. "Yes," he told her, pointing to the shadows. By now, Rosie and I were able to make out the bent top ends of a cluster of trees tied together in an overlapping fashion. Over this rough, crude hemisphere, Louis now proceeded to drape a large piece of canvas slightly split on one side. "There, it's perfect," declared Louis. Turning to me, he said, "I'd ask you to join me if you wish."

I wasn't prepared for this invitation. But I half suspected that this was something of an honour. I looked at Rosie for help in making up my mind.

"Go on," she whispered.

The fire and the rocks were at a spot only slightly higher than where Louis had set up his sweatlodge. The two spots were no more than six feet apart.

Rosie asked her father, "What will he do while you sing your songs?"

"Why, he'll listen."

"Well, I'm going to go inside. I'll let you change and get on with it." She brushed my arm gently as she turned away. A dark flock of birds flew overhead, pumping the air with their wings, cutting through the silence with their muffled cries. Even as Rosie turned away, they were gone, dark specks swallowed by the stars.

There was work to be done. First, I helped Louis roll the stones inside the lodge. He warned me to be careful as the stones had been in the fire for at least four hours. With the slope in our favour, it was easy to roll the stones. Louis lifted up an edge of the flap and pointed a flashlight at the spot where he wanted them gathered. Once the stones were in place, Louis brought out a shovel from his everyday tent and lifted a shovelful of glowing embers from where the stones had heated and carried them inside the lodge. He went out a couple more times, brought in more embers, and made a neat pile of them all. Louis then made sure the outside edges of the canvas lay flat on the grass. Even in the dark, he moved quickly, coming up with small stones to press down the edges of the canvas. Then we undressed outside in the light of the moon.

Standing naked, pleasantly chilled by the air, I felt a little awed by the prospect of the ceremony. But gradually, I began to think I might enjoy it. From where we stood, we could see a small slice of bay swimming in the moonlight. That was enough to remind me of something Rosie had said. Somewhat half seriously, I repeated it to Louis. I said, "Rosie told me about your theory on Henry Hudson and his son John.

"Theory?" asked Louis, a slight touch of annoyance in his voice. Then he pointed to the bay. "See the half-moon reflected on the bay?" he asked. "It's on nights like these that I hear them most often, prisoners doomed to remain here forever, hostage to the spirits who loved Donnacona."

It was beyond my understanding. I kept quiet.

Louis carried a small bucket of water inside. At the same time, he picked up a braid of sweetgrass that had been lying, unnoticed by me, beside it. The glow of the embers gave enough light to see the outlines of objects inside the lodge. Louis lifted up the flap one final time and asked me to get in. There wasn't much space inside, just enough for the two of us to face each other, rest against the slender trunks of two conveniently placed trees outside, and pull in our knees and feet away from the embers. It was warm inside. As Louis proceeded to secure the flaps together, it began to get warmer still.

A peculiar sensation of chill and warmth, each contending against the other, worked through my body. Louis broke off a piece of the dried grass and placed it on the live embers. A soft fragrance rose with the coils of smoke and swirled inside the lodge. "Close your eyes and clear your mind of every thought," said Louis. "I'll sing my songs now. Breathe deeply of the sweetgrass and you'll find windows opening to a new world not much different from ours, except in time."

There followed a long lull in the conversation during which I tried to follow Louis' instructions, emptying my mind of all thought, focusing only on the smell of the sweetgrass. As the fragrance of the sweetgrass intensified, I found my head feeling lighter. Louis spoke, "You can see time pass, you can hear the footfalls of spirits." At this point he began to sprinkle water on the hot stones. As the snake-like hisses of the blistering steam subsided, the space inside the canvas-covered tent swelled up with moisture.

It was only then that Louis began his songs. His high-pitched voice rose and fell, kept rising and falling in identical patterns of sound. I suppose he was droning an invocation to the Spirit. Louis never explained the words to me. Over a period of twenty minutes or so, he sang four songs, their words a mystery to me to this day. The steam and the smoke from the sweetgrass filled the lodge and worked their way to the innermost recesses of my mind. A peculiar numbness began to come over me. Louis opened the flap a little, allowing some of the steam to escape. Then he pulled back the cover once more, threw some more sweetgrass into the fire, and sprinkled more water on the stones. The hot stones hissed angrily once more. I too began to hear voices:

'We must have crisscrossed the ocean a million times.'
'What's there left to discover?'
'What's there left to conquer?'

'There's a restless longing that drives us on.'
'We've rested here as long as the sun and moon
have been around. Unblessed. Unpardoned.
How much longer must we wait?'

Slowly, strange forms began to take shape in my mind. No, perhaps they stood right in front of my eyes. The smoke from the sweetgrass and the steam from the hot stones lifted like a mist and it was fair, sun-shining weather once more. I saw a boat on the bay carrying several men, all but two wilting with listlessness. In their faces, I could read fear; in their hearts, hope.

It was the Captain. "The Lord be blessed," said Henry Hudson. His son, John, looked up at him and smiled bravely as if he felt some courage trickling back into his heart.

"Aye, Captain," moaned one of the sick men in the boat. "He has delivered us before, and so He will again." The man's neighbour, also sick and with delirious eyes, nodded his head. The Captain's ship, the *Discovery*, loomed larger than life as it came out of the fog. But she was sailing away — there was no question about that — away from the Captain and the eight others they had abandoned with him. There was nothing melancholic about the ship any more. The air of gloom that held her in its grip all winter long as she lay trapped in the ice vanished in the sunlight pouring into the bloated sails. The ship was gliding away from them.

"There was a Judas for you, that Juet," sighed Thomas Wydowse, Student in the Mathematickes. Fever racked his brain and he could barely open his eyes. "But for the vengeance of God," he muttered.

"She was a good ship, the *Discovery*, though not as fleet as the *Half Moon*," said the Captain, stroking his beard, smiling. Then he added, "In a while we'll secure the boat on land and go searching for food."

John pulled on the oars a little harder, perhaps shuddering at the thought of the vanishing savages they had tried to track down across the ice so often, so fruitlessly. "They must be there somewhere," said John. "Remember the last voyage when they actually showed us their hoards of maize and beans, when they went out and shot pigeons for us. We had even started to skin a fat dog with shells from the water's edge before you decided it was time to go."

"I remember," said the Captain. "Never forget Dyre-Fiord, my son. Remember Breyde-Fiord."

"No, sir," said John. "In my mind, I keep going back to Iceland all the time. The hot springs we bathed in every day for the seven days. All the wild fowl, the geese, the mallard, the teal, and the curlew we took. And the fish that overflowed the sea. One gun blast could kill enough to feed the whole company. Twenty three seamen we were then. We only stopped the hunt because you thought we might run out of salt."

The muffled groans of one, then another, of the sick men rose above the swishing of the waves and the wind and stopped John and the Captain in the midst of their conversation. The Captain gestured with his hand for John to keep rowing. Then he poured a few drops of water for the seven sick men, offering each a mouthful with words of gentle encouragement. Afterwards, wrapping his cloak tightly around himself, he spoke softly to his son, "We'll be out of the water before the day is done."

The *Discovery* had vanished from sight. The sunshine began to fade and the little boat seemed close to being smashed by floating islands of ice, some tiny, but others which dwarfed the men in their drifting craft. There was a strange quiet in the heart of this pack ice even as a sudden gale began to rage overhead and the surf broke heavily about the edges of the pack. The fog was moving back in. But the Captain persisted. "We can't be too far from land," he said. "In my heart of hearts I'm certain we are close to the Pacific we've been dreaming of."

"What makes you say that, sir?" asked John.

"Did you not see the Mexican knife one of the savages had on? One of the terrified Indians we saw before the ice surrounded us last winter."

"Aye, sir, I remember the chase, as futile as the others we set upon last summer. It was sad that we would see the savages, see the fire from their villages. But just as we thought we were upon them, the savages vanished and so did the village. Like a mirage on ice. It was like the seals and bears we tried to hunt off Iceland, stalking the animals, scampering from floe to floe, only to lose them as they jumped off the ice and swam away. They seem to share some strange, secret knowledge, the savages and the animals they hunt, knowledge denied to us."

The moon crept slowly over the ridges and floes, driving away the mist, smothering everything in white. "We were mad to be scouting around the ship last winter," mused the Captain. "It grew more and more reckless as the howling wind and blowing snow gathered strength and all signs of life turned into dreams. How graceful the fox, secure in its warm white coat, trotting silently on furry paws. And the ermine dancing among the rocks—white, except for the black tip of its tail—stopping only to listen for lemmings. The ptarmigan, white in its winter plumage, sailing on feathered feet among the stunted dwarf willows, snipping off buds and pausing warily to sense the solitary fox lurking in ambush. The deer and fowl we had seen late in autumn, they too were gone. But the musk-oxen, majestic and war-like, cloaked in their dark, thick furs, wandered in the shadowy patches over fallow grass and around the dwarf willows. In the sky, blue-black ravens darted about in excited flight and fell silent as flocks of snow geese came down from above like a twisting blizzard. Juet and the mutineers, their infamy will never take the memory away from us."

"But tell me about the mermaids, sir," pleaded John.

"They who saw her remain to this day under her spell, I am sure. From the navel upward her back and breasts were like a woman's, her body as big as one of us, her skin very white, and her long hair hanging down behind, of colour black. But then a huge swell crashed down upon her. In her going down they saw her tail, which was like the tail of a porpoise and speckled like a mackerel."

"She must have been so beautiful," murmured John.

"I remember them well," said the Captain, "they who saw her first; Thomas Hill and Robert Rayner they were called. The Lord have mercy on their souls. I wish I had seen her again myself. For, in truth, I have lived only for the unknown. Oh! to break out of this womb, this bay, some day. I'd gladly sell my soul to Circe, lace my voice with hers, unchain myself for the sirens."

Time passed, and the rest of the men were gone. Their features became one with the grey mist. The

Captain crossed his heart and said, "May God grant us the strength to give these men a decent burial."

Perhaps time was repeating itself, for again the fog disappeared. If the night was short but luminous, the dawn seemed bright and promised never to end. The boat had drifted close to land. Silent ridges of sand and gravel rose from the water's edge, step by step, one sweeping layer followed by another. The topmost tier touched the sky which suddenly burst into life with the cries of fulmars, murres, guillemots, and gulls. Belugas and narwhals joined in the chorus. Armies of seals slithered down the rocks into the icy waters. The Captain and his son paddled their boats with the ebbing strength of desperate men within sight of land or—it was difficult to tell—perhaps the sight of God.

The boat touched land, and father and son stood at last on solid ground, entranced by what they saw. In a lagoon beyond the sand, eider drakes sang over the water, transfixed by the reflection of their black and white feathers and the olive-green napes. They crooned their songs of love and the sounds floated hauntingly over the incessant hiss clinging like the embroidered foam on the churning waters of the bay. Further down, at the mouth of the estuary, a herd of beluga whales nosed noiselessly down to the sound, and twisted back to the surface with a dozen fountains spurting into the air, accompanied by soft, fragile screams of glee that faded but refused to die away.

Beyond the lagoon, male old-squaw ducks filled the air with chattering hoots and whistles as they courted their mates. Their sounds trailed into the bugling calls of sandhill cranes and the lilting songs of honed larks invisible to the eye.

"My discoveries," said Captain Hudson, looking around with undisguised pride.

"Only rediscoveries, sir," whispered John. "Only rediscoveries." The fog seeped through the cracks in the sky once more and snuffed out the phantom voices.

"Oh-h-h! give us back our garden," cried Louis, as if in a dream. His voice sounded like a drawn-out moan.

I was cruelly shaken out of my trance. Anxiously, unconsciously, I blurted out, "We must find him."

Louis was wide awake now. He opened the flap a little to clear the heavy air. "He is one of us," he told me. "He is one with us. Some day, the Spirit will point us to the sons and daughters of John Hudson. But why search for what we know is here?"

Afterwards, Louis and I came out of the lodge and lay down on the ground to cool off. And I found myself echoing, "Why? But why?" as I looked up at the night sky and heard the faint sound of music in the distance.

Larry had promised to meet me with his skidoo at around noon at a certain bend on the road where a tamarack tree perched precariously on the side of a shattered rock. But I had second thoughts about leaving the car parked by the side of the Chisasibi Road for days while I visited Larry in his trapline. The times were changing, they told me. The car would vanish into the bush. So I asked Rosie to drop me off and keep the car herself. I was disappointed she was not coming with me to the camp, but felt infinitely better the night before I left when she agreed to visit over the weekend. This meant that I felt committed, even if it be to myself, to stay at the camp for at least a week. I felt excited and apprehensive at the same time.

Rosie stuck out her cheek at me to kiss her goodbye. "Don't do anything crazy with that Larry," she warned me. She told me that while he had spent many years in the bush with his father, over the last four years he hadn't done much except grow big and fat.

I assured her I would be careful, but that I'd be happier if she was there too.

After she was gone, I looked around with a fresh sense of wonder. I was reminded of my weekend trips with my father, as a boy. But soon the sub-arctic nature of my surroundings and the gut-wrenching ride, clinging to Larry with a backpack bouncing on my shoulder blades, drained much of the enthusiasm out of me.

A thick blanket of snow covered the land. Fresh snow from the night before lay over the spruces and the poplars so that there seemed hardly any landmarks to go by. Yet, the speed with which Larry hurtled his skidoo across the open undulations, knowing exactly when to slow down and when to accelerate, suggested that he either knew the route very well or that he couldn't give a damn. I opted for the first possibility for it seemed less disturbing. The blowing snow gathered over my eyebrows and eyelashes. I was afraid to let go of my grip on Larry's shoulders to brush it off, so that after a while I was forced to keep my eyes closed, which seemed to make the trip scarier still.

After only about twenty minutes of what seemed like an age, Larry throttled down to a surprisingly slow speed. I forced myself to open my eyes a little, in time to catch sight of a couple of camps, grey smoke curling out of them. A few minutes later, the skidoo came to a halt.

"Here we are," cried Larry, over the sound of the engine. "Hope it wasn't too rough on your bones."

Larry's wife came to the door to greet us. "This is my wife, Emily," he said by way of introducing her. "And this is my *muhtukan*. "

Emily was pleasant, cheerful, and happy, and I thought she complemented Larry admirably. The longer I stayed in Larry's *muhtukan* the better I understood how closely their lives were intertwined in the bush.

The *muhtukan*, as I discovered, was a permanent sod house. Its rectangular frame is made up of split whole logs, placed upright. The cracks between the logs are ingeniously filled with sphagnum moss compacted into them. A second layer of sod covers the entire house from the outside. A main beam in every corner provides the strength against which the entire structure appears to rest. It was perfectly windproofed and a mild smell of spruce filled the air at all times. The fragrance came from the spruce boughs placed on the cleared ground as a form of disposable flooring.

From the moment Larry brought me in from the roadside, there seemed not a second to lose from the daylight hours. As soon as I had thrown the knapsack into one corner of the floor, Larry said, "My uncle has a cabin close by. He has promised to show me how to make a wolf-trap. Maybe you'd like to come along."

With a quick goodbye to Emily, I was out of the camp in a flash. Larry was at pains to let me know how happy he and Emily were that I had decided to visit. This was a different world from the other, and he had tasted both. Larry said he had no idea how long the

Cree would be able to keep it this way. He said to me, "I own the land on which I hunt, but it's a different kind of ownership. The land and the animals I hunt cannot be bought and sold like they are personal property. The land will still be there after you and I die. It really belongs to the Great Spirit, and He put the animals there."

Larry was in a talkative mood. "A few years ago, before I went to college, my old man said he was going to hand the land over to me. He asked me to look after it, to take care of it as a white man would his garden. It was up to me to protect, preserve, make rules where necessary, and enforce proper hunting practices. He wanted me to look after the land as he had shown me how. He wanted me to look after my people and to share with them what I found on the land if they were prepared to practice this way of life. There are five camps close together here, and we all cooperate. My uncle's the oldest, he's kind of a head-man."

I met up with the old man soon enough. I called him Uncle Snowboy which the old man liked. There wasn't too much time wasted on pleasantries. We walked some distance from the camp and got down to business right away.

It took us most of the morning and part of the afternoon to dig the wolf-trap. In between, we stopped only briefly to eat the lunch Emily had packed for us. Part of the digging seemed already to have been completed in stages in the past, to help the ground soften under whatever strength the sun could muster during daylight. But there were rocks and boulders encrusted in the soil which made the work more difficult. Uncle Snowboy showed us how to pile the rubble along the edge of the pit. This pile eventually took the shape of a strong, stubbly wall. Resting on a large boulder during a brief pause, Uncle Snowboy told us, "Got to make the wall strong or it won't support the branches and leaves we'll use for a roof."

We cut the leaves and branches for the roof, arranged them carefully in a precise pattern, and finally set the trap door under Uncle Snowboy's directions. Then it was time to do something else.

On the way back to his camp, Uncle Snowboy pointed to a spot and said how, several years earlier, he had passed by that bunch of trees many times. But he didn't see that there was a black bear den there. One day, he found a set of lynx tracks that crossed his. The tracks were about a day old. He followed them and found that they led to the entrance of the den. The lynx had been standing at the entrance all night. Uncle Snowboy looked at us and asked, "Why did he do that, the lynx?" He waited for an answer, then said, "The answer is that the lynx wanted me to see and check out what he had found."

The lynx, a friend of man, was actually showing him what he had missed. Uncle Snowboy told me that the bear was very powerful too, spiritually speaking. Bears could withhold game and spoil a hunter's chances of success. People believed that if a bear did not allow one to find him, one wouldn't be able to. Uncle Snowboy explained, "They say the bear is putting his paws over your eyes." It was like that with beavers too, he said, adding, "If beaver are not caught, there is a meaning to that. So we just let them be and come back later when the beaver are ready to be caught."

After leaving his uncle, Larry went around to check some of his snares. Sure enough, he found a snowshoe hare in one. "This is excellent," said Larry, "now we have supper for our guest." He apologized for not having given me time to eat upon arrival at the camp, for that was the custom, a show of respect for the visitor. It was assumed that the visitor was tired and hungry as he would have had to cover a long distance through the bush to get from one camp to the other. "But," said Larry with a smile, "I knew Rosie would've made sure you had a decent breakfast at the motel or her trailer."

Emily heard our footsteps and was ready inside the camp to meet us. The first thing she did was to take the bag off Larry's shoulder. I discovered that it was not proper for women and children to rush out of the camp when they heard the hunter approaching. The hunter is bringing them food, and they were expected to wait respectfully inside the tent.

Then Emily quickly went about skinning and cleaning the rabbit. There was already a wood fire going in the middle of the tent, and it wasn't long before the skewered rabbit was cooking over it.

Strangely, the conversation was all about bears as we ate the rabbit with large chunks of bread and butter, and bottled cranberry juice which I could swear tasted better than the best Chateau Lafite. Larry told us about the time his father saw a female bear up on a tree. It was the black bear mating season. His father was standing just under the tree, and all he had in his hand was a small axe. Larry's mother warned him that there might be another bear nearby. She was right. Just then they saw the male, up on its hind legs and starting to charge towards his father. Seeing such a dangerous situation, Larry's father spoke to the bear. "I am unarmed," he said. "You should not be attacking me like this." At which the bear paused, got down on all four and, a little later, walked away as if he understood. Larry said he truly believed that, when confronted by men, some animals would make a stand and force men to step back. The Cree had learnt methods of preventing attacks in such a showdown. A hunter, for instance, talked to black bears and tried to reason with them.

In ages past, said Larry, animals talked to people too. In a sense, there was still communication between animals and hunters. For example, in some cases one could predict where a black bear was likely to den. Even though the bear zig-zags before retreating into his den to hibernate, trying to shake the hunter off his trail, the hunter can still predict where he is likely to go. Often, when approaching the den entrance, the bear will make tracks backwards, lose his tracks in the bush, and then make a long detour before coming into the den. The hunter tries to think what the bear is thinking, and their minds touch. Hunters and trappers know about animals as animals know about them. The knowledge is detailed and intimate. The details and intimacy are a personal science, a system of understanding that reveals and secures a peoples' absolute dependence on the land and its creatures.

At night, I slept in the same cabin as Larry and Emily. I simply put down my sleeping bag over the spruce boughs at the back of the tent, a place customarily assigned to people who deserve respect.

Over the next couple of days, I made many other discoveries. For instance, when a hunter gets up in the morning, the wife gets up too at the same time, like it was in Rosie's story to the children. She packs lunch for him. When the husband is gone, she goes out too and chops wood, cuts spruce boughs for the floor of the cabin, and prepares animal skins. Emily described to me how chopping wood was especially important because it was believed that when a wife chops wood, the husband sees many animals in the bush. If she stays in bed, he sees nothing at all. So the act of chopping wood was an important responsibility, a way for the wife to take part in the hunt. And if her husband came home empty-handed, said Emily, it was no big deal. He still deserved respect, and got it. That's how, she said, old people — man and wife — built up a special bond through sharing in the bush over many good and difficult years.

Rosie couldn't come that Saturday. She sent a message from the village the night before. So I resigned himself, happily, to spending one more day following Larry around. We checked the snares for rabbit. There was nothing. Larry told me, "We did all our beaver trapping last month. From now on till Christmas, it'll probably be some grouse and ptarmigan. But there's enough food, so don't be alarmed."

In the south, in the direction of the airport, a flock of crows kept circling the sky. Larry looked grimly at the dark spots as if they were a patch of infection on the face of the sky. He spoke with a grimace, "There's something dead out there, or the crows wouldn't be going crazy. Whatever it is, it has no business being there."

With me behind him, Larry gunned his skidoo towards the hovering crows. After a half hour journey, as exciting as the most hair-raising roller-coaster ride I have ever been on, Larry found what we were looking for — three headless moose carcasses piled into a shallow gully. Flies, thick as bees colliding for space in a hive, covered the necks where the heads had been hacked off. The shine was gone from the coat of the animals. The stench was awful.

Larry shook his head in disbelief. There was disgust in his voice as, pointing to the wide wheel-marks in the snow left by a pick-up truck, he said, "Hunters from the south. Could be Americans, could be from Quebec, Ontario, who knows? Once they used to hire Cree guides who would take care of the carcass even if the tourist hunters wanted only the heads for trophies. Now they seem to know it all, don't need guides no more. They just shoot at whatever's moving and take away whatever they want."

It took Larry the rest of the day to arrange for the carcasses to be burnt.

On Sunday morning, shortly after he had brought Rosie over from the wayside on his skidoo, Larry announced that he had had a dream a couple of nights ago. "I know what you'll think, Charlie," he said. "That we have been talking about bears every evening, so what was one to expect."

The dream, naturally, was about a black bear. Larry explained how Cree hunters often made contact with their prey in their dreams. Men and women who showed proper respect for animals could leave their bodies at night and move along dream trails in the bush. The dreamer meets a bear or moose. The hunter notices a distinctive mark that identifies the animal. During the days that follow, whenever the hunter decides that conditions are auspicious, he goes into the bush, finds the trail of the dream and follows it until he discovers and recognizes the animal in his dream. Just as the animal allowed itself to appear in the dream, it now agrees to be killed. The hunter collects the prey, as it were, in fulfilment of a contract agreed upon in a dream.

Larry hauled out a couple of pairs of snowshoes and a shovel. Then he and I set forth after breakfast. My credulity had been tested once before by Louis, now Larry was putting it to the test again. Along the way, we came across a porcupine up a tree. Larry made a careful note of which way the animal was pointing with its head. He said, "It's a good sign. We go in the direction he was pointing with his head. Notice that the porcupine is only half way up the tree, which means big game is not far." In his father's days, Larry told me, one could kill the porcupine and bring him to camp, and some of the old men could tell if the porcupine was really pointing or not.

About two hours later, we came across a slight but sudden elevation of the land. Since everything was covered under a thick layer of white, it was only Larry's practised eye that picked up anything unusual. We had almost walked past it when Larry asked me to stop. He began picking around the mound with his shovel until he thought he had found what he was looking for. There were signs of vegetation and some broken boughs underneath the snow. Larry knelt down and brought his nose close to the ground. He sniffed deeply, he sniffed in short bursts, and finally raised himself off the ground. "This is it," he said to me.

I went down to sniff, but got up admitting that I couldn't smell anything more distinctive than vegetation.

Larry pulled out a small piece of rag from his hunting bag and planted most of it in the snow. Then he covered up the spot he had explored so that the leaves and branches did not show. I was surprised to see him turning back. Flashing his customary smile, Larry said, "We now go and tell Uncle Snowboy what we've found."

Larry sat down in front of the fire inside his uncle's cabin and faced the older man on the other side. Then he picked up a pipe, lighted it, and gave it to his uncle. This was a sign that he was passing on a black bear to his uncle, a sign of respect. He didn't have to say it in words; it meant that he had either killed the bear or found the den and now the bear was his uncle's.

Uncle Snowboy smoked deeply and nodded his head in understanding.

The following morning all three of us set out for the den. I noticed a curious look of satisfaction and amusement in Rosie's eyes as we said goodbye. Since I didn't see Larry kiss Emily goodbye, I didn't wish to kiss Rosie either. I was becoming more and more sensitive to the social rituals of bush life and had no intentions of violating any.

As we plodded along in our snowshoes, I was surprised how none of the hunters betrayed the slightest emotion, certainly no hint of exuberance. In fact, they seemed positively subdued. Even when they approached the den, it was without any sense of heightened expectation. Uncle Snowboy told Larry where to shovel off the snow. Before long, the entrance to the den was exposed, and so was the bear. Uncle Snowboy said simply, "*Nitakushin*," and, as it tried to shake itself off the ground, shot the bear straight through the head. Later, he explained how *Nitakushin* meant 'I am here', and it was the same way that a visiting hunter would announce himself at a camp. The hunter shows as much respect to the bear as he shows to people. It is almost as if he is arriving at the den as a visitor, hoping that the bear will accept him.

I helped them pull the bear outside. Then Larry took out a knife and cut the warm skin in front of the chest, just over the breast-bone, to check the fat. There was a fair layer of fat, and both Larry and his uncle declared it to be a good, healthy animal. The more fat the better.

With amazing swiftness, Larry fashioned a pole out of the trunk of a nearby tamarack tree. Then they tied up the bear's limbs so that the animal lay suspended as Larry and I picked up the two ends of the pole. I heard how Larry's uncle had, in his youth, carried bears on his back—paws over the shoulder, legs held under his arms, like a child's, and the limbs tied in front over his chest. The uncle also told me how carrying a bear can have a symbolic significance for the hunter. Once, when he and a friend had killed a black bear, his friend gave him the bear.

Uncle Snowboy told me what happened next. "I tried hard to lift it, but I stumbled and fell down. Then my friend told me that now the bear was really mine." The point of it all, said the uncle, was that the human hunter is not all powerful. "Even though I tried hard," he said, "the bear finally prevailed over me. With the stumble and the fall, I had really earned the bear the hard way. Now it was truly mine."

Hunters from the neighbouring tents also joined us as we hauled the black bear into the back of the uncle's cabin. This too was not without meaning. The area was known as *waaskwaataan*, or the old man's place. By bringing the bear to *waaskwaataan*, one showed respect not only to the bear but also to the 'old man' for his past accomplishments as a hunter. Then we all sat down in a circle, the black bear in the middle. Larry's uncle started smoking a pipe and made a gesture of offering the pipe to the bear. After that, we all smoked a little more and then tried cracking the bear's knuckles, all four limbs, hand and feet. Some of the knuckles did crack, and the hunters smiled. The sound told them that the bear had been hiding or withholding some game from the hunters. The cracking of the knuckles meant that the animals were released from the power of the bear. Their spell was broken, and they could be hunted.

Before butchering the animal, Larry's uncle cut some patterns on the bear, indicating to the women how he wanted the animal skinned. The bear looked like a slumbering Sumo wrestler, enjoying his handlers rubbing the knots out of his body.

Emily, Rosie, and Larry's aunt were now joined by two other women, the other hunters' wives. While they bloodied their hands in skinning the bear, Larry's uncle discussed how they were to divide the animal. Everyone from the four other cabins would receive an equal share. If there were young children, even those who could not eat solid meat, they too would receive an equal share. The infant's share would be left aside for a day, and after that it would be redistributed among the others.

Rosie watched my reaction to the slaughter from the corner of her eyes. I caught her looking and merely smiled back, marvelling at the casualness with which the women attended to the gory task. I tried to learn to be casual from them, but it was difficult.

Once the bear was skinned to a shining red and white apparition, Larry carved out a chunk of meat and threw it into the fire. It was an offering to thank the Provider.

Larry's uncle asked him to keep the skin covering the chin of the bear. Larry thanked him and promised to keep it in a pouch. He would use it as a charm. Strictly for my benefit, the hunters explained some of the customs peculiar to the meat of black bears. For instance, only men would cook black bear meat. The head, they said, was primarily for male consumption; the backbone, primarily for women. Bones with the attached meat and marrow were exclusively for men over forty. Children were not allowed to eat the backbone and the four limbs. If they did, they would age too rapidly. As a sign of respect, all black bear bones were to be hung on trees or placed on top of wooden platforms. Oh yes! and one mustn't forget, said Uncle Snowboy amidst playful laughter, that the male organs of the animals belonged to the women.

Even though I had played no larger a role than help Larry carry the animal back to camp, I felt unusually high. Five thousand years and more of this, I thought, and the bear was still around, and the caribou and the lynx. At last, I was beginning to understand the close, intricate relation between the hunter and the hunted. Here, in the land of the Cree and the Inuit at least, the relationship was one of equals. The eternal principle, when they explained it to me, appeared so simple— NO MAN CAN BE SUPERIOR TO THAT UPON WHICH HE DEPENDS. Uncle Snowboy pointed out how humans have souls and spirit powers. But since humans and animals are equals, it follows that animals must also have a place in the spirit world. It also follows that animals too must depend upon the hunt, they must agree to be killed. All northern hunters, he said, insist that if animals are not treated with respect, both when alive and dead, they will not allow themselves to be hunted. Seen in this light, the hunt too is a form of contract between partners, in which it is not always clear who is the prey.

Uncle Snowboy insisted that the contract was not simple, for animals have to be found in vast terrains and difficult bush. Or else, they must be intercepted in a trail that herds elect to follow each year. Under such difficult conditions, how can the hunters find the animals? How can they be sure that the animals will let themselves be killed? This is the Cree's problem of knowledge. I could never imagine such problems existed.

Back in Larry's cabin, Rosie volunteered to make some coffee for everyone. Larry asked me if I had seen enough excitement for a day.

I replied, "Sure, but how come you guys didn't seem all that excited?"

"That's the way we were taught to live our lives in the bush," replied Larry.

I found myself shaking my head in admiration. "I think you are so lucky," I said. "It seems the power of imagination has fled our lives."

With a curious half smile, Larry said, "Actually, to help you along the way of imagination, we thought you might like to sleep in the canvas teepee outside. You won't recognize it. Rosie cleaned it out, cut some fresh boughs and laid them out on the floor. There's even a small fire which should keep it fairly warm. Hope you don't mind, but we took the liberty of placing your sleeping bag in the other teepee."

"Not at all," I replied, flattered by all the attention. "Maybe I snored and kept you all awake last night, that's why you're throwing me out, isn't it? I asked. I let the laughter die down and then asked if I could go and take a look.

"Certainly," said Larry as he accompanied me outside. Larry lifted the canvas flap and let some of the smoke escape. After the smoke had cleared, I took in a deep breath and was immediately filled with pleasure. "Look at you," said Larry, "you're like a kid." He observed me carefully and said, "Yes, you can actually breathe the sweet fragrance of the forest. But it is we who breathe life into it. In destroying us, you also destroy nature."

I really didn't mind Larry lecturing me. Much later, I finished my coffee in silence. I wanted to say goodnight to Emily and Rosie, but Larry said he'd tell them on my behalf. I said I was sorry I had hardly had time to talk to Rosie, but Larry assured me I'd have all day to talk to her tomorrow.

I put out the fire and lay down on my sleeping bag. It was warm inside the tent, and it felt good on the fresh, springy boughs of spruce. The night was full of strange whispers, sounds I could not name. Then I realized what I wanted to hear was Rosie's voice. I imagined there were uncounted spirits outside and in the teepee with me. But I wanted Rosie. Rosie, standing over the fallen bear like some elemental creature, blood dripping from her hands.

Just then, the flap of the teepee opened once more revealing a shadow framed against the clear blue triangle of the night sky. Rosie came in and lay down beside me without a word.

She took me on a voyage Ulysses would've envied. Rosie was Helen, Penelope, Circe, and the sirens all rolled into one. Achilles didn't fall, Cassandra didn't utter a sound.

We held each other in our arms for a long long time. After what seemed like an eternity during which the tide of happiness refused to let up, I finally broke the silence, and—inadvertently—some of the magic. I whispered in her ear, half jokingly, "I hate to break it to you, but I keep seeing bears all around us."

"It's quite possible," said Rosie, snuggling close to me. Then, nibbling at my ear, she asked, "Will you be bored if I tell you another bear story?"

"Tell me," I said eagerly, drawing her closer.

"The story starts when a woman goes out to pick berries one day. She takes her young son along. While she picked berries, the child wandered around here and there, eating berries, as children do. He was quite a distance away from the mother when he heard a voice calling, "Come over here." It was a bear calling for the child to come. There was nothing unusual about this because, a long time ago, animals like the bear and caribou—all things that we eat—spoke. The bear willed the child to come to him, and the child came. The child cried out when the bear took hold of him. "Hush, hush," said the bear, "come and sit on my back." The bear then ran off with him.

The woman soon came looking for her child. She kept calling out to him, and rushed over to where she had seen him last. There, she saw the tracks of the bear and began to fear the worst. She went home, grieving loudly, telling how she thought a bear had taken her child. In the camp, there was a man who knew how to divine through the shaking tent ceremony. He was asked to find out what had happened to the child through his shamanistic powers. At first, he didn't come up with anything. Then his Spirit, *Mishtaabaau*, told him, 'The child is alive. He is living with someone. A bear has taken him and that's where he is living. It will be that the child will return.'

"The bear who had taken the boy got a lot of help from him. The bear could not see very far, so he would have the boy warn him if there were people nearby. The boy would say, 'Grandfather, the people are close by.' And the bear would ask the boy to go to the edge of the forest and hide. Later, the boy would get on the bear's back and the bear would carry him away. If the bear was sighted, it always seemed there was someone on the bear's back. Hunters were unwilling to shoot their arrows at such a bear.

"Time passed and winter came. The bear said to the child, 'You will not go hungry all winter, grandson. I will make a place for us to live, a place during the winter.'

"The bear eats all the animals that are on land—ptarmigan, porcupine, beaver, even the rabbit—just as people do. It now gathered all the food that they would need for the winter and dried it, just as people do.

"When the bear wants to prepare his den, he looks for a hill-like mound of earth, sometimes with sand. So now they moved on until the bear said, 'I will make a home.' The boy watched as the bear started the den, a place for them to live. And the bear said, 'Grandson, you will never be cold all winter, for here we will stay. I never go out during the winter. When the weather turns warm and the snow melts, that's when I go out.' The boy watched until the bear finished the den. 'Grandson, bring some boughs,' said the bear. 'Break off some boughs that we can lay inside the den.' The boy did as he was told. When he was finished, he said, 'Shaash!'

When the bear saw the boughs the boy had gathered, he asked him, 'How did you break them off?' When he saw where the child had broken the boughs off—for it was very noticeable—the bear said, 'Oh! this will not do. We will be found. People can see where you've broken off the boughs.' Then he showed him the proper way to do it. 'If you break them this way, upward instead of downward, the break will show only on the underside of the branch and it will not be noticeable.' This is why a bear would leave a finished den sometimes, because of what the child did, breaking off the boughs from the wrong side. Then the people would look for a bear in a different place. So, this time, the bear did leave, saying, 'It will not do. We must leave, or we'll be found.'

"The boy lived with the bear for many summers. He grew up. Over the winters, whenever people got too close, the bear would say, 'Grandson, set out some of your food.' Then he would put his front paws up to his face, and the people wouldn't be able to sight any bear. If the boy didn't do as his grandfather told him, they would've been found by the people.

"One day, the bear said to the boy, 'The time has come when your father will claim you.' But that Fall, the bear once again made another den. When they moved into the new den, the bear said to the boy, 'Go and find a tree stump. This is what we will burn all winter.' That is the only piece of wood they used that winter. When the stump burned in half, the bear said, 'Grandson, it is the middle of winter.'

"Time passed, and one day the bear said to the boy, 'The time has come for your father to claim you. I will not be able to prevent him. He will find you, he will find us.' The bear could not see everything very clearly. So he said, 'Today is the day that your father will be able to find you. Your mother has finished the clothes that you will wear. Your snowshoes are finished. I see them hanging up.'

"The father had told his wife to make some clothes for their son. He said, 'The time has come for me to claim our son.'

"And the boy's grandfather said to him, 'He is coming. I see him bringing your snowshoes. He is coming out of the lodge now.' The bear said to the boy, 'Grandson, set out some ptarmigan.' The boy's father saw the ptarmigan and said, 'I will shoot them on my way back.' The boy continued to set out more food. Each time, the man said, 'I will shoot it on my way back.' Next, the man came upon a beaver dam. Again, he said, 'I will kill the beaver on my way back.' If he had shot and killed any of the animals he had seen on his way, he would have failed to do what he had set out to do. He would not have found his son.

"This is the way it was, long ago, that when a man was hunting bear, he would shoot at the first thing he saw. This is where he went wrong. The bear willed him to do this.

This man, the boy's father, did not shoot any of the animals he saw on his way and was not overpowered by the bear. Soon, the boy had set out all the different food they had, as his grandfather told him to do. 'The time has come for your father to take you home,' said the bear once more. 'I will speak to you, grandson, of what you will do. I will be the first one to go out. But remember, when there is a need for food, and you go out hunting in the wintertime on a beautiful day, go to a high hill and climb it. Look in all directions—north, south, east, and west. Look for some smoke drifting upwards. You may see the smoke very faintly, or you may see thicker smoke rising. When you want me, say this as you go outside: 'Grandfather, where is it that you said you will be?' touching your chest as you speak. Say this whenever you want me.' And the bear ended with this, 'The smoke that is faint will be a small bear and the smoke that is thick will be a big bear. You may go to the one you want.'

"The bear did not tell the young boy, now a young man, to always go to the thicker smoke. Sometimes, the young man would go towards the faint smoke and kill a small bear. He did not want to be greedy or frivolous with what had been given to him by the bear, and go always for the thicker smoke.

"Shortly after the boy's grandfather had finished instructing him, he said, 'He is almost upon us.' Soon they heard noises at the entrance to the den. The entrance of a bear's den looks grey. This is from the breathing of the bear.

"Then the boy heard the sound of blows landing on his grandfather. These were the arrows striking the bear. Then the boy's father dragged the bear outside. Next, he poked his head in, looked around and saw his son. And the boy heard his father say, 'Why did you not tell me that I killed your grandfather?' He gave the boy clothes which he put on. They went home. The son was a young man now, and the family was all together.

"From then on, and only once in a while—because he did not want to be frivolous with the knowledge given to him—the young man would do as his grandfather had told him to when he wanted to hunt bear. And he was always successful in his hunt. He was able to provide bear meat for the people and everyone was fed. But one day his father heard him speaking as he was leaving, and he wondered what he was saying. And other young men who were also his friends asked him one day: 'Why is it so easy for you to kill the bear in the wintertime? Is it because you lived with a bear?'

"He did not answer. Other boys kept asking him the same question, and still he wouldn't answer. His friends kept after him, kept asking him the same question many many times, sometimes after a kill. Whenever there was great hunger among the people, the young man always seemed able to kill a bear. Sometimes he would kill one bear, sometimes two. He did not want to use his knowledge frivolously.

"Finally, one winter, he decided to answer his friends' repeated questions. And so he did. From then on, he was not able to do what he used to be able to. Only once in a while would he now kill a bear. The power given to him by his grandfather was weakened because he had spoken of it to others.

"This happened a long, long time ago when animals still spoke. To this day, if a new, finished, unused den is found, people know that it's because of what the boy did long, long ago.

I kissed Rosie for the beautiful story, for the knowledge she had chosen to share with me. Soon I was fast asleep in her arms.

In spite of my earlier misgivings about John Gage, I dropped by to see him at Woody's one Wednesday evening when I knew he would be there. In the pale light of the smoke-filled room I was surprised to see the change that only a few months had brought upon him. He appeared drawn and haggard, with a melancholy air which was accentuated by a straggly beard. I immediately felt a pang of guilt over the distance I had maintained from him for some time. But then I began to wonder if I might have ever noticed slight and gradual changes in John if we had met week after week. Maybe I would have, had John gone out of his way to open his heart to me. Maybe I wouldn't.

Tonight he did, explaining how he thought his life was a mess after he had broken off a relationship going downhill for months. I said I was truly sorry to hear it, and I think I was being sincere. That was not all — John was beginning to have departmental problems over funds, staff performance, student standards, and class size. I said it was too bad. To crown it all, John had put his house on the market since he no longer needed such a big place, only to find that the value had actually fallen below the price he had paid seven years ago. I felt compelled to offer him my sympathies for this misfortune too.

I too had my share of problems at work. Almost unwittingly, I had put my finger on a conspiracy of silence and deceit spreading through my world of ships and their voyages. A casual computer search through the marine claims register of my company, world-wide, had come up with an alarming incidence of claims affecting certain specific ships and the cargo they carried. By a curious coincidence, many of these ships were built in British shipyards in the nineteen seventies. By another curious coincidence, most of these ships had initially been registered by Lloyds of London but had, over the years, taken on flags of convenience by registering in countries with secret and inscrutable codes of engineering standards for ships.

I had probed deeper, only to discover that every year Lloyds de-classified dozens of ships without disclosing — as a service or courtesy to the rich shipowners — the names of the ships that were being struck off the registry because they had failed to meet the more stringent British standards. So the shipowner simply took the ship to another country.

John interrupted me at this point. He said, "I think they call this the comparative advantage of nations, a new buzz-word. Bring us your castaways, your leaky tubs, and we'll help you set sail with confidence."

I continued. In rummaging through the literature, I had found unusual structural failures in British-built ships of the seventies. Entire welded sections of the hull had come unstuck. I had discovered that the welding of these ships had been contracted out on a piece-work basis, and welders — in order to complete the job quickly — had often placed welding rods along the seams and welded them over. The machinery of the time wasn't advanced enough to properly monitor the strength of these hurriedly, and often incorrectly, welded joints. I believed some of these ships were absolute death-traps and many were already lying at the bottom of the sea, mossy wrecks marking the unnamed graves of hapless sailors.

I tried not to get carried away by my passion. But I had to tell John. "You don't know Pentland Firth, north of Scotland, like I do. Can you imagine these creaky buckets trying to butt through the meeting of waves from the open ocean and tidal currents from the opposing direction? With easterly swells and a flood tide it's hell at the Bore of Duncansby in the east end of the Firth. And it's sheer madness with ebb tides and a westerly swell at the Merry Men of Mey on the western end of the Firth." I told myself not to get too excited as I remembered the heaving seas from South Ronaldsay and Hoy.

I caught John looking at me with amazement. I'm sure he never thought an insurance man capable of strong emotion. This was a side of my life I had tried desperately to hide from others. What I had done, following my very private discoveries, was put together tighter underwriting requirements which had made life difficult for a lot of people. My detractors told me that my principles might be sound, but they would only drive business away to other companies.

"Ah!" said John at the end of all this, "your conscience has driven you to a crossroads—a very serious problem in some societies, though not others." I had to laugh as I reminded John of something Louis Bearskin once told me: "The white man is problem-solving. He sees problems where others see the ordinary and the inconsequential. Not so with the white man, who dips his hunches into the alchemy of science and reshapes the inconsequential as problems."

"Yes, Louis is wise," said John.

After we had each knocked down a couple of drinks, something of the previous warmth returned to our meeting. John said he couldn't explain why he had felt and acted so foul earlier in the evening, why he had to be whining and groaning upon seeing me after such a long time. And I apologized too for my long absence from Woody's. Now I was quite eager to tell John how much more had happened in my life that year.

"Where are you with Isabel Gunn?" asked John.

I tried to explain that La Pointe a Callieres, or Place Youville, or the street where I lived, none of it would be the same for me again. They had taken on a life much larger than the names themselves. I wondered what had happened to make me accept Louis Bearskin's words as the truth and put aside all the material John had gathered for me from the archives. How could I afford to reject the written word when I allowed it to put its stamp on just about everything else I did? Could it be that I had wanted to believe Louis all along?

By the time I had finished, John Gage was very drunk. Still, he made a brave effort to summarize what he had patiently heard over the previous hour. He began, "Let me see if I've got your story right. From what you say, Isabel Gunn has been temporarily rehabilitated in your mind. Or should I say permanently?"

I said that Louis Bearskin had appeared to be quite credible. In fact, Louis had given me more information than my parents ever had.

"Yes," said John, drawing out his words, "but you seem quite prepared to disregard all the information that came from the archives in Winnipeg. Is that right?"

"No," I replied, "but I am beginning to believe that the difference between a slut and a saint may sometimes only be a problem of the imagination."

"Brilliant," said John. "Brilliant," he repeated, mockingly. "My dear Charlie, this time you have a bigger problem on your hands. The problem you are facing is a problem of knowledge. We so-called intellectuals face it all the time, but we're supposed to be able to handle it. Your salvation can only lie with a shrink. All I can say is that you're facing a major crisis of knowledge. Good luck."

I think I made my irritation quite obvious. "Why should everything be a crisis?" I asked. "A crisis of knowledge. A crisis of identity, crisis of conscience."

"Yes, I was coming to that," said John, ignoring my annoyance. He forced an angelic grin across his face. It lit up the wisps of his greying beard. "A crisis of identity most certainly when you start hallucinating with Cree elders about Henry Hudson and his son."

I found John nod his head understandingly, patronizingly, at me. I had hoped for John's ostensible sympathy for the Cree and their cause to lead him to a kinder understanding of my stories. Although I was certain John was speaking half in jest, I was beginning to feel uncomfortable once again. I had heard so often that one believes what one wants to. I wondered if that was really true. I suspected that I had been carrying in my mind for a very long time the pathetic figure of my father trying to reform the world with fiction, which was nothing but a pack of lies. It was a cruel image, one that grated harshly against the deep love I had always felt for my mother and for Malcolm Gunn. Could it be that my easy acceptance of Louis' story had something to do with a chance to restore and fortify my love for my parents, especially my father, rather than a need to believe in Isabel Gunn's saintly legend?

I kept looking long and hard at John and finally asked him, "Don't you ever hallucinate? Don't you ever speak with unseen people?"

"Only when I am drunk," replied John. "Let me tell you something. Perhaps the most serious crisis of identity is that you seem to be in love with Rosie."

I was determined not to let him off easily this time. In fact, I noticed a touch of envy in John's voice. Eventually, I decided to try and clear the air a little. I said to John, "If I had been married and fell in love with Rosie ten years from now, I suppose you would call it a mid-life crisis."

'Hell, no," he cried adamantly. "No, you'd be so guilt-ridden I'd probably call you suicidal." He paused for a sip of beer and continued, "You've gone over the Eastmain River, haven't you?"

Yes, I had, I replied, unsure of what to expect next.

John explained how alcohol sometimes made the memory so crystalline and clear. He said, "In 1760, the master of Eastmain Fort, a man by the name of James Hester, had to be returned to England because he had gone crazy and attempted to castrate himself with a knife 'for fornication that he had committed with an Indian' woman. That's what I was suggesting by suicidal—near-suicidal."

I honestly felt the comparison in bad taste. I couldn't find it in me to brush it off as a silly joke. So I told John, "You're a bit of a cad to be bringing up that story, aren't you? Especially when you know I really love Rosie."

John was contrite and apologized right away. But he did move on to what he thought would now begin to bother me anew—the suspicion that my apartment was spooked by the ghost of Marguerite d'Youville. "I fear you're going to continue being suffocated by saintly influences," he warned me. John left the table conceding that life was perhaps like the Babushka doll he had once given to a lover—one and many forms of the doll hidden inside the other. "You always get more than what you see." Adding, with a long sigh, "But never more than what you paid for."

Instead of feeling spooked, I felt almost energized in a curious way at the thought of Saint Marguerite having perhaps walked through the space where I lived. It was a special feeling because the apartment was such a private place. It's different in a cathedral or such other public places. I almost had a private saint all to myself. Kechechowieh's story was the rounding of a circle which gave a little more space to my life than the narrow confines marked simply by birth and death. I thought I had made some progress in becoming a part of events around me—events that happened when I was neither memory nor hope. A little more than before, although nowhere near the extent to which Rosie or Louis appeared to be.

I lay awake at night and the faces hovered over me, dissolved and picked up substance and shape. My mother, Malcolm Gunn, Barry, Rosie, they all stepped out from behind the veil of sleep and then left. I felt surprised and a little disappointed by John's scepticism over the images I had seen, the voices I had heard, in Louis Bearskin's company. How was that any different from what I was experiencing at that hour in my silent apartment in Jardin d'Youville? Why should the other be any less real? Kechechowieh had probably seen the shaft of light over the very building in which I now slept. Like the ebb and flow of tides, combining with or resisting waves large and small, I saw my memories and experiences forming unexpected combinations, resonating with unheard-of mysteries.

No longer was Marguerite d'Youville just a name which a clever property developer had found for his over-priced apartment complex. I thought it likely that the quay where the big ships lay moored was precisely where the twenty nine-year old Paul Chomeday de Maisonneuve and his band of forty five colonists came ashore in their canoes and flat-bottomed boats after their voyage from Quebec City. Where the fountains now stood outside my apartment might have been the very spot where Father Vimont set up an altar in 1642 and finished his first mass with the words: "You will rise and grow till your branches overshadow the earth. You are few, but your work is the work of God. His smile is on you, and your children will fill the land."

Father Vimont was the only priest in the group, committed—like the sponsors of the Montreal adventurers, Jerome Le Royer, Sieur de La Dauversiere, and Pierre Chevrier, Baron de Fancamp—to saving Indian souls. The rest of the group was made up of masons, carpenters and farmers who cleared the trees and built the first houses and the first palisade fort, all crowded around the present spot I had paid handsomely for.

I learnt that among the members of the original group was Jeanne Mance who set up a hospital near the new encampment, on a corner which I passed everyday— St. Paul and St. Sulpice Streets. This is where the first casualties of the skirmishes with the Iroquois began to come in. Iroquois—what a word! To call a whole nation rattlesnakes and adders. But the colony multiplied in spite of the Iroquois attacks and numbered a thousand people thirty five years later. The place really took off when Louis Hector de Callieres came as the ninth governor of the colony in 1684 and built himself a beautiful house on the site of the first defensive ring of stakes. Soon the stockade was replaced by a much larger one surrounding the growing town around Pointe a Calliere—protection against marauding Iroquois as well as drunken Huron traders.

It was during Callieres' term of office that the philanthropist Francois Charron helped build a new hospital, thirty feet by ninety feet, and for men only, on the land south and west of the governor's house. Charron died in 1719 and the hospital slipped into neglect until it was taken over by a wealthy and generous lady, Marie—Marguerite Dufrost de La Jemmerais, widow of Seigneur Francois d'Youville. Marguerite restored the building and founded the nursing order of the Grey Nuns to help with her work. When the great fire of 1761 swept through the town it destroyed the hospital but not Marguerite's courage. She rebuilt the hospital.

I always felt a sense of reverence in knowing that some of the walls of the rebuilt hospital stood surrounding me to this day. My bed might well be on the very spot where other beds lay, where many of the settlers had perhaps breathed their last, feeling the touch of Marguerite's benediction on their brow. It occurred to me in the midst of a dream that history did not lie locked in the pages of books. It lay in objects one could feel, touch, see, and smell, words that one could actually hear. One could read and read and read history and be a fool. One had actually to live in history to be truly a part of it. One needed to dance, to sing, to smoke and drink. There is such wisdom in dreams.

And I remembered Barry and began to understand the passions unleashed at Oka when a golf course suddenly seemed more important than the buried bones of ancestors. I understood Louis too. I saw how powerful leaders were busy creating new history with the towering structures around James Bay, crushing the history of the Cree. Not the history in their history books of which they had none, but the history that was the

Requiem for the Last Indian | 209

stones and pebbles now submerged, the animals now banished from the land submerged, the ancestral bones now crumbling under the land submerged, or floating away to the sea like debris—a way of life doomed to extinction.

Strange that my thoughts left me not in turmoil but in peace. Perhaps it was the nearness of Marguerite d'Youville and Kechechowieh. Yes, and Isabel Gunn too, for who was I to pass judgement on her?

I brought my knapsack out of the trunk of my car and pulled out a cardboard cylinder in which I stored some of my most treasured maps since childhood. As I spread out a roll of paper on the flat rock, its smooth surface reminded me of the hand of Nature, patient and uninterrupted, brushing over it for a million years or more. On this sheet of paper, a bleached and crumpled map, the La Grande River existed as a thin blue line that stretched from east to west across the pale green surface of the map. Along the way, it grew fat, took on the shape perhaps of an insect or animal, or worse, a blue smudge where rivers had been forced into lakes. In the most recent maps, I knew the blue lines disappeared altogether, thanks to some grand design which willed them superfluous, locked them upstream, and choked off the run, the surge without which the miracle of a river's life is desecrated.

I had taken three weeks' leave to come and see Rosie, to feel the throb of the new life I had helped create in her. Rosie's classes had recessed for the summer, so she too was able to join me in wandering across trails, marked and unmarked, up and down the river and around the many new lakes. A week into our holidays, this day had turned out to be somewhat frustrating so far.

We had wandered close to the mouth of the river where work crews were blasting for the new LG1 powerhouse. There was an acrid smell of explosives in the air. For some reason, the water in the river looked unusually murky. Rosie had never seen it that colour before and wondered if someone had dumped chemicals into the river. A light brown haze of dust and salts rose from the blasting area and spread onto the river. Within the haze, scores of gulls lifted and settled, lifted again, picking at the scraps of fish and eels chopped up by the blades of the turbines.

We decided to move away from the rimrock from where all this was visible. Rosie thought it was unhealthy for her unborn child to be so close to the raw, smoking scars on the rock, the piles of rubble, rusting tin shacks, and miles of unwelcome orange fencing. Carefully clambering down sudden slopes of jackpine and juniper, we found ourselves in a small canyon Rosie didn't know existed before. Nor did I. Though the canyon was still tight and wintry, spring lilies, white and pale blue, grew abundantly in the edges where the sun could warm them. Rosie picked up a fresh tail feather of a ruffed grouse glistening with the shiny moisture of the early morning. She looked just a little tired, so I drew her gently in my arms. Rosie relaxed and dropped her head on my shoulder and closed her eyes. We stood there a long time, breathing the fresh smell of flowers and pines.

At the foot of the slope was a group of boulders so harmoniously composed they might've been set there for worship or some other ceremonial reason. In the centre of this arrangement of stones, there rose from the canyon floor a strange round dome of rock and pine. Like the Ring of Brodgar, I told Rosie, promising her for the umpteenth time that I would soon arrange to take her there.

We returned to the car after a long, slow walk. Rosie looked closely at me and said, "You look less than happy today, Charlie. What's the matter?"

"I've been thinking about us," I replied. "Won't you consider coming back to Montreal with me?"

She too had a problem, she said, of how to divide her life between me and Chisasibi. She was looking for answers all the time, she assured me, but she didn't have one for me.

Just then, we drew near the gleaming camp which housed the hundreds of construction workers and engineers from the province. I turned to Rosie and asked, "Could we go in for a look around?"

"Sure," said Rosie. "If I were to go alone, they'd probably stop me, thinking I was a Cree whore looking for business. But I guess we'll be okay with you at the wheel."

We were.

I had often passed this way, but had never ventured into the camp. There seemed no reason for me to. I was amazed at the shining and spotless living quarters and other amenities that lay behind the unassuming facade of the cluster of prefabricated buildings. A supermarket, Caisse Populaire, swimming pool, bowling alley, skating rink, gym, restaurant, all bore evidence of the most meticulous care and maintenance.

Rosie, a touch of sadness in her voice, told me, "Some of us imagined we'd be inheriting all this some day. We were fools. Among the five thousand or so working here for Hydro Quebec you won't find more than a dozen Cree."

I didn't know what to say. What I did remember was that we had skipped lunch. Now we were both famished, and so we headed for the restaurant. We ate hot dogs, then fooled around in the gym, and wasted time examining the supermarket shelves. Walking through the aisles, I was surprised to run into Pierre quite unexpectedly.

"What are you doing here?" I asked.

"Another stupid claim." He shrugged his shoulders and cast a withering glance at Rosie.

I was surprised by the look of sheer contempt in his eyes. He walked by us with three words, slowing ever so slightly, and I didn't even have a chance to introduce him to Rosie. He looked drunk, and I convinced myself he was.

I didn't want my rising anger to spoil the evening. I wanted to forget the incident. "Let's go for a swim," I suggested, finding ourselves near the pool. I even sweet-talked the solitary attendant to bring us a couple of swimsuits. Rosie's was smaller than her size, and it squeezed her body and moulded it into soft ripples. Mine was an extra-large, and Rosie burst out laughing when she saw me come out of the locker room. We plunged into the warm waters together.

Inside the pool, shut out from the world outside, we hardly realized that evening was upon us. There was a dance and a big party in the camp that night, and we were startled by the passage of time when the music suddenly came on. We dried ourselves quickly and wandered over to the edge of the lake. Happy in our closeness, it was as if there was only this single lake on the face of the earth and we the last lovers leaving our footprints in the sand.

The sound of music rose and fell near the water's edge as the wind darted forward, stopped, and discovering us locked in each other's arms, wheeled around like a curious, restless child, uncertain of the next play. Neither the music nor the wind caused the slightest ripple across the waters of the dam, the river's fury sucked out of it forever, its resounding springtime roars silenced by the dykes like a hangman's noose.

A soft, purplish mist rose stealthily from the water's edge where the evening sun lay bathed in wine of uncertain and impatient blush. Soon the waters of the lake began to turn a dark, bluish green. The air grew moist. As darkness fell, the lights from the camp turned brighter — throbbing, pulsating lights throwing a soft glow against the sky and the water's edge. The music spilled out of the open doors of the Recreation Centre and flowed down to the grassy lookout where Rosie and I shivered delightedly in our embrace. She whispered to me again and again how amazed she was with the new life inside of her. Her tears bathed my face, for she was so happy the life was mine too. I found it difficult to believe it was all happening to me, to her, this ultimate experience, this unstoppable renewal of eternal wisdom, without which passion would be a mirage, like drowning in an empty ocean. Time stood still for us as we drained every drop of love out of each other and struggled to take hold of the wild, careening pangs of joy before they slipped out of our reach.

"It was such a beautiful river once," Rosie whispered in my ear.

For me no river, no ocean, no mountain could be more beautiful than the warm, living, breathing woman I held in my arms. It also occurred to me how foolish I had been in setting imaginary ideals for women, like setting targets for my sales force. One day, out of the blue, it would dawn on me that each one is an ideal. When Rosie told me, "You know, I've been with many men before you," at first I thought it was my mother cautioning me, or Isabel Gunn chastising me for my passion. But when her love left me in profound peace, complete as never before, I knew Rosie was a healer too.

Quite suddenly, the mist veered away, and the La Grande River lay blinded by a final flash of the sun melting at the edge of the sky. It was gone in a moment. But in that brief space, the river raised itself like a wounded serpent goaded to fury, exposing its raw, jagged banks and its pitted bed. Briefly visible in its distant reaches, it stumbled along its rocky path, exploding in spray, smashing against the concrete wall in an orgy of self-destruction. The wet haze leapt up in sparks from a hundred thousand bubbles and wrapped the silent hillside of spruce and fir in a damp, heavy cloak of sleep.

If the distant hills suddenly appeared to move, was it only an illusion? Was it fall, and ten thousand doomed caribou headed south once more out of the northern wilderness? The animals gathered as if in answer to their deepest instincts, their numbers growing by the minute, and soon they became a living tide on the land. In the quivering haze of the evening, entire hillsides and sweeping valleys shook and headed implacably towards the horizon, scattering clouds of dust in their wake. But the clouds froze in mid-air and came suddenly down on the caribou like a shroud. The river froze around us and the earth stood still. The image was like that of a child's playroom floor, carefree, strewn with toys. But the air was tinged with horror.

It seemed certain we were sharing the experience of this phantom vision spread across the hillside. Both of us lost it at the same time. Rosie broke the silence, saying it was springtime she loved the most, when the river swept into the bay in an irresistible surge, colliding against winter's shrinking strength, smashing the blocks of ice into little pieces etched with the frozen blue from a fire's heart. Such power, as the thick waves climbed up like syrup against the nodding eelgrass and waited for the next sweep of the river's arm to fall back. Rosie thought of spring as she clung to me in the dark, conjuring childhood memories to tell her child. When the baby comes, she told me, she would want to feed it fish like her mother used to. Crush the fish to juice it, place it in a container made of pike stomach, and stick in a goose quill as a nipple for feeding. Of course, she added with a nervous laugh, I would first have to find a river which mercury hadn't polluted.

Rosie kissed me long and hard. "I love you Charlie," she said. As she drew away from me, the darkness deepened around us. The wind, colder now, steered a fresh flood of sounds towards us. We heard the frenetic music, the sound of a hundred feet stomping on the dance floor, the sounds of drunken laughter. The sounds all but muffled the approaching footsteps of three revellers who had had enough dancing, enough drinking, and were now searching for some fresh air in which to cool their brains.

The men walked out of a clump of juniper and stumbled over us sitting on the grass. One fell on Rosie, maddened by her warm and supple body. The remaining two fell upon me, beat me fiercely about the head, then gagged and tied me with strips from my shirt and my belt. They gagged Rosie too, and twisted her arms behind her as she struggled like a wild animal. Then they started to drag her back into the darkness. I tried to scream, but I couldn't. I gave up as I felt rocked in and out of a nightmare with every jolt of pain shooting through my head.

Something must have happened to make the men change their minds. They returned dragging Rosie to where I lay. One of them spoke in a rasping voice, "We thought you'd like to see what we do with this slut."

With vicious, jerky movements he started to rip the shirt off her back. Naked, Rosie writhed helplessly on the grass while two of the men held her down.

The air awakened me. Lying on my face, I tried to loosen my hands bound so tightly behind my back. It was an impossible task. I lifted my head and turned my face to get a closer look at the three. The baseball caps the men wore made it difficult to make out their faces. They got busy shooting cocaine up their veins.

"This'll make you high as a kite, bitch," said one of the men, deftly filling a syringe. "You'll love us for it, and it's all free." Then, waving the needle in my face, he taunted me. "You'd love a shot, wouldn't you, fucker?" he asked, adding, "But then we won't have any left to pump into the whore."

"Get on with it," ordered his companion impatiently, unzipping his trousers.

"Here, I've found it," said the third man, holding Rosie's twisted arm. The other jabbed the needle into her vein. She struggled for a moment or two, then quietened down.

Softly, gleefully, one of the men cried, "She likes it, give her another."

So they prepared another needle and emptied it in Rosie.

I hadn't been inside a church for ages. But in my moment of desperation, I now muttered a childish prayer under my breath asking for, of all things, a miracle. Just one person to come out of the Recreation Centre. Just one security guard making his rounds. I imagined myself kneeling before the altar at Saint Magnus Cathedral. I thought of the spirit of Saint Marguerite d'Youville I had once felt so close to in Montreal. I'd do anything to save Rosie. Search for the remains of Isabel Gunn. There must be a gravestone for her they never found. I'd go back to my mother's grave in the Highlands. Oh God! I didn't want to have to write an epitaph for Rosie. We're in the midst of monsters here, I prayed. Healers, save my Rosie, I cried. Isabel, make her whole. Mother, bring her back to me.

The men were waiting. I moved my head to see what they were up to. One of the them noticed the movement and kicked me squarely in the face.

"Right, untie her. I think she's ready for us."

Through the pain, and the blood trickling into my eyes, I could barely make out the outline of her face as they untied her and rolled her over in the grass. Rosie lay absolutely still.

The men tossed coins over who would have her first.

"I knew it was my lucky day," said one as he pounced upon Rosie. "I want to feel her mouth," he said. "Let's take the gag off."

"You sure she won't scream?"

"Naw," said the man, throwing away the gag. "She's like a baby."

But the very next moment he gathered himself violently off the ground. "Fuck, man," he cried, "the bitch is dead."

I thought I recognized the voice, but I wasn't certain until much later. I went cold inside, straining at my bonds till I had no strength left. The three men were over Rosie's face, feeling her neck, searching for signs of life.

"Mother of Christ! She's dead all right."

"Let's get outta here."

Hurriedly, the men straightened out their clothes and moved away into the shadows behind the line of bushes. They reappeared a moment later and I began to fear—no, welcome—a similar fate for myself. But the men ignored me, and picked up Rosie's body instead. Then they hurled her over the edge into the still waters of the dam. There was a splash, and then, only the distant music was left to weave hollow patterns of meaningless sounds in my ears.

"Cree shit," muttered one of the men as they all walked away.

It was early morning before anyone found me. "She's in the water," I kept saying over and over again. But the local security seemed more interested in testing me for drugs.

Divers kept going down into the lake all day, but they came up empty-handed. A stone-faced Louis Bearskin sat on the water's edge from morning till dusk, watching the water break into ripples and then be stilled until the next diver broke through the surface. Larry had brought him over to the dam the moment he got my senseless message. At day's end, Louis said with an air of finality, "They'll never find her down there." Then, pointing to the east, he said, "The Spirits will have taken her to Kaniaapiscau where her ancestors lie buried. I know she's with her own people."

"So, monsieur, you say they threw her body into the water?" the officer, a faint smile of disbelief curling his lips, asked me. "But so far we haven't found anything. You say there were three men, but you haven't been able to describe them."

"It was too dark," I pleaded. Then, in a feeble attempt, I added, "They spoke with French accents."

The officer, now a little sombre, stared straight into my eyes, and said, "Mr. Gunn, there are five thousand people in this camp who all speak with French accents."

Of course, they never found any drugs on me. Yes, they had picked up needles and pieces of torn clothing, most probably a woman's. Everything had been sent to the forensic lab in Montreal. The police seemed a little more amiable during subsequent meetings. One of the officers went to the extent of gently patting me on the back, and said, "Don't worry, we believe you, and we'll get to the bottom of this."

I suppose I did the regular things one is expected to under such circumstances. I phoned my office in Montreal. I phoned John Gage. Everyone was full of understanding, sympathy, and shock. John was beside himself with impotent rage. I decided to stay on in Chisasibi for a few more days, to help the police if need be. Larry got me a room at the motel in the Community Centre.

A week later, I was still trying to come to grips with the swift turn of events that had overtaken me, shattering my wild hopes of a life with Rosie. I couldn't think of what had happened to me without the tears exploding behind my eyes, eyes that threatened to fly out of their sockets. Sometimes, when I looked out of the window at the singularly depressing view outside, I wondered whether mixed with the tears there weren't some tears of gratitude for the saints, for Isabel Gunn, for being so merciful during Rosie's final moments. Then, doubts began to rise in my mind — were they truly merciful? But, if my prayers had been answered, surely it was a strange, tortured answer, as I saw it. If there was an answer, it probably lay in the covenant of love and intimacy between Rosie and me, a covenant no one would be able to break. And if what Louis said about the body was true — a body that seemed to have vanished without a trace — Rosie's covenant with her own people had been preserved too.

That day, I had an unexpected visitor, Pierre Tremblay, who said, simply, "Come, I'll drive you over to the police station. Let's see what else they've got so far." We didn't exchange any further words during the car-ride.

The police had found nothing. Nothing, except that the needles contained a very powerful concentration of cocaine, enough to kill a horse. But the body, there were still no signs of it, and they had decided to call off the search. The officer offered me an apologetic smile and said, "Look, Mr. Gunn, your cuts have healed. Why don't you return to Montreal and let us handle the matter." He looked expectantly at me, and finding me silent turned his eyes to the bare landscape framed by

Requiem for the Last Indian | 221

the window and added, "We hate to remind you, but she was only a Cree. You can spend a night with these women, maybe even a few weeks. But anything more permanent -?" The officer stopped in the middle of his sentence, turned away from the window, smiled, and nodded his head doubtfully.

Pierre was on his feet instantly. "Officer," he said angrily, "you're not allowed to speak like that. I will report you to the Ministry of Justice." I was on my feet too. We left the room without another word.

Back in the car, Pierre apologized for the officer, "I'm sorry, terribly sorry." Again, we rode in silence for a long time. "It was a terrible death, a terrible death," murmured Pierre ruefully.

I was filled with a strange sadness as we passed a vast field being worked over by backhoes and front-end loaders. Light snow lay in random patches in a jungle of brown stubble, dotted with warts of boulders and craters from knotted roots. I heard myself speaking. Maybe I was only speaking to myself. But Pierre heard me in silence. I said, "Dying is easy. It's much harder to face the pain of living."

That evening there was a phonecall from Officer Marcel of the Surete du Quebec requesting a meeting at the LG2 camp. He had some information he wanted to share. Pierre had flown back to Montreal only hours earlier. Larry was sitting with me, silently flicking through the pages of a discarded issue of *Vogue*. He said he'd like to come along with me.

Officer Marcel looked a little uncomfortable when he saw Larry walking in with me. He shook my hand and said, "I'd rather we discussed this alone."

"He's a friend. He'll stay," I said firmly.

"Well, I don't want to upset you, Mr. Gunn, but is it true that earlier on the said evening you and Rosie were in the gym, in the pool, and in the bar?"

"Yes, that's true." I nodded.

"Well, we have succeeded in speaking to an engineer who claims he saw someone diving into the lake about the time you say the attack took place."

"Diving? I cried, incredulous.

The officer shook his head, and I couldn't help asking, "I suppose the engineer also saw Rosie tie me up and gag me?"

The officer, unfazed, continued. "We don't know about that. But we do know that you pressed two hundred and eighty pounds in the Nautilus Room, that Rosie swam no less than twenty laps across the pool, and that you had six Labatts between the two at the pub."

Larry interrupted him angrily. He appeared ready for a fight. "Didn't your informer tell you," he asked, "that they got the coke and the needles under the counter at Guy's Gym Shop within the camp itself?"

Officer Marcel turned a little pale but said nothing. Larry wasn't ready to give up. "What you're telling us is that you are going to do fuck-all over Rosie's death. So what's new?"

Back in Chisasibi, Larry recounted how Marcel considered himself the hero of Oka and was now a point-man in every sensitive case involving the police and aboriginals in Quebec. He told me how Marcel openly boasted that the Surete du Quebec had finally and conclusively put down the Great Indian Conspiracy of the nineties, thanks to a clandestine operation he had helped mount seven years ago. Marcel did infiltrate the Warriors to a point and his friends believed he would soon be honoured with an Order of Canada. Larry said he wouldn't be surprised by such an honour since Marcel had a powerful friend in Ottawa, Officer McWilliams of the R.C.M.P., who had just returned to his home in Provo, Alberta, a haven for White Supremacists. Larry marvelled at the web of power that people like Marcel and McWilliams had woven across the land. Stretching all the way from Chisasibi to Provo where — so Larry had heard from his friend, Milton — McWilliams had accepted a position as chief martial arts trainer at the Aryan Nation headquarters. Their plan, as he understood it, was to clean out the natives, then go to work on the Jews, the Vietnamese, the Chinese and the East Indians.

The inquest into Rosie's death a few weeks later was equally bizarre. There had been a lot of speculation among the Cree as to what would take place. But there were few surprises. The Hydro Quebec engineer who claimed he last saw Rosie thought she had been engaged in what he chose to call 'l'activite sexuel' near the dam which he chose to call 'forebay'. As a result, many observers at the inquest were confused and amused when the travelling judge asked the engineer to describe what he meant by sexual activity. The engineer blushed slightly, and said: Foreplay. His French-Canadian accent was such that, to many in the audience, foreplay sounded like forebay. Between repeated interruptions during his testimony as to when he was referring to foreplay and when to forebay, the frustrated judge and the audience succeeded in getting a laughter-filled if totally unclear picture of what might have happened. In the end, there was no reference to anything criminal other than to a vague suggestion of possible drug use on the part of the victim.

Pierre came to see me in Montreal a few weeks later. He looked drawn and shaken. "I'm sorry, he said, I'm so sorry." I was surprised by the depth of his continuing remorse for Rosie. It almost seemed there were tears in Pierre's eyes as he spoke sadly of the many lives she could have touched had she lived. It was quite a change from Rosie's last passing encounter with him in the camp. We talked idly of this and that, the weather, the language bill, about Mordecai Richeler, the English-speaking Jew and perpetual thorn-in-the-flesh of Quebec. Pierre wondered if I had heard anything further about the investigations.

Of course, I hadn't. I knew, however, that as a claims adjuster Pierre had fairly close contacts with the police. So I asked Pierre instead, "Have you?"

Pierre replied that he had, but that I would be most unhappy. He himself felt terribly distressed. He had been to several levels of the government, right from the premier's office down. During the first go-around, the focus everywhere seemed to be on the fact that Rosie was Cree. What was one to expect? Or rather, what wasn't one to expect? Sex. Drugs. Jealousy. Revenge. They kept going back to the findings of the inquest, even though Pierre insisted they lacked credibility. He admitted that he thought all along he was talking to friends, when in fact he was speaking to a brick wall. But the interesting thing was that everyone seemed to know something about the case. "But there's worse news," he said. "There has been a murder."

"Drugs?" I asked. "I thought that issue had at least been taken care of." Pierre probably sensed my anger. He asked me if I wanted him to go on. "Go on," I said.

He started to describe his second go-around. He had paid good money into the political campaigns and felt he deserved some better answers. This time, each department pointed to another department that seemed to be intently studying the file. Actually, this time Pierre was surprised at the amount of revulsion he found over the senselessness of the act if — as the departments took care to qualify it — Rosie was indeed a victim of foul play. Some sort of a breakthrough came when, early on in the third time around, he armed himself with a letter from the Premier. At this point, Pierre actually received an admission from the police that they had no doubt now that she was murdered, that the concentration of cocaine in the needles was absolutely lethal, and that the fingerprints on them clearly did not belong to Charlie Gunn. They counselled patience and suggested that Pierre return in a week's time.

During Pierre's third visit, the police admitted they had three suspects, and that some sort of action was already in the pipeline. The next thing Pierre heard was that all three had vanished. Everything, all their possessions, remained as before in their quarters in Radisson, except that the men were gone. The police now had a theory that the men may have been the victims of a revenge killing. Rumours started to fly about a strong suspicion that the Crees had carried out the killing.

Pierre was sorry, but that's where matters stood. He wanted me to know that he didn't really believe the police story but that he himself had come to the end of the road. Then, in a rare moment of candour, Pierre admitted, "It might have been different if you had been a Francophone."

I spent the weekend in Chisasibi. When I returned to Montreal, there was a message from Pierre. "There has been another killing in Radisson." His voice was shaking.

I knew that very little was happening with the investigation. I lay awake all night and worked myself to a fury. Should I go to the English-speaking newspapers as John Gage was urging me to do? Should I hire a private investigator? I suddenly felt totally overcome with disgust for everything around me. The system, the system, I kept muttering to myself. Work at the office had become unbearable. The system, the system, my mind kept repeating, until disgust turned to self-disgust for was I not a part of the system as well? I had to teach the system a lesson.

It was not that simple, John Gage told me with his usual scholarly profundity. Systems were inescapable, explained John, and that in the present state of society only another system or several systems could possibly replace one or more systems. The system-less system of the North—to the extent that the aboriginals relied on primitive folklore and less on modern science—was gone the day the missionaries started to move inland from New France, the day Groseilliers and Radisson persuaded the Indians to bring them beaver pelts by the thousands, the day the Hudson's Bay Company decided to set up shop in Rupert River having "formally purchased" land from the Cree. Now there was no going back.

I called Louis Bearskin to find out how he was. Since there was no telephone in Louis' trailer, I had him call back from the Band Council offices. Later, when Louis finally got through to me, he said, "I don't expect anything from them, least of all justice." Louis said he was all right. He ended the phone conversation with his characteristic expression, "This too will pass."

Larry called me to say he was coming down to Montreal on some Band Council business, and I promised to pick him up at the Sheraton. When I met him at the suite, there were no less than five other aboriginal officials there, in deep conversation with two television producers from the CBC. The number of times they came in with food and liquor during the twenty minutes or so I was there — while Larry put his things in order — convinced me that the Sheraton's entire room-service staff had been pressed into service to attend to this single suite of rooms.

"Get me out of here," said Larry, assuming an air of mock helplessness.

Right away, I asked him to move in with me. As we left and I took one more look around the hotel-room, I had a sneaking suspicion that John Gage, however pompous his explanations, might after all be right.

Larry couldn't control his disdain when I told him what I had found out from Pierre. Disappeared? Revenge killing by the Cree? Larry suggested an alternative, "They're probably lying drunk in some whorehouse in Matagami. You've not been in Canada long enough to know, so I must tell you something about the nature of the beast, the one we call Hydro Quebec."

I knew of course that it was the vision of Robert Bourassa, one that would bring Quebec to the forefront of Canadian provinces, if not the assembly of nations.

But who would build his dream? Workers had little interest in coming up to James Bay. Val d'Or, Chicoutimi, or Matagami was about as north as they knew. The Quebec government worked out deals with prisoners serving criminal sentences to have them come up as labourers. Larry stopped in the middle of the story to ask me, "Now you see why the place is so unsafe for women, Cree or Francophone? Check out how many women there are in LG1 or Radisson."

"But Hydro-Quebec's biggest consumer," continued Larry, "its knight in shining armour, was to be the U. S. of A., and Bourassa was forced to make an agreement with American companies involved that the James Bay Project would go to American unions. Given this situation, and the riff-raff who had come to work for Hydro Quebec, there was bound to be trouble. The Quebec Federation of Labour wanted the contracts for itself.

"Trouble came on March 21, 1974, when Yvon Duhamel got into a bulldozer left idling by the cafeteria at the LG2 site. He pushed a pickup truck out of the road with the dozer blade, then climbed the hill to the generator trailers. Duhamel overturned the nearest generator, dismounted, got into a jeep driven by a steward of the Q.F.L. and drove back to camp. There, fired by rage and a sense of drama, Duhamel drove a payloader into two thirty-thousand-gallon fuel reservoirs, one containing gasoline, the other diesel fuel. The fuel flowed down a hill in between the garages and the barracks. Five minutes later, oil from the punctured tanks started a large fire which practically destroyed the camp."

Larry went on to describe the two detachments of riot-equipped Quebec Police Force who came up to help the hopelessly inefficient James Bay Municipality Police Force. All night, a half dozen aircraft and buses sent up from Matagami carried out non-stop evacuation in a snow-storm with temperatures dropping to ten and twenty below.

Duhamel, a business agent at the LG2 site for the International Union of Heavy Equipment Operators, an affiliate of Q.F.L., was arrested and detained. He boasted that he was ready to take five to ten years for what he had done, and proud of it. "But do you know what happened to Duhamel?" asked Larry, interrupting his narrative.

I said I didn't.

Larry laughed and said, "You would've guessed right if you said 'nothing'. At the bars in Matagami, amidst the beer and cigarette smoke, the workers weren't talking. There was little evidence with which to nail Duhamel."

"The truth," continued Larry, "was that Hydro Quebec was running LG2 like Churchill Falls—fifty hour work-weeks with no overtime. They said trouble started because Q.F.L. labour union stewards had accepted five hundred to five thousand dollar bribes to whitewash worker grievances about food, housing, Sunday work, and vicious supervisors. But most people believed that Hydro Quebec management provoked the violence to pressure a not-too-reluctant government into granting a ten-year no-strike contract.

"Ever since then, Hydro Quebec workers had been held sacrosanct. Hydro Quebec management had become powerful gods. Everything had worked so well, except for the Cree, that no one was interested in disturbing the status quo. Not the police, not the Premier.

Who wanted to create waves over the death of a slut of a Cree woman, daughter of a known trouble-maker?" Then Larry's face darkened and a note of bitterness crept into his voice as he asked, "Do you suppose we can take over the reins of justice? Did you see what was going on at the Sheraton before you rescued me?"

Larry thought it possible one of the murderers would kill himself or another. Maybe one of them would rat on his friends. Short of these two remote possibilities, he didn't imagine I could count on anything further happening to the investigations into Rosie's murder. But Larry warned me not to count on even that. "They might still nail me or some other Cree bastard," he said, "over the disappearance of the three suspects. In a den of criminals, no one dares to point a finger at the real murderer."

Larry expected a feeling of total helplessness to come over me. It didn't. But that's because I spent hours during every visit to Chisasibi in the LG1 bar. I would go there alone. The bar was a goldmine of information, and my imagination worked wonders. "I feel so powerless," I told Larry, insincerely. "I feel like an alien in this country."

"Join the party," said Larry. "You are, unfortunately, all aliens in their eyes, just like Rosie and me. And, sadly, the law is'nt on our side. Only *Ijjan*, the self-consuming monster, can ever correct the injustice, when the old order implodes from its burden of sleaze and lies."

In moments less savaged by self-pity, I would've believed Larry to be wrong. But now something in my heart told me I was one of them, and nothing could change it, for Rosie had put me to sleep in her arms with a child's story. And I had listened. Oh! how I had loved and listened. And had I not planted a new life in her, a life she had taken with herself into the mysterious heart of the lake or perhaps to the rock at Kaniaapiscow which saw everything, remembered everything, and lost nothing.

Then they found the third body. It looked the same as the first two. The same knife. The same incision. The same serial killer, they concluded.

The discovery sent shivers through the village of Chisasibi, a small Cree village on the shores of James Bay. When word got out that the dead man was an insurance adjuster from Montreal, the news hit the close-knit white community like a bomb. Pierre was a friend to me, and I had to admit his death brought me some public grief. But it was less than considerable because there were aspects of Pierre that I despised. Especially his hatred of the Cree.

The Surete was showing an unhealthy interest in my movements. They had visited me twice in Montreal already. So I decided to slip into Chisasibi as inconspicuously as possible. I was pleased the flight from Montreal had been delayed. It meant it was late afternoon by the time I drove into the village.

Only a few kids were playing in the open fields. The shadows were lengthening and no one took any notice of me as I drove past. At every turn on the way to Louis's trailer, I felt Rosie's presence. The more I remembered her face, eyes that sparkled all the time, lips carved in smile, the more unbearable became the pain within.

Little seemed to have changed since my last visit except the final bit of the gravel road leading up to the trailer. There were a few more empty drums and cartons stacked on both sides of the path. Nearby, the 1950's Pontiac firmly embedded in the ground with its door wide open looked just as rusty as in the past. Everything else was the same.

Louis wasn't home. There was a note written on the side of a brown paper bag taped behind the window. "Away," it said, "Check Band Council office for emergencies."

I could remain anonymous no longer. I drove back to the Community Centre and walked up the stairs to the Council's offices. The woman at the front desk recognized me right away. She explained indignantly how Hydro Quebec, the utility, had cut off Louis' power because he hadn't been able to pay his electricity bills. Voice shaking with emotion, she asked, "Can you believe it? They steal our water, wreck our lands in building the James Bay Project, force us to move from the island, then they cut off our electricity. It's happening all over the place. Where can we find the money to pay their rates?"

She told me I would find Louis at the Monster Rapids where a group of young men had helped him build a camp. She warned me as I got up from the chair, "Be sure you have a four-wheel drive before trying to get near the place."

I thanked her and said all I thought I needed was a pair of hiking boots from the Northern Store on the floor below the offices. I knew how to get there.

Before I left, she said, "We still can't get over Rosie. We're so sorry, so angry. We miss her all the time. The children miss her most of all. She was the best. She lighted up the whole place. She was an angel." Then the woman broke down with sobs.

I put my arms around her and waited in silence till she had wiped the tears off her face and was ready to return to her desk.

Looking through the shelves for my size of boots, I couldn't shake off the feeling Rosie was walking along the aisles with me. We had come here so often, bought seemingly useless things so often. Now every possession seemed so meaningless, all the more since I had no one to pass them on to.

I caught a fleeting glimpse of the lake just before I hit the dirt road leading towards Kaniaapiscow. I also passed the project settlement which now looked so innocuous, so peaceful, that I found it hard to believe it might still harbour some of the men who had played a part, however small, in Rosie's death. With three dead bodies floating in the water, I seemed to have been purged of anger. I was not surprised that I no longer felt any resentment against the three killers.

Much of the pain I had felt in stepping off the plane was gradually ebbing away in the face of the unaffected serenity of the land. I felt much more at peace with myself than I had been in a long long time. I was also in familiar surroundings. This familiarity now led me unerringly to where I knew I would leave the car, then clamber over rocks and ridges and gulleys before reaching the Monster Rapids.

Winter still had a few weeks to settle in. Already, there were patches of snow in folds of the earth which seldom saw the sun. The river, when I saw it, also proved to be something of a surprise. Parts of it, close to the banks, looked like delicate layers of icing where the river was beginning to freeze. Tempted to run my fingers over the ice, I walked pensively along the sandy bank. Up close, the icy sheet looked so much like crinkled folds of human skin that I had to stop myself from touching it. Before long, I turned slightly inland to avoid a ledge of massive rocks piled in the shape of an amphitheatre. In doing so, I was astonished to find myself looking at a field of daisies and yellow buttercups swaying and dancing with a final burst of life in the face of the approaching winter.

This seemed most unusual, and for a moment I wasn't sure where I was. Surely, I couldn't be dreaming of the wild heaths on the Orkney's Papa Westray. But here were birds too, boreal chickadees, warblers and crossbills. Darting in and out incessantly from their nests in the rocks, birds that looked like snow buntings searched for insects for their ravenous young. There were countless numbers of them skipping around the meadow. In one corner, a young boy circled them warily, trying to net them for food. As I looked at him, I was filled with an intense desire to hold him in my arms. I don't know why, but tears welled up in my eyes.

I skirted the field and returned to the river's edge. I was now standing on a narrow bluff from where I was able to look upstream for quite a distance. I saw a solitary hunter paddle down the river in a canoe and stop abruptly at the head of a terrace of menacing rapids which had so far escaped the ravages of the construction gangs. The hunter stepped out of the canoe nimbly and stood for a moment gazing at the masses of ice — only just starting to grow in form — heaped in confusion down below. The river flowed underneath, around, and over the blocks of ice. There'd be no turning back on the rapids.

The young man stepped into the water, hauled his canoe onto the land, and disappeared behind a clump of spruce trees.

I had found my bearings and knew exactly where to go. I needed to get close to the first visible strands of sagging transmission lines straining to touch the river under the weight of *nimischuuskutaau*, the fire that shakes the land. During our first meeting when I had seen part of his arsenal, I remembered Louis telling me that one could only fight fire with fire. I had wondered then if Louis was contemplating war with the white man, and Louis had read my thoughts correctly. He told me, "We could plunge Montreal into darkness if we wanted to. We are hunters. We can use the very guns the white man gave us to blow away vital links in the transmission towers. We could blow them up as fast as they could repair them. But what's the use? All this will pass too."

I remembered the sadness in the old man's eyes, the note of resignation in his voice. I was to discover later that, in a matter of moments, Louis's moods could swing from dejection to anger. So I wondered how I would find Louis on this visit, for he had not bothered to answer any of the letters I had written on my return to Montreal after Rosie's death. Larry had also dropped out of sight. I wasn't inclined to approach anyone else in John Gage's new class for information on Louis. John himself had become somewhat distant.

I felt closer to the land this time. I realized I had grown to love the land in a way I would have thought impossible only a few years ago. I wasn't sure though if I loved it enough to pick up Louis Bearskin's fight. I didn't know what, if anything, there was to fight for? And yet, now that Rosie was gone, I also wondered if an inner hunger to find an answer wasn't somehow ultimately behind my wish to see Louis one more time.

Up close, the rapids seemed less wild than I remembered from my earlier visit. Just below the rapids, on the sunny side of the river, Louis Bearskin had found helpers to build him a log-moss teepee. The slow rhythm of a drum wove tremors in the air around the cabin.

Louis didn't show any signs of resentment or hostility towards me, but he didn't greet me with much warmth either. He sounded tired and short as he told me, "I've camped out here to see Rosie, but I don't know if you should stay here."

I felt my face turn red with confusion and disappointment. "But why?" I asked Louis, not knowing what to expect for an answer. Then it occurred to me that Rosie's loss might be driving Louis mad, for he was certainly not his usual self. At the same time, an inner voice reminded me that Rosie was around, watching my every move, protecting me, silencing the voice of reason that kept saying I would never see her again.

Louis did answer my question. "You know we call this place Monster Rapids," he said. "What you don't know perhaps is that the place and its legend are sacred to the Cree. This was a fearsome place long ago. You couldn't shoot the rapids. There was a man who used to camp here on his way up the river; he lost his son in the rapids once. Many years later, he and his wife were going up the river. The old man was thinking of his son, wishing he could see him one more time. So he made his camp at the bottom of the rapids.

"The place looks different now. In those days there was a lovely sandy beach, much wider than what you see today. The old man pulled his canoe ashore on the beach. Nobody had been on this beach recently, or he would have known. But the old man saw two sets of children's footprints. He decided to stay there a few more days.

"One night, he heard a noise outside. It sounded like footsteps. So he got up, lit a candle. Then the door flew open and the old man saw his son. He recognized him right away. The son said to him, 'Father, I have a house, a very nice place. That's where I live with a woman and our two children.'

"The old man got up and made a fire. By now his wife was up too. He asked his son if it was possible for them to see his woman. The son said he would have to ask her first. Then he took their leave to go and ask the woman.

"A little before dawn, the old man and his wife heard the noise of footsteps again. Then the son came in and said, 'She is here with me.' Behind him was this young woman with their two children. The old couple were so happy. The man asked if they could kiss the woman and their children. 'Yes,' nodded the son. The parents kissed their daughter-in-law and the two children. Asking them to sit on the other side of the teepee, the father wondered if they could eat the food they ate. The son asked his wife and said it would be all right. Then the mother offered some food to everyone.

"The young man told his father that it was only because they were alone that they were able to see him and his family. If there were others with them, they wouldn't be able to come and see the old man. 'If you set up camp here for a while,' said the son, 'we'll always come to visit you.'"

Louis turned to me and said, "Our people come here to be with those they think of continually. Others have seen their loved ones the same way the old man saw his. But even though their son and family came to see them, they never slept in their teepee. The old man couldn't get over how beautiful his daughter-in-law was. The last time he saw them, just before his death, their son had a third child, a new-born baby girl. During this visit the son told him the rapids would grow calmer. 'Tell your friends about it,' said the son. 'They won't have to portage the Monster Rapids any more.'

Louis ended his story and poured me a cup of tea. He looked more mellow than when I had entered his tent. As I took the cup away from his hands, Louis closed his eyes and seemed to sink into a deep meditation. His voice sounded from afar as he spoke slowly, "That's why I am here. Rosie will come, and so will her child. We'll have all the ceremonies for the child, all the feasts. The Walking Out ceremony when the child comes out of the teepee and walks for the first time. We'll make a circular path of spruce boughs, in a circle around a pile of wood. We will dress the child in animal skins. If it's a boy, we'll sling a bow and a quiver of arrows on his shoulder. If it's a girl, we'll give her a carved axe, small pieces of firewood and cooking sticks. Then we'll feast. Later still, we'll have the First Kill ceremony. Maybe the girl will catch a fish. Maybe the boy will pierce a goose with his arrow. We take the fish-head or the beak, decorate it, and place it in view of people to admire and applaud. Then we stick it in pemmican and pass it around the circle for everyone to share the food. I want Rosie's child to experience it all. Our life never ends, Charlie."

For some unaccountable reason, I felt a shiver run through my body. I felt nervous. It was at the tip of my tongue to ask if I would ever be a part of these ceremonies as I once was — or felt I was — at the pow-wow on the island. But the question remained frozen on my tongue.

Quite abruptly, Louis said he had forgotten to tell me something. "Do you know, Charlie?" he asked, "the child is not expected to taste the food he has killed the first time around. For he is the provider then." A deep sigh escaped Louis. "And who do you think will provide for me but Rosie's son?" he asked. "Death doesn't scare us, Charlie. Death doesn't separate us. When the night hangs long and heavy on the earth, when winter locks its door to the glaring sun, that's when our land is most alive. You see, it's the same God that makes storms and weaves the magic of stillness."

We tasted the stillness surrounding us for a long time. Afterwards, Louis picked up the drum and began to beat a slow rhythm on it, singing softly all the while. He stopped after a few minutes and told me he was trying to re-learn the drum. "Before I die," he said, so the Spirit can hear me coming." Louis went on, "When I play the drum, I think of my father all the time. I remember him playing the drum in our tent one day when I was a child. And a priest came inside the tent. He had such a kindly face. He sat down next to my father and gently grasped the drum and pulled it out of the old man's unresisting fingers. 'It is evil. This is where it belongs,' said the priest, as he placed the drum over the glowing logs in the centre of the tent. Moments later, flames shot up from the logs, licked the sides of the drum and roared upwards in fury. When the fire started to die down, my old man turned his face away from the drum. He looked the priest straight in the eye and said, 'Now you have nothing more to fear, Father Gastineau. Fire has turned evil to dust.'"

In the evening, I went back to the water's edge to think, to wander through my memories, to quieten the pain that kept returning. A narrow dirt path led again to another bluff overlooking the river. Here, the hills were barren, the occasional clumps of trees scraggly. One could see long distances. Suddenly, I caught sight of the same young man I thought I had seen earlier in the day. Now I saw him haul his canoe down to the water and paddle away upstream. The spot where the man had come out of wasn't far away. I kept walking in that direction, skirting boulders and sometimes walking on sand. When I came to the spot, I noticed a curious thing. On a flat slab of rock, two candles burned side by side—one larger, bigger than the other. The flames from the two seemed impervious to the wind. They burned steadily without a flicker. It looked strange in the twilight and it made me somewhat fearful, if only for a brief moment.

I stood there a long time, watching the flames in amazement, waiting for the wind to rise and snuff them out. The place was deserted, there was no reason for the candles to be there, no reason for them to be burning in the open, unaffected by the wind. It was as if the wind had carved out a vast hollow of stillness around the flames. The flames hypnotized me. My amazement gradually gave way to a calm that flowed out of my heart and pushed fear and sadness out of me, away from me. I heard no sounds, except the sounds in my head, clear and sharp as the sounds I heard each night when my head rested against my pillow and sleep refused to come.

Overhead, the wind swept away the last remaining clouds. It stilled the water and reflected the precise shades of the sky in the river. Elsewhere, the river moved. Elsewhere, the clouds rolled in. But not where I stood. The silence wrapped itself around me, and fired my imagination to rejoice in the quiet intensity of this experience.

Louis showed no surprise when I came back to his teepee and told him what I had seen. He said that he too had seen the two candles, one bigger than the other, two flames untouched by the wind, any evening that he went that way. If he was early, before the sun went down, he would also see the lone Cree paddling away upstream in his canoe.

"What is one to make of it?" I asked.

Louis thought for a while, the whites of his eyes shining like onions in the pale light. He said, "Nothing, really, except that it is a place of reflection, perhaps even of divination. The ways of men," he added, uncertainly. And then he fell silent.

Like a breeze gathering strength and then changing its mind, another deep sigh broke loose from Louis. "I know Rosie will come out of the water," he said, "but I don't know about the others."

Later, in the darkness of the tent, he told me, "In a sense, our people have all been drowning for the past four hundred years, so there's nothing to keep Rosie apart from her people. But I don't know, don't know if the people will ever raise their heads above the water.

Rosie, I've seen her footsteps on the sand. Even in the depth of winter, I know I'll find her footprints again in the icy heart of the world."

Then Louis closed his eyes and whispered, "Get the cops off your back. It was I, I who sent the three to their hell. I have failed in just about every thing I tried to do. But I had to avenge Rosie, and I'm glad I succeeded. I have sent the police a letter with the people who came fishing here last week. The police should have it now. Feel free to return to Chisasibi and don't think of me anymore."

It was early Wednesday morning and the ale was beginning to extract its price, its *scot* as Sven had pointed out, for etymological correctness. I could barely keep my eyes open. Sven put his face in his hands and lay slumped beside the glasses on the table, fast asleep. I left some change at the bar, helped Sven to his feet, and then slowly walked out of the room together.

The sleepy town of Lerwick was worn out from the festivities. The parties had quietened down. The few remaining customers were ready to leave the bars, but found it difficult to move. "Why is it," asked Sven, resting his head against a lamp-post on the street, "that the prettiest women I see are always on the other side of the bar?"

I said to him, "That's because they aren't drunk, and you are." Just then I caught sight of my dishevelled self in a large mirror in a store window and had to admit, "Boy, I look horribly drunk too!"

We stumbled up the stairs of our hotel amidst much thumping and banging, punctuated by occasional curses from the rooms lining the corridors. I opened Sven's door and helped him on his bed. He didn't even open his eyes to say goodbye, but promptly went off to sleep.

Back in my own room—Number 222 (how could I have ever forgotten it and tried to barge into someone else's room?)—I took a long time splashing my face with cold water. Pain and longing returned. My heart began to ache for Rosie. No, I reminded myself, it had been aching for her from the day I had landed in the Shetlands amidst the howling gale sounding, it seemed, the end of the world. The inescapable presence of the sea around me was a continuous reminder of Rosie.

It was certainly the end for the good ship *Braer*, and its cargo of crude oil destined for the Ultramar refinery in Quebec, clients of my company. What a business to be in, I thought. I could live with it as long as I persuaded myself to grapple, half in an attitude of jest, with accounts that would never really balance, greed that knew no limits, and logic that was at best absurd. After all, was this not the final residue of the business I was in? But the emptiness that surrounded me after the day's business was over, that was something that depressed me most. That's when I missed Rosie most of all. Often, when I saw a pretty young face—and the girl behind the bar was certainly pretty—I was filled with infinite longing and sadness.

I changed into my night clothes and stood in front of my window. One would've thought there was never a storm that touched the silken waters. It was a quiet moonlit night on Bressay Sound, something I had thought I would never see during my stay in Lerwick. A single boat was crossing the sound, a pale light moving into the harbour to my left. All else was quiet, except that the sound of the band and the rhythm of the marchers singing the *Up-Helly-Aa* song and *The Norseman's Home* kept ringing in my ears. As I kept staring at the half-darkness framed by my window, the flaming torches from the night before appeared to rekindle and brand their reflection into the sky. The light of the torches lifted the clock from the Town Hall tower and pinned it above the flames like the face of a full moon. The guizers were all but invisible until the line of marchers turned past the War Memorial and King Erik Street into Saint Olaf Street. Then an eerie glow climbed over the outlines of roofs along Saint Olaf and on Hillhead beyond. Smoke from the thousand torches curled up and lay down over the rooftops. It was as if the town was on fire, as if the Vikings had come a-harrying again.

Suddenly, all hell broke loose. The night erupted with the sound of clashing armour, horses rearing up in battle, and fiery galleys cris-crossing the waters. Hamish Duncan, owner of the Lerwick Pub, gilded helmet on his head, girt with a sword, a great spear in his hand, every inch Thorfinn the Skull Splitter, rounded up his bodyguards and other men of rank for dinner, there to ply them with meat and ale as he did each night through winter so they would leave the ale-house alone, too drunk to cause trouble.

Sigurd, Dr. David Cox from Public Health, the grisly head of Maelbrigte fastened to his saddlebrow, whooped with delight as he spurred his horse with his feet and charged across the horizon, oblivious of the victim's gaping teeth tearing into his flesh.

Iain Pottinger, of Pottinger's Accountancy Services, sombre as Havard Harvest-Happy, murderer of his brother Arnfinn, sated with ploughing his brother's wife Ragnhild, whistled nervously as he walked to Stennis, unaware of the shifting winds of Ragnhild's affections, careless of death waiting for him at Havard's Field at the hands of her new lover, Einar Buttered Bread.

In the far distance, John Lawrie of the *Shetland Times*, suffused with the new-found faith of King Olav, watched Sigurd the Stout rise from the waters of Scapa Flow. Under a magnificent standard with a raven's image, his mother's needlecraft, Jim Burgess as Sigurd the Stout, now baptized, watched his son he would never see again embark for Norway.

Erland the Younger, lithe as an arrow without his coat of mail, relaxed with his new wife, the mother of Earl Havald, on the Broch at Mousa. Earl Havald, a pharmacist from Burra bathed in a shower of blood, cut out the tongue from the Bishop of Scrabster and plunged his knife into his eyes. But the sexiest of them all, the tall, handsome, golden-haired Jimmy Irvine, Rognvald Brusi's son, exempted from the twelfth oath by King Jaroslav, now scoured the land for the prettiest girls who watched the parade the previous night.

Head bowed before Lifolf, occasional help at the Chip Shop on Commercial Street, Mike McNeil, unemployed, shorn of helmet, shield, and axe, privy to God's will as Magnus Earl of the Isles, pure and clean of all carnal sins, treacherously seized, awaited the stroke to the middle of the head that would send him to Paradise. His mother Thora's barely audible voice pleads with a tired and unhappy Haakon—Johnny, head-waiter at the Skipdock Inn—who answers, "Bury thy son where it please thee." Moments later, green sward covers the moss-grown, stormy spot where Magnus falls, and a heavenly light begins to shine on his grave at Birsay.

Tall Einar with the eye-patch—alias Jimmy Burnett, temporary librarian at the Islesburgh Community Centre—who gave Tree-Beard to the trolls, was now an artist carving a bloody eagle on Halfdan's back. One might say he was a poet among butchers, as he hacked Halfdan's ribs to the loin.

In Pentland Firth, blood streaked the sea, blood fell on the shield-rim, bespattered the ship, black blood oozed from the yielding seams of fallen heroes. Only Magnus Erland, Math teacher from Hillswick, trapped in the shining armour of a reluctant Viking, refused to fight or duck for cover.

Jarl Ronnie Gair, smiling only hours before for the network cameras, resplendent as Earl Rognvald Brusason, the poet brandishing his pole-axe and his shield with the Maeshowe Dragon, helmet glistening in the flames of the torch-laden *Vagsoy*, now betrayed to his enemies by his lapdog's bark, awaited his death on the rocks at the hands of Thorkel, the amiable lawyer from Levy and McRae. His ships, *Arrow* and *Held*, lay floundering at Gulber Wick. Meanwhile, at Sumburgh Voe, a nameless crofter waited another day, hoping that the man in the cowl, Earl Rognvald, would join him fishing one more time before the laird had his way and drove him off the land.

The grey wolf was gaping over each bloody corpse even as the bells started ringing in Saint Magnus Cathedral, forever bathed in red. In goes Ogmund, head swathed in rags where a cross-tree fell and smashed his skull. Out comes Alan Ogden, retired policeman, a whole man. And the Bishop of Scrabster too, his tongue and eyes restored, and a motley host of lepers, lunatics, the sick and the maimed—all whole. Each one seeking a miracle and finding it. Only the unrepentant Sigurd the Mighty, writhing from the poison in his blood, a parting gift from Maelbrigte's teeth, wilted gangrenously green in the distance.

I stood transfixed before my window. It took David Bedborough of the Marine Pollution Control, masquerading as Earl Thorfinn the Mighty—leaping from a burning broch with Ingibjorg, his wife, and escaping Rognvald—to break my spell. Lucky dog, thought I.

The light faded from the sky, the sounds from my ears. But the pain and shame returned as I wondered why I hadn't leapt into the lake with Rosie in my arms, away from the grasp of our pursuers. I had failed, never really had the courage of my ancestors. Blind rage filled my mind, driving pain and shame away.

Timid waves from the boat crossing Bressay Sound lapped against the walls of the hotel. I could hear the waves, but couldn't see them. I strained to catch sight of the line where the water touched the wall. And that's when I saw the seals, climbing on the ledge below my window. The sea was as still as a sheet of beaten copper. First one, then another, then another, there rose an endless procession of seals. They looked more like bears drenched in the brown filth pouring out of the *Braer* impaled on the rocks. First there were the seals, then the otters, and schools of fish that could only squirm on their sides, and flocks of shags and kittiwakes who had lost the gift of flight. Past the pier, up the Esplanade, they marched slowly and mournfully towards the north. They rose from Burra and Esha Ness, from

Mousa Broch and Muckle Green Holm, and from the cliffs of Yell and Unst. And from the distant sounds of Scapa Flow there rose a hundred ghostly whales to join the rest.

Then the Spirits of the North, the land of icefields and floating mountains and silver bears, started to reclaim their own. The sea began to move back, laying bare a floor littered with fresh carcasses and bleached bones and rusted skeletons of ships ensnared in limp seaweed, all silent reminders of crimes against man, of crimes by man. And I heard my mother cry, "Where's the music in your voice? Be a shame to lose it, Charlie."

The music, it seemed, had left me. I had no answer for my mother.

As I looked at the dry shoals of Bressay and beyond, I began to understand what my father meant when he called the seas the highways of an earlier age. There was enough carnage here too, but nothing more fearful and ugly than anything I had seen in the present. They seemed to tell me that, in the real world, there was nothing to fear except that which sprang from the imagination. Whose words were they? thought I.

Gentle valleys of the deep entered Frobisher's Straits and went past Cape Desolation towards Desire Provoked and Isle of God's Mercies, past Cape Cornmouth, Earl Bristol's Island and the Sleepers Dozen, through Hudson's Bay, and into James Bay. Wind, waves, and pirates, all magically dispelled. But imagined or not, the fear was real when its reflection entered the hearts of sullen mutineers or crept behind the fearless brow of the cruellest, harshest captains.

If I had wanted to, I could've almost touched the craggy slopes beyond the Germane Sea where stood the land of Olaf and Erland and Rognvald Kali. Flagstone coffins, their lids blown away, lay scattered on the beaches, the shrivelled bodies inside spread with red ochre, surrounded by spears of slate and quartz arrowheads in some vain hope of continuing life beyond death. From the ocean bed came the ugly whiff of dead seals stacked one on top of the other in the North Sea. From the west, the wind brought the unforgiving smell of ten thousand drowned caribou. The south I could not bear to look at—an entire continent turned into a smoking charnel house.

Distances shrank to the measure of a hand. From Mongstad to Quebec City seemed nothing. Only the distance of a few city blocks separated Stromness and Radisson. A child could walk the distance and return on a single lazy afternoon. I thought I could see the twinkling, dazzling lights of Montreal. And Radisson, where the beast was first chained and transformed, and from where it was let loose through the beaded necklaces strung across the sky. The sky glowed over Radisson. But to what end? I wondered. All this, to what end?

Even when the oceans surged at full tide, I could understand how inviting these highways might have been to another age. After all, mariners know the power that creates a wave can also destroy a wave. Unfamiliar highways may buckle without a warning as a friendly wind suddenly whips up and gathers in the direction the waves are going, striking them to satanic fury. But so can heaving oceans be flattened to gentle, rocking motions when fresh Atlantic trade winds begin to blow and crush the might of swells that come rolling from Iceland and head for Africa.

The cover of the ocean blown away, rocky ledges and shoals of sand and clay stood naked and claimed the forgotten kinship of the land. George's Bank loomed along New England, as gentle as the highlands I had known as a child. The treacherous crests of their highest hills, forever lurking under the surface like a hidden knife over the Cultivator Shoals, now took on the warm and inviting look of the brighter folds of sunny valleys. It was easy to see how these unvanquished hills — aided by the tidal currents that swirled around and across them — robbed the power of the ocean swells and led them to such a tender meeting of surf and land so frequently.

The sky was dark over Sullom Voe. Yes, I could see right to the northern tip of the Shetlands as thousands of birds threw an umbrella over the refinery stack spouting fire and towering over the village. The spotless highways leading to the island's heart scudded under the march of dead fish, dying seals, and other birds, flightless birds. I came down from my room, stopped on the ledge for a moment, and stepped onto the rocks once covered by the sea. I walked past Garths Ness to where the remains of the *Braer* lay scattered around a new eruption of stacks hidden from my view earlier. I kept walking and walking and walking until I reached the eastern shores of James Bay. I stood at the mouth of the La Grande River, staring in awe at massive walls of stained concrete that looked like so many headstones to giants.

But the real headstones lay in the dam behind the spillways, and I knew that's where I would find Rosie. "Sing, Charlie, sing," I heard my mother cry again, leading me with her love, leading me to my own. I started to sing 'Stay, my Charmer' to please her. Even before I had gone on to 'Sweet are the banks o' Doon', there started up the sound of bagpipes and bugles from the west. A ghostly band, this must've been the one that had played to Sir George Simpson two hundred years ago. Now they shook themselves up from their sleep and the sound of their music ringed both bays. They came marching to the dry ocean bed from Forts Churchill and Nelson, from Albany, Moose, and Slude River. They were followed by Cree fiddlers playing tunes I remembered, with surprise, from my childhood days in Stromness. I felt happy. I sang of love, cherished or forgotten, love betrayed or unrequited.

I sang as I walked up the river. I walked past the rock at Kaniaapiscow that Louis had told me about, recognizing it by the slime-covered Hudson's Bay Store that stood nearby — walls still lined with barrels, shelves with jars, stacks of blankets piled on the floor. As soon as I had left the store, I knew I was in the burial grounds. One after another, the graves swelled up like dough inside an oven and cracks appeared on their crests.

Then I saw her. Still glowing as she did in life, she lay stretched on one side of the valley away from the graves. Through the delicate green veil that covered her body, I could see her fair skin, her face masked in peace, and knew it would still be soft to the touch. The wide open eyes, all movement stilled, reflected in their emerald mirrors memories of our brief life together. Her lips, I saw them red. Red like the wisp of red trailing away from two tiny wounds over a vein in her hand. The trail grew pale as it disappeared over her breast and became one with the colour of the veil jealously guarding her against . . . . . against what? It seemed only yesterday when the sound of her laughter skimmed bird-like across the water as she lay in my arms on the banks of the dam. Silence might have saved her life, I thought. Was it her laughter that gave her away?

Risen from the dead, they were now gathering around me. They had watched Rosie's body floating down like a leaf with a gentle to and fro motion, her hair now clinging to, now billowing away from her body. She must have looked perfectly at peace—as I remembered her—as she dropped lower and lower to the bed of the lake. Some of the shadowy figures now started to sing softly in Cree around Rosie.

"I'm Pegleg's father. The jester, the jester, the fool. I'm the one who let all these dead folk out," said a voice. "When we heard Rosie's body crash into the water," he continued, "we thought we were getting another barrelful of shit. Pureed to perfection like we've had pouring down on our heads ever since they put up the camp at La Grande II."

Now a toothless old woman joined in. "Early mornings before the workers go to work, usually the worst," she chuckled. "Filet mignon and creme caramel mixed with Grand Marnier or Kahlua just isn't the most wholesome combination, if you know what I mean."

"Give us caribou and porcupine any day. Isn't that right, son?" asked an old man, turning to a somewhat slimy figure seated at his feet.

The man closest to Rosie looked down at her, as her veil moved slightly in the wind blowing down from the rock. For a single foolish moment, I thought she was coming back to life. "They'll never let us be," mused the man. "They messed us up in life, they torment us in death. The Captain, Henry Hudson, rants about his grandfather's funeral, but look what they've done to us?"

From out of another mouldering stone building near the store, Father Gastineau walked out with a limp, his arthritic fingers clutching a large, rusting crucifix. "Poor girl," he said, hobbling up to Rosie. "Won't you look up once and accept our Lord into your heart?"

"Truly, in their hearts there's only pity for us," said the man nearest Rosie. "Full of pride, full of lies, they come crowding into our lives and leave us poisoned with their crap, the crap of civilization."

Just then, a thunderous explosion shook the ground where we stood. The very next moment, it seemed the river was rushing towards us, past thunderous cataracts upstream that had been silenced. The soft, monotonous singing faded away in the background.

"It's Louis Bearskin blowing up the dam," said Pegleg's father, laughing. "The Spirit's not with him of late, or he would've been stopped. It's stupid. It's no use."

"But I've come for Rosie," I cried.

"She'll forever be a part of you, Charlie," explained Pegleg's father, "as she is of us."

We heard a roaring sound gather over our heads. The water started to rise at our feet, touching my ankles in a flash. Soon the water covered Rosie and the veil turned a darker shade. Her hair began to sway like eelgrass in the wind.

"I want to take her back with me," I pleaded. I went down on my knees and started to gather her up in my arms. She was still warm and soft as I remembered her. I trembled with joy.

"You're a fool to think you can get back what you've destroyed." Pegleg's father's voice was soft and mocking. He grinned at me. "Out here, possession kills. Didn't you know that, young man?" The voice trailed away. The figures disappeared. I tried to lift Rosie but came up empty-handed. She was gone.

Enough, enough, I repeated to myself, trying to regain some form of control. If I was tired of the past, I felt frightened by the future. Maybe the answer lay in burying the present in something like amber, to see but not to touch, for the pain was still there like a throbbing nerve, goaded by my familiar longing. Little by little, my mind cleared. Peace returned to me.

The sea in front was strangely, unusually calm—an oiled-silk smoothness rippling to the music of unhurried swells. I remembered how divers in an earlier time carried oil in their mouths to release beneath the surface when rough water made their work difficult. The mountainous flow of oil might have calmed the ocean off Sumburgh too, I thought. My heart went out to the Greek captain, caught in the wrong place at the wrong time. He had stumbled into a roost at the feeding time of monsters, and the frantic, bursting, tumbling sea had devoured and spit out his ship. All that now remained of that wild feast was the bow of the *Braer* jutting out of the water at Garths Ness like the lower jawbone of a creature stripped of all flesh.

How the world had changed, changed in a way my father would never have understood. The sense in which my father saw the permanence of things was falling apart at the seams. It was so sad.

I also felt sorrow for the thousands of modern-day seafarers, driven by hunger and poverty in their lands rather than love of the sea and its romance, whose ships, I knew, were doomed. It was only a matter of

Requiem for the Last Indian | 255

time before they too were called to the terrible, final banquet of tides and waves and consumed like the *Braer*. I couldn't help feeling a surge of anger since I knew that those who least deserved a call to the table—grubby owners of patched up ships—would probably still be feasting on Mediterranean islands, in Amsterdam, London, New York, or Connecticut.

Yes, the oil was gone. The smart TV people had feasted too and were now leaving Sumburgh. It seemed Sven and I were the only two left on the island. Sven would go too, on the afternoon flight to Aberdeen. It was as if the storm had never blown, and the *Braer* just a tourist commercial, an event staged for TV.

One can't get into Booth's from the front. A faded and wholly inconspicuous sign suggests that one use the side entrance. The first side entrance is a black door without a door handle. It wouldn't open. The next door was locked as well. It was smart of Sven and me not to have given up. The third door, heavy and painted white—without any indication that it might lead to what we were looking for—did open once I pulled it hard enough. We walked straight into the bar, a single step or less for the thirsty. The ceiling is low, and one can touch it easily. Parallel to the bar, behind us, were a half dozen tables and chairs with a couple more thrown in to the left of the bar. A bunch of music makers came in through the white door, followed by a motley group who could've been from anywhere and everywhere in the world, from Porsche-driving oil executives to unemployed seal lovers.

In between short speeches and folksy music, a fisherman seated next to us seemed at pains to explain how Shetlanders could make a virtue out of any necessity. "Like Sullom Voe," he said. "We'll work there long enough to make the money we need, not a minute more. We can shrug off the oil companies. We know this'll pass too. Maybe not in the eyes of the rest of the world, but for us, most certainly."

The crowd had slowly filled up the little pub. I looked around and saw, immediately behind me, four long-haired Shetland beauties drinking what looked like clouded lemonade. Sven and I were both afraid to start a conversation with them for they looked like they might be Greenpeace activists. Of course, we had nothing against Greenpeace. In fact, I remembered seeing in my dream the night before the *Solo* lying on its side on the dry sea-bed. The truth was that we simply didn't want to be accused of being snoopin' lackeys of greedy capitalists in case they found out we worked for the hated insurance industry. A short while later, the women got up and went inside through a door behind the bar to our right. Maybe they were Jan's daughters. I never asked. The drinks that looked like clouded lemonades remained an enigma to the end.

"I expect you folks aren't reporters," said the fisherman standing next to us. "But this is what they didn't do. Never spoke to folks like us, never really listened. Just told us what they feared most."

"But will the Rain Goose come back?" yelled someone from the back of the crowded room. The fisherman just shrugged his shoulders, smiled and pushed his glass forward for another pint.

That previous Saturday, at the fundraiser at Booth's in Hillswick, this big, jovial fisherman drinking next to us confessed how terrified he was at the height of the storm. "Sat up all night, scared stiff. 'Twas like a flamin' Tornado parked on top of my roof, throttling up to fly off. Except that it didn't, just kept revvin' and roarin' on top of my head." He told me of the gale that blew for twenty infernal days at a stretch. "For what it stood up to," said the man, "the *Braer* was one mighty tough ship. But they didn't look after it—Liberian flag and all! You should've seen the waves, fifty feet high, sometimes a hundred. They just kept pounding away at the hull, impatient for the kill. On the fifth night, the ship's heart simply gave out. The next morning, the stack, the decks, everything was covered in black, and I knew it was bunker oil. The funny thing is that the ship wasn't carrying enough of it."

The fisherman continued after renewed refreshment. "That stuff is hard. After it's dried up you can pound the tar with a hammer and the hammer'll bounce up. A ship that size would be carrying eight hundred to a thousand tons of bunker oil. Where did it disappear?" Our friend smiled mysteriously. "I can understand the light crude breaking up," he added, "but you can't do magic with bunker oil."

"Monkey business perhaps?" chimed in Sven mischievously with a wink. There were rumours that the ship might've been tapping its cargo to run its engines, that it didn't have all the bunker oil people imagined, the amount it was normally supposed to have been carrying.

"Ha, ha ha!" laughed the fisherman. "You strangers are too clever for us." Then, lowering his voice, he said, "Between you and me and this post, sir, there's much that goes on in them tankers ordinary folk know nothing about."

The sea was too calm, too unreal, speckled with silver tongues that seemed to have frozen that cold morning. But the sun began to stream down through the grey clouds and lit a path for itself all the way to Sumburgh Head. There, surrounding me, a light cover of snow lay over the rocky ledges and mottled patches of grass, mostly brown, but with a handful of blades still defiantly green. Only the faint spoor of some gulls and shags lay on the snow — creatures who had left behind, for a moment of respite, the shrill excitement of the cliffs below the lighthouse.

Up here, the odd, solitary shag, gull or guillemot floated around in leisurely circles, or plummeted downwards in a free fall, or simply sat in stony silence contemplating the sea. Much like a flat, finite, pebbled garden reflecting nothing less austere or more dramatic than itself, the sea stared back at the birds and me. The waves stood still, letting three jagged stacks lift their heads to the sun. If only life could be a little less even-handed, I thought. But no, that would be too simple, too easy.

It was strangely quiet behind me too. In the crofts stretching over the headlands, some fenced with wire, others dyked with stone, even the sheep stood still, staring seawards. The pyramid shaped stacks in the ocean wove a hypnotic spell I found difficult to ward off. They held the promise of a timeless harmony quite like the sea in front of me. For reasons I cannot recall, I remembered the story of the white-tailed sea eagle that had carried the baby Mary Anderson, some three hundred years ago or more, from the island of Unst to the eagle's eyrie on the island of Fetlar, three miles away, to a place called Bustapund. A Fetlar lad named Robert Nicholson had been lowered down the cliff to the eagle's nest, where he found her being guarded by two eagles. He saved the child. Years later, on a trip to Unst, he met and married Mary Anderson.

Mute, the sea promised nothing of the sort, no fairy tale endings. I could be free, but it wouldn't make the slightest difference. The present would simply remain locked in amber. No difference at all to the party of pensive cormorants that seemed to be always sitting on the distant shingle bar near Scatness. No difference to the fields of red campion and white and yellow wild flowers just waiting for Spring. Not to anybody. A brief splash and the sea and the sea-washed stacks and skerries would all return to their meditations with no more concern than if an egg had rolled down from a nest in the cliffs and shattered in the water below.

But the eggs always defied such a fate. Pointed at one end, they rolled in circles and seldom fell into the sea. How remarkable! It seemed to belittle the possibility of my lying broken on the rocks below, picked at by scavenging gulls piece by piece, or smothered by buzzing flies. I couldn't help laughing to myself, feeling more defenceless than an egg. Was that why the ancients made the egg the source and origin of the universe? I recalled some of my father's earliest maps where the earth and the universe were both egg-shaped. In comparing myself with an egg, I was quickly struck by the irony of the analogy. But I have arms and legs, I reminded himself. I am a grown man.

There was a certain excitement, a vague sense of terror, in the thunderous waves I had seen earlier from this very spot, smashing themselves into a million slivers on the rocks below. Now the sea was tamed, content, noiselessly licking the salt off the foot of the cliffs. The birds seemed rebellious and unconcerned as always, screaming as before, floating carelessly away as fancy moved, wherever, whenever. Behind me, in the distance, the softly rounded hills powdered with snow like the faces of Noh dancers, eyed me like a silent audience waiting for my next move. All this was sentimental, yes, but Rosie was like a red rose to me after all. The oceans could stand still, they could disappear. But I had lived, and so had Rosie. Yes, and in her own way, Isabel Gunn as well.

And now to my unfinished needs. The whole world. I still wanted the whole world. I would settle for nothing less. I would try to get on that afternoon flight to Aberdeen. Maybe I could still find a seat next to Sven. And in the Spring, perhaps a long visit with Louis Bearskin in his camp near the Monster Rapids. This time, I knew he wouldn't mind.

The sky was full of stars and I could feel Louis Bearskin's presence filling the emptiness below the rich blue dome from which they shone. The stars were questioning, persistent. The most persistent of all seemed the Great Bear. Why? it seemed to be asking me. Why? why? echoed the other stars, glowing, pulsing in anticipation. The wind carried the sound of Louis's laughter, and the Milky Way drifted like smoke from his celestial pipe.

Yes, Louis Bearskin was gone. His cabin was empty. His footsteps led curiously to the river's edge and then disappeared. As I stood by the river in darkness, I was surprised by the heavy wings of a nighthawk whirring in flight from tree to tree. Suddenly, a flame appeared nearby, shuddering in the wind, springing from a cluster of rocks which reminded me of a stone altar during an earlier visit. In the pale light I saw one face, then another. Isabel Gunn, still in her flowing patchwork cape, stood on one side of the stone altar, and my mother on the other. Isabel's face was sombre, no longer did it reflect any signs of the agony I remembered from Sumburgh Head. My mother's eyes held the tenderness I have always associated with her. Both women held out their arms towards me. What did they want from me? Was it a welcome, an invitation to their world?

I had no time to think. All my life I had lived in awe of Isabel Gunn, forever imagining her censure dogging every move I made. Here she was holding out her arms to me. I rushed forward. My mother took a step in my direction. I craved her embrace. The faintest hint of a smile lit both faces.

The flame trembled as I drew near. Then it leapt upwards and swiftly went out, sucked up by the stars' inhalation. Puzzled and full of expectation, I came to a halt in front of the rocks, my arms outstretched, the cool air swarming over my face. For an instant I felt like a fool, until the air in front of me seemed to freeze and the space between my arms filled up with a supple lithe figure. Even in the darkness, I could recognize every curve on that lovely body. She was cold, cold as ice. But not her lips. They were warm, warm as the blood of the three men that ran through my fingers and dripped down my arms as I sliced the life out of their veins. It was Rosie. Yes, it was.

"Charlie," she whispered as her lips crushed mine. "Charlie, Charlie, come home to me," she said. "Your job is done."

I held her in my arms, afraid to lose her again. I experienced a strange sensation of being lifted off my feet, of floating in air. The icy blue of the sky engulfed me, the stars were white sails bobbing gently over the blue swell, thronging to welcome my arrival. I revelled in my exhilaration.

I never knew when Rosie had slipped out of my arms, becoming aware of her absence only when the wind whipped across my face and rippled through my clothes. I was still floating, but the lights went out one by one, and I soon became aware of a blue that was the blue of the sea and, in the place of the stars, there now was a pale glow of light that shone above me and lit up the ocean floor, bare and spotless except for silvery swarms of fish that flashed back and forth like lightning. A loon drew close to my eyes, then darted upwards like an arrow. I could hear it break the surface of the blue, and thrash along the water as it lifted into space again with a wailing, quavering laughter.

In that instant, I half sensed what lay at the heart of my romance with the sea. Could it be a desire to unlock the secrets locked beneath its surface? Possibly. Ships and sailing offer only a poor substitute, merely skimming the surface. I felt lucky I had shared the secret with Rosie. She was a part of the secret.

She needn't have been. Suddenly I felt ready to lay bare my own secret without regret, without guilt, and certainly without fear. This was the other half of the revelation. I was finally ready to shed my concern about whether it was a crime to avenge a crime with whatever means available to one? Such profound questions seemed beyond me. All I knew was that Rosie, wherever she might be, believed my work was done either by me or by Louis Bearskin. What's more, even Isabel Gunn seemed to be off my back. That's all that seemed to matter to me.

"So here I am, officer," I said, looking through a haze of cigarette smoke at the face pinned like an egg yolk to the wall and the body rounded like a pig's against the table. "Let Louis Bearskin rest in peace, the last Indian there was. As for death, did I not tell you that the absurdity of certain deaths is a secret between man and his God?"

The officer sat in silence, looking impassively at me.

We sat staring at each other a long time. Finally, I said, "I am your man."

END